W9-BZP-370

Always the Designer, Never the Bride

"*Always the Designer, Never the Bride* shows yet another angle of the journey from 'I think I love you' to 'I do' and all the side adventures that keep her readers begging, 'Tell me another story!' "
—Cynthia Ruchti, radio personality and novelist, author of the Carol Award finalist *They Almost Always Come Home*

"Sandra Bricker has done it again! Like every book in this series, *Always the Designer, Never the Bride* made me laugh, made me sigh, made me root for the heroine, and made me cry. No way I'm loaning this one out, because—gasp—what if it isn't returned!"
—Loree Lough, best-selling author of more than 80 award-winning books, including reader favorite *From Ashes to Honor*

Other Abingdon Press Books by Sandra D. Bricker

Always the Baker, Never the Bride
Always the Wedding Planner, Never the Bride
The Big 5-OH!

And coming soon . . .

*Always the Baker, **Finally** the Bride*

Always the Designer, Never the Bride

Sandra D. Bricker

Abingdon Press fiction
a novel approach to faith

Nashville, Tennessee

Always the Designer, Never the Bride

Copyright © 2012 by Sandra D. Bricker

ISBN-13: 978-1-4267-3223-2

Published by Abingdon Press, P.O. Box 801, Nashville, TN 37202

www.abingdonpress.com

All rights reserved.

No part of this publication may be reproduced in any form, stored in any retrieval system, posted on any website, or transmitted in any form or by any means—digital, electronic, scanning, photocopy, recording, or otherwise—without written permission from the publisher, except for brief quotations in printed reviews and articles.

The persons and events portrayed in this work of fiction are the creations of the author, and any resemblance to persons living or dead is purely coincidental.

Published in association with WordServe Literary Group, Ltd., 10152 S. Knoll Circle, Highlands Ranch, CO 80130

Library of Congress Cataloging-in-Publication Data

Bricker, Sandra D., 1958-
Always the designer, never the bride / Sandra D. Bricker.
p. cm.
Includes bibliographical references and index.
ISBN 978-1-4267-3223-2 (book - pbk. / trade pbk. : alk. paper) 1. Women fashion designers—Fiction. 2. Female friendship—Fiction. 3. Weddings—Fiction. 4. Brothers—Fiction. 5. Atlanta (Ga.)—Fiction. I. Title.
PS3602.R53A51 2012
813'.6—dc22

2011050025

Scripture taken from the New King James Version®. Copyright© 1982 by Thomas Nelson, Inc. Used by permission. All rights reserved.

Printed in the United States of America

1 2 3 4 5 6 7 8 9 10 / 17 16 15 14 13 12

Deepest thanks to my rock star agent and friend,
Rachelle Gardner.

Also to my editor Ramona Richards,
and to my cheerleading section:
Marian, Jemelle, Debby, and David.

And special thanks to Barbara for taking the lead and rallying the troops. If one MUST have a near-death experience, there's no one better to have by your side. I'm forever indebted.

The next best thing to being wise oneself
is to live in a circle of those who are.
—C. S. Lewis

Prologue

"That's not ivory, Granny. It's ecru."

"Is it?"

"Yes. And I needed crystal beads, not these iridescent ones. The crystal is much more showy, and I need them to make a statement."

Beatrice leaned forward in her rocking chair and smoothed the white-gold hair of her grandchild, perched like a bird at her feet. "Are you sure you're just nine years old?"

"Granny, please. Just help me look through these cases for the crystal beads? I knew not to let Carly alone in my room with my cases open. She must have mixed them all up."

She pushed two matching plastic boxes into her grandmother's lap. Beatrice flipped the latch on one of the pink gingham-patterned cases and tipped open the lid before glancing down at the little girl who seemed to be surrounded in light amidst hat boxes, organizers, and immaculate containers.

Audrey's innocent porcelain face crumpled like a grape left out in the sun as she continued her search. Without missing a beat, she raked back her spun-silk hair and fastened it with a pink sequined band. When she glanced up to find her grandmother watching her instead of engaged in the search,

Audrey cocked her head to one side and heaved a laborious sigh.

"Granny? The crystal beads?"

Beatrice nodded, fingering through the separated compartments of the tray, each of them bearing a red vinyl label with raised white letters.

Glass beads.

Seed beads.

Sequins.

Beatrice, at the tender age of nine, hadn't known the first thing about various types of beads, much less having thought of asking for a label maker for her birthday to better differentiate them inside organized plastic cases! While Audrey's other nine-year-old friends played with accessories for their Barbies, she designed and created haute couture for every doll in town.

"Her wedding is scheduled for this Saturday afternoon," the child announced. "She can't get married without any crystal beads on her gown."

"Of course not," Beatrice sympathized.

"And Granny, will you make the wedding cake? We're going to have the ceremony here on the sun porch."

"I think I can do that," she replied, and the corner of her mouth twitched slightly. "Oh, is this what you're looking for?"

She stuck out her hand, several shiny beads rolling on the palm.

Audrey's amber eyes ignited, and she gasped. "Granny, you're wonderful! Where did you find them?"

"The second tier. Under these thingies." She tapped one of the compartments with the tip of her finger.

"Thingies!" Audrey said, chuckling. "Those *thingies* are just the last of my wooden barrel beads. I used them on the bracelet I made Carly for her birthday, remember?"

"I think I do." She nodded. "Yes, that's right."

"Once this wedding is behind me, I'm going to have to go through every one of my cases to put everything back in its right place."

"Yes, I suppose you can't have shiny sequins in a compartment marked as something else."

"You can see what a disaster that could be, can't you, Granny?"

"Clearly."

Audrey took the cases from Beatrice's lap with caution, gingerly setting them on the carpeted floor beside her.

"That Carly," she muttered as she began plucking crystal beads from the tray. "Sometimes she's like a gorilla at a tea party."

1

Audrey, the car will be here any minute. You're going to miss your plane."

"Shh. I just need another minute."

She leaned down over her sketch pad, nibbling the corner of her lip as she put the finishing touches on the train of an elaborate A-line wedding dress.

"Oh, Audrey! That's beautiful. Is it for Kim?"

She didn't reply for another moment or two; not until she felt perfectly secure in the fact that she could lay down her pencil and be done with it.

"There are two others in the leather portfolio in my closet. The messenger will be here at three o'clock to pick them up and get them into Manhattan by four." She handed her assistant the finished product, pausing for an instant to admire the drawing. "Be very careful about it, but put this one with the others, and be sure to zip it all the way around so they aren't wrinkled. Just give him the whole case, and call Kim once he's on his way to give her a heads-up that they'll be delivered to the penthouse."

"Will do."

"My plane lands in Atlanta at five-something, and it will take me an hour or so to get out to Roswell where this hotel is located. You've shipped—"

"And confirmed. Carly's dress is safe and sound at The Tanglewood Inn, awaiting your arrival."

Audrey sighed as she cast a quick glance toward the door where Kat had lined up her pink plaid luggage. One oversized rectangular case and one large round one, both on wheels, both packed to full capacity.

Audrey applied a glaze of Cherry Bliss to her lips while Kat added the final sketch to the leather case. She paused with the wand in mid-air until she heard the *vvhht* of the zipper. As she slipped the tube into its compartment inside her purse, the buzzer sounded.

"That will be your car," Kat announced. "But before you go . . ."

Kat grabbed Audrey's hand and placed a compact little cell phone into it, closing her fingers around it. "Now this is the simplest cellular phone available."

"Kat, I do not want one of these. I told you that."

"I know. But you have to."

Audrey stared at the strange thing on her palm. "What do I do?"

"If it jingles, you open it. Like this." Kat demonstrated. "It will either be a phone call—in which case you press the blinking green button—or a text, which will come up automatically."

"Ah, maaan . . ."

"I know. But it's the best way to keep in contact. You want to keep in contact with me, don't you?"

Audrey groaned. "Yes."

"So put this in your purse."

Audrey reluctantly tossed the thing into her bag as Kat pressed buttons on her own much more complicated-looking cell phone. An instant later, Audrey's purse began to . . . *sing.*

"It sounds like a harp."

"That's your cue to pull it out and open it." Kat stared at her for a moment before nodding at Audrey's purse. "Go on. Answer it."

"I already know who it is."

"Audrey."

Audrey groaned again as she produced the cell phone, unfolded it and stared at the thing.

"The green button," Kat prodded.

Audrey pressed the button and held the phone in the vicinity of her ear. "Audrey Regan isn't available right now, but please feel free to take a flying leap at the tone." As Kat opened her mouth to reply, Audrey interrupted with a "*Beeeeeep.*"

Kat shook her head as she pushed the button on the wall intercom and she told the driver, "Come on in. We have a couple of bags." Back to Audrey, she remarked, "Text me when you arrive. Do you want me to show you how?"

"I'll call. Let me know the minute you confirm the sketches have reached Kim."

"Will do."

"The very minute, Katarina. *We need this.*"

"I know. She's going to love them."

"As long as she loves them more than Vera Wang and Austin Scarlett."

Audrey paused in front of the full-length etched mirror propped against the wall. She smoothed the straight pencil skirt and adjusted the corset belt around her waist.

"Car for JFK," the driver announced, grabbing both of the bags.

"How much, by the way?" she asked as she followed him down the stairs.

"Ninety-five," Kat called out from the doorway. "Already charged to your card."

"Ninety-five dollars, from Soho to JFK?"

"You can grab a taxi for fifty bucks, Princess," the driver snapped, letting the street door flap shut in her face.

Audrey turned and looked back at Kat, standing in the doorway at the top of the stairs. "Charming."

Kat chuckled. "Have a good flight."

"One can only hope."

As she climbed into the back seat of the dark blue sedan, Audrey appreciated the good sense she'd had to hire Katarina Ivanov. Staring blankly out the window, Audrey sighed as the driver took a left on Kenmare.

She'd held interviews on a Tuesday afternoon in the corner booth at the Village Tart, and Kat had arrived fifteen minutes early. She'd ordered a coffee at another table while Audrey finished up with the design school student who looked like a cross between Buddy Holly and Kramer from *Seinfeld*. When they were through, the young man stood over Audrey, tapping his shiny patent leather shoe.

"So let's cut right to it, shall we?" he'd said, glaring at her over the bridge of thick black-rimmed glasses. "Do I have a shot at this or not? I'm only asking because I have two more interviews after yours, and I need to know whether I can blow them off."

"I think I can answer that," Kat told him as she transferred her espresso to Audrey's table and sat down. "Go on the interviews. I think we've decided which candidate is the best choice. I'm so sorry, but good luck to you." Her smile emanated a ray of pure sunshine.

The boy grimaced at her before he looked back at Audrey. She only shrugged. Twenty seconds later, the front door of the café thudded shut behind him.

"Did I go too far?" Kat asked her as she crossed her legs and wrinkled up her nose, flipping short dark waves of hair. "I know. Sometimes I go too far. But he was wasting your time. You weren't going to hire him."

"I wasn't?"

"No," she said confidently, sliding her résumé across the table, only a slight trace of amusement in her dark brown eyes. "Even if you don't hire me, you certainly can't hire him. He's high maintenance; he's a drama a day, at least. And you don't need that."

"I don't."

"No. You need stability. Loyalty. You need a take-charge, organized fashionista who makes her workday all about you."

And Katarina Ivanov had been doing just that for more than a year since. Two parts Mother Earth and one part All-Business. Audrey had no idea what she would ever have done without her.

"Where are you going?" she suddenly asked the driver. "Are you taking the Van Wyck Expressway?"

"I got an idea," he tossed back at her over his shoulder. "You worry about your hat and gloves, and I'll take care of getting you to JFK."

I'm not wearing a hat and gloves, you Neanderthal.

When he glanced into the rearview and noticed Audrey seething at him, he sighed. "Don't worry your pretty little head. I'll get you there, Princess. Deal? Okay. Deal."

Audrey dug her bright red fingernails into her palms.

I despise New York.

But she knew it wasn't the city so much as the energy of the place. Ten million people crammed into jam-packed streets, everyone trying to get somewhere, all of them convinced that their particular mission trumped everyone else's. If her driver worked in another city, say St. Louis or Abilene, she felt certain he'd be far less disagreeable. Audrey, on the other hand, just wanted to survive long enough in New York to catch the tail of her dream.

Nearly out of money, and fast running out of steam, she had just enough of both to carry her through Carly's wedding in Atlanta. If she didn't score the job designing Kim Renfroe's wedding dress by the time she returned, Audrey would have to start thinking about throwing in the towel. Perhaps she could rustle up a job working for one of the other design houses. Her stab at venturing out on her own hadn't been the starship success she'd been convinced that it would be.

Two years and three months.

That's how long it had taken her to run through the inheritance Granny Beatrice had left her. Twenty-seven months, almost to the day. When she'd left Atlanta for New York, she had such high hopes of making a name for herself as a designer. Marginal successes along the way had not contributed much toward soaring, only toward staying afloat. And even that was in jeopardy now.

Audrey nibbled on the corner of her lip as she stared at the scenery beyond the sedan window. A mist of emotion rose in her eyes, blurring the passing cars. She really needed to figure out a way to tell Kat that she wouldn't be able to pay her much longer.

She wondered if Carly knew how much it cost her to drop everything and head home for a week, not to mention all the time and resources she'd spent on designing and creating Carly's dream bridal gown. By the time the Atlanta trip came to a close, she would find herself up against the final wall. She would say good-bye to Kat, convert her design studio on the other side of her apartment into a living space, and advertise for a roommate. Then she would go begging for a job with low pay and long hours in support of someone else's design reverie.

Unless Kim Renfroe chose to wear an Audrey Regan original for her spring wedding; in that case, the air in the tires of her dream would carry her on a little farther. Not much, but a little.

"You gonna answer that, Princess?"

"What?"

"Your cell phone. It sounds like God is calling."

The jingle of her harp-phone nudged her as she wiped a tear from her cheek. "Oh. I didn't hear it."

She pulled the phone from her purse and fumbled with it. Finally, she heard Kat's muffled voice, and she held the thing up to her face.

"Audrey? I'm just checking on you. Audrey, are you there?"

She held the phone like a walkie-talkie she'd seen the night before in a late-night rerun of *Star Trek*. "Yes, I'm here, Scotty. Now either beam me up or quit bothering me. And Kat? Can you change the ring? Apparently, it sounds like God."

"I can't change the ringtone remotely, but—"

"I have to go now, Scotty. But only use this thing in an emergency, okay? It's annoying."

"Here we are. Terminal three."

She blinked, and a lone remnant of a tear wound its way down the curve of her face and dropped off her chin. Brushing its path dry with the back of her hand, she tossed the cell phone into her bag and inhaled sharply before cranking open the door and stepping out.

J. R. pulled off the black helmet, instinctively running a hand through his mane of shaggy brown hair, shaking it out. He glanced down at the CL Max helmet and noticed a tiny nick in the polycarbonate shell.

He unzipped the cuffs of his leather jacket and pulled off his gloves.

I paid a hundred and fifty bucks for this helmet just so this wouldn't happen.

He paused to tuck the helmet between his knees while he stuffed his gloves into the pocket of his leather jacket. He took another close look at the nick, then ran his hand over the flip-up shield before fitting the helmet under his arm and stalking through the brass-plated glass door of The Tanglewood Inn.

His brother Devon had called him early that morning to ask him to come straight to The Tanglewood rather than meeting up at the house, and J. R. had been glad for the change in plans. He hadn't been back in Atlanta for a while now, but he looked forward to catching up with the people he'd met there on his last pass-through with Russell.

Carly saw him first, and she hopped to her feet and rushed toward the entrance of the restaurant. With her honey-blonde hair pulled into a messy little bun at the back of her head and her glistening blue eyes dancing, his brother's fresh-faced bride curled her arms around his neck and placed several kisses on his cheek.

"I'm so happy you've arrived safely!" she exclaimed. "You and that motorcycle of yours—well, we just never stop worrying. Devon has been itching to see you!" She looped her arm through his and led him inside.

It struck him as funny that Devon and Carly worried about him riding his Harley when there had been so many more pertinent safety concerns with which to concern themselves.

J. R. had to admit that relief over someone returning to Atlanta in one piece was something he knew all too well. He hadn't seen his little brother since before he left for his last tour of duty, his second in Afghanistan in just three years.

Devon, the same old twinkle in his eye, stood up as he approached the table. As J. R. drew his brother into an embrace, he exhaled for what felt like the first time in months. Relief washed over him, and he smacked Devon's back twice. "Good to see you, bro."

"Good to be seen."

Truer words had never been spoken, and J. R. sent up a quick prayer of thanks for the fact that his brother had come home from war virtually unscathed. Physically, anyway.

"Thanks for doing this, man."

J. R. chuckled. "There's no one else going to be your best man."

"J. R., I want you to meet my wedding planner, Sherilyn Drummond," Carly said.

Her familiar laughter took the form of music, and J. R. rounded the table and took a much smaller Sherilyn than he remembered into his arms.

"Oh, of course! You two have met."

"How's Dr. Andy?" he asked her.

"Wonderful," she sang. "You have to come to the house while you're in town. We'd love to have you over, maybe after these two leave for their honeymoon."

"Sounds like a plan. Maybe we'll get a good snowstorm out of season so we can barbecue."

Sherilyn's turquoise blue eyes glistened and her laughter warmed him to his soul. She tossed her copper hair over her shoulder before she sat down again.

"You look amazing," he told her.

"Doesn't she though?" Carly added. "She's lost forty pounds!"

"Forty-eight," Sherilyn corrected with a grin. "But no one's counting."

"Well, you were already a stunner, but—"

His words were sliced in two by the high-pitched shriek Carly released, and everyone's attention followed her as she raced from the table and into the arms of . . . a *knockout!*

The platinum blonde pin-up girl had curves that pushed the boundaries of her straight skirt. A thick leather lace-up belt cinched her small waist, and the thin fabric of the ruffled blouse tried—and failed—to camouflage all that God Himself had endowed.

"Who *is* that?" J. R. whispered to Devon.

"That's Audrey."

J. R. had heard the name often, but it had passed without much notice. If only he'd realized the embodiment of two simple syllables looked like this—

"Come and meet everyone!" Carly cried. As she dragged the vision toward them, J. R.'s own pulse began to thump in his ears. "Audrey Regan," she announced. "This is Sherilyn Drummond, my wedding planner."

"It's such a pleasure!" Sherilyn told her. "I love your designs."

"You know them?" Audrey asked with a chuckle.

"I saw your runway show at the bridal expo in Chicago last year. You're a genius with beading and tulle."

Audrey grabbed Sherilyn's hand and shook it vigorously. Tossing a cute little glance back at Carly, she wrinkled her turned-up nose and added, "I like her."

J. R. couldn't take his eyes off Audrey.

Carly giggled. "And you know Dev."

Audrey planted a kiss on Devon's lucky cheek while J. R. took a deep breath and pulled himself together.

"And this is Devon's brother, J. R."

"Hi, J. R."

He had no idea what he said in reply, only that the pin-up's light brown eyes reminded him suddenly of a sugar crumble on top of a tart apple crisp.

"Let's all sit down and order some lunch," Carly suggested. "And then the ladies can go upstairs to the suite and admire my dress!"

Audrey felt a surge of blessed reprieve as she, Carly, and Sherilyn left the restaurant. Devon's brother made her uncomfortable the way he kept gawking at her. Did he think she hadn't noticed? While everyone else focused on the conversation and the marvelous food, J. R. Hunt had fixated unapologetically on every move Audrey made. At one point, she'd dabbed the corner of her mouth with the linen napkin, thinking perhaps a forkful of spinach salad had missed its mark. When he wasn't deterred, she compulsively ran her tongue over her front teeth in hopes of dislodging some stray piece of food that might have held the guy's attention in a vice grip.

"I think J. R. was quite taken with you," Carly said as they rode the glass-enclosed elevator up to the second floor.

"I noticed that too," Sherilyn added.

"Please."

"Aud, J. R. is a catch!"

She groaned. "Please!"

"No, she's right," Sherilyn told her. "He's a wonderful guy."

"Did you put her up to this?" Audrey asked Carly. "Because this is not what I'm here for."

Carly sighed, exchanging a look with Sherilyn that irritated Audrey to no end. She was always doing that. Since the time they were in the first grade together, Caroline Madison could push Audrey's buttons like no one else. And yet somehow they'd managed to remain best friends from then to now. Over the years, she'd come to equate it with sibling rivalry.

The bridal suite at The Tanglewood Inn, tucked behind double oak doors with large brass handles, smelled sweetly inviting. Fragrant bouquets of roses and hydrangea in low crystal vases graced the round claw-footed dining table as well as the oval coffee table in front of the green chenille sofa. A large arch with a sliding door of etched glass ushered the way into the adjacent room. A breathtaking king bed draped with a sheer violet canopy hugged the corner of the room at an angle, set against muted moss-green walls and flanked by antique nightstands with crystal knobs. The bellman had left Audrey's luggage against the foot of the bed in a neat little line.

"Good grief," Audrey said with a sigh. "This is lovely."

"Isn't it?" Carly cried. "I know we're already technically married—and don't tell Devon this—but this room is why I convinced him that we should live apart again for three days before the wedding. Isn't it exquisite? And we're going to have so much fun here until then. It'll be like living in Barbie's Dream House for two days!"

Audrey chuckled; such a *Carly* thing to say.

"You sit down out here," she told Audrey, her finger wiggling toward the sofa. "Sherilyn will help me get into the dress, and I'll make an entrance."

"Shouldn't Sherilyn sit out here?" Audrey asked with a grin. "I mean, I've seen the dress."

"Oh, so has Sherilyn!"

Sherilyn nodded, one side of her mouth turning upward in a lopsided grin. "Three times already."

"Besides, I made some additions. I want to spring it on you!"

"Additions?"

"So just sit down—"

"You changed the dress?"

"—and I'll go put it on for you and—"

"Caroline! You changed the dress?"

"Not really changed it. Just . . . *enhanced* it."

The horror rose slowly, like a pot coming to a boil on the stove. Leave it to Carly to have the audacity to revamp the wedding dress Audrey had designed! Her eyes darted to Sherilyn, and the pretty redhead shook her head reassuringly.

"It's okay," she mouthed. "Really. It's okay."

"Just sit down and make yourself comfortable," Carly told her. "There are drinks in the mini-fridge. And I'll be out in two shakes."

Resisting the urge to press her nose against the glass door standing between them, Audrey stalked to the window and looked out over a stunning brick courtyard.

Enhanced it. She enhanced it.

Audrey slowly paced back and forth along the length of the large window, breathing deeply and exhaling in controlled little bursts as she recounted myriad *enhancements* Carly had made to Barbie doll gowns and one-of-a-kind prom dresses over the years.

"Please, oh please," Carly had begged the night she called to tell Audrey that she and Devon were getting married again. "We were so rushed the first time around, but we really want to have the big formal wedding, so we're going to start planning it now. You just have to design my wedding dress, Aud. You have to! We're more like sisters than best friends, aren't we? How could I walk into a bridal shop and buy someone else's design to wear on the most important day of my life? Will you do it? Please?"

All of Audrey's alarm bells had sounded in those seconds between the request and her reply, but she'd ignored them.

"Of course I will."

It's my own fault, after all, isn't it? She's probably cut off the sleeves and used the fabric to make a longer train, just like she did to Barbie's gown when she married Ken on Granny's sun porch when we were kids!

"Are you ready?" Carly called out from the bedroom.

"Not at all," Audrey replied dryly. "But come on out. Let me have a look at what you've done."

Sherilyn slid open the glass door and emerged first, rushing tentatively to Audrey's side while Carly used both hands to beat out a drumroll against the wall.

"Ready?"

"Get out here!"

And then there she was, wide-eyed and hopeful, standing before Audrey.

"Well?"

Audrey blinked, and instinctively smacked her hand over her mouth with a gasp. "Caroline Madison!" she managed between her fingers.

Audrey needed to sit. Fortunately, Sherilyn pushed a chair underneath her before she went down.

"It's okay, isn't it, Aud? You don't mind?"

"Are you all right?" Sherilyn whispered. "Can I get you some water?"

"Audrey, say something."

Audrey leaned back against the chair, cocked her head, and pressed her lips together for a moment before bursting into tears.

"Audrey?" Carly exclaimed. "Is that a good cry, or a bad cry?"

Audrey pulled several tissues from the box that Sherilyn extended to her and dried her eyes with one of them. She hadn't even thought of the veils in years! But there stood Carly, in the bridal gown Audrey had made just for her, and the elbow-length wedding veil Granny had given Carly as a gift on their high school graduation.

"Aud?"

"Sorry. It's a good cry."

"Oh, thank God. I thought you were going to be upset with me for wearing your granny's lace."

"Upset?" she repeated, and she blew her nose. "I'm overcome."

"Audrey and I used to stage these elaborate weddings for our Barbies," Carly explained to Sherilyn. "I would style the ceremony with flowers and candles, and Audrey would make the wedding gowns."

"Of course," Sherilyn added with a grin.

"Of course," Carly repeated. "And her granny used this little . . . What was it, Aud?"

"Tatting tool."

"Right, a tatting tool to make these intricate, exquisite lace veils for our brides. We begged her to make life-sized ones for us to wear when we played dress-up, never realizing of course what it would take, or the level of skill and effort involved . . . But before she died, she presented both of us with these beautiful wedding veils." Carly took an edge of the veil carefully into her hand and showed it to Sherilyn. "She did her thing with tatting to create the designs for the edging, and she appliquéd it to the fabric. Isn't it beautiful?"

"Exquisite," Sherilyn replied as she examined it.

"Nottingham," Audrey sniffled.

"Sorry. What?"

"The fabric. It's Scottish Nottingham lace."

"Oh. Well, you should see Audrey's!" Carly cried. "She and her granny added crystals and beads to it, and it turned out so pretty. You looked like a queen in that veil. Do you still have it?"

"Of course," she answered with a smile. "I haven't thought of it in years. I'd almost forgotten about it until—" Her voice trailed off to silence, and Audrey sighed.

Carly had attached the veil to a stunning rhinestone tiara. With her hair twisted upward and piled on the top of her head, she looked like a regal, all-American princess. Audrey thought it sort of remarkable that the veil seemed to match the dress perfectly, even though she hadn't thought of it when she sketched out the designs for Carly's empire-waist organza ball gown.

"Carly, you look exquisite," she told her friend, a mist of emotion clouding her thoughts. "The veil makes it perfect. You look just like the princess you always wanted to be when you got married."

"I thought it looked sublime with the dress, like it was just meant to be. And did you recognize my mom's pearls?" she asked, fingering the three-strand choker.

"Is that your mom's?" Audrey moved toward her for a closer look.

"Audrey and I used to play dress-up," Carly said.

"A lot," Audrey added. "Carly's mom is so glamorous, and she had all this amazing jewelry."

"Yeah, my mom does love her bling."

"You two remind me so much of Emma and me," Sherilyn told them. "We've been friends forever too."

"Emma works here," Carly chimed in. "She's making my wedding cake. You'll meet her tomorrow night at the Jack-and-Jill."

"At the what?"

"You tell her, Sherilyn. I'm going to get out of my dress before I cry all over it. It's bad luck for a bride to shed tears on her dress. Wait. Or is it good luck?"

"Do you need help?" Sherilyn asked her.

"Are you kidding? I'm becoming an expert at getting in and out of this thing. I've probably tried it on ten times since it arrived."

"Well, at least let me unclasp the buttons for you."

Once Carly stepped into the bedroom, Sherilyn and Audrey sat down at the round table with a couple of bottles of water.

"Carly said she didn't want the traditional bachelorette festivities, and Devon didn't want a bachelor party, so they decided to combine things," Sherilyn explained. "They've rented out a place called Happy Days over in Sandy Springs. It's a fifties diner with a bowling alley, a karaoke lounge, and great old drive-in food."

"Aside from the karaoke, it sounds like fun."

"It is. My husband and I teach Sunday school to the teenagers at our church, and we took them there once. We had a ball! Everyone has to go in costume."

"Costume?" Audrey scowled.

"From the fifties. When we went, I wore this great poodle skirt I found at a vintage shop."

"She should have told me. I don't have anything like that with me," she said.

"We've got you covered. Tomorrow, a group of us from the hotel are taking you and Carly for a morning at the spa. One of the people joining us is our friend Fee, and we're going to her place afterward to raid her closet. She'll have a ton of stuff to choose from."

"Just hanging in her closet," Audrey clarified.

"You'll have to meet Fee to understand, but she's very . . . unique."

"After my own heart. I can't wait."

"It's going to be so much fun," Carly said as she joined them at the table and twisted the cap off a soda. "I can't wait for you to meet everyone here. We've all become very fast friends."

"Sounds like it."

"Oh, I wish you still lived here in Atlanta, Aud."

She wished Carly knew that New York had been such a disappointment to her. However, she saw no good coming from admitting that out loud. Things could still work out somehow, couldn't they?

"Hey, do you want to see where we're holding the ceremony and reception?"

"Sure."

"Let's take a walk. And maybe Emma's in the kitchen. You're going to love her."

Carly had brushed her hair loose again and wore skinny jeans and a floral blouse with butterfly sleeves.

"Sherilyn told you all about the Jack-and-Jill?"

Audrey nodded. It didn't exactly feel like Audrey's cup of tea, but if dressing up and drinking a milkshake was how her childhood friend wanted Audrey to spend the night before the big wedding, who was she to play Party Pooper? Sure, she'd don a poodle skirt and bobby socks. But she vowed to draw the line at black and white saddle shoes.

Jack-n-Jill went up the hill
to shout, "I love you madly!"
Jack, he bowled,
and Jill rock-n-rolled,
and all their friends sang badly.

Join us for a Jack-and-Jill bachelor/bachelorette party
the night before our wedding.

There will be bowling, dancing, great food,
and——YES, FRIENDS——
there will be karaoke!

Happy Days in Sandy Springs
Friday night at 7:00

It's a 1950s sock-hop theme, folks,
so everyone should come in costume!

Dig out your saddle shoes and grease up your pompadours.

BE THERE OR BE SQUARE!

2

Before they headed for the door, Sherilyn received a call on her cell phone from someone in the hotel. When she hung up no more than a minute later, she announced that Emma wanted to see her right away, and the group of them headed downstairs.

"Ooh, I'm so glad you're both here!" Carly cried as she led Audrey through the swinging kitchen door. "I want you to meet my BFF, Audrey Regan. Audrey, this is Emma Rae Travis and Fee Bianchi."

Emma greeted her with a broad and welcoming smile. "We've heard so much about you, Audrey. Glad to meet you."

"Dude," the more solemn of the two declared, looking at Audrey over the bridge of square black-rimmed glasses. "The dress you made is smokin'."

"Is there anyone you haven't shown it to?" she asked Carly with a giggle. "Do you not care in the least about the element of surprise?" She tilted her head and sighed as Emma grinned at her. "So she's modeled it for you both as well?"

"Twice," Fee divulged.

Emma chuckled. "Speaking of dresses," she directed at Sherilyn, "you'll never guess in a million years what has arrived."

Sherilyn grimaced. "I don't know. What?"

"Wait for it," Fee remarked as she moved a tray holding several unassembled cake layers to the refrigerator. "She'll catch up any minute."

Sherilyn thought it over for a moment. Then a light began to dawn, and she gasped. "Are you kidding me?"

"Nope."

"No way!"

"Way!" Emma blurted. "It arrived this morning, all packaged up in plastic and folded up like nothing more delicate than a beach towel."

"How weird is that?" Sherilyn cried.

Carly looked from one to the other curiously. "What? What's going on?"

"Sherilyn got married last New Year's Eve." Fee looked like that should explain everything.

"Oh." Carly and Audrey exchanged quick glances. "Congratulations."

"In the weeks leading up to the nuptials," Sherilyn chimed in, "I was somewhat . . . *bridal gown-challenged.*"

"It was freakish," Emma explained. "She had the first dress—"

"The first?" Audrey clarified with a chuckle.

"—shipped from Chicago, and it never arrived. So we went shopping for a second dress, which was altered and delivered, *supposedly*, but—"

"No!"

"Yes! And no one could locate it. Pearl finally found it a month later, hanging on the back of the door in the restaurant office!"

"It took them a month to find it there?" Carly asked.

"They never close the door, so no one ever saw it hanging there."

"Why the restaurant?" Audrey inquired. "That's a strange place to hang a bridal gown."

"That's the question of the year!" Sherilyn chuckled.

"But Sher wore her mother-in-law's Dior when she and Andy got married," Emma told them, "so—"

"Bridal serendipity," Audrey said with a grin, and Emma nodded. "I love when that happens."

Carly moved over to the counter and plucked a flower-shaped cookie from where it cooled, plopping it into her mouth. "My dress is one-of-a-kind," she announced, curling slightly as she leaned back against the counter and grinned. "Aud took it straight out of my dreams and made it a reality. The one thing, the only thing really, that I've ever truly wanted is to have a wedding gown that was completely unique to me. No one else ever had or ever would wear that very same dress. And she made it happen for me. It's the best wedding gift I could have gotten, from the best friend I've ever had."

"Carly is very once-upon-a-time," Audrey told them as her friend beamed at her. "She's been planning her wedding since we were kids. When Devon got his orders and had to ship out, they rushed down to city hall and got married. I seriously couldn't believe it when she told me! This, from the girl who had been planning a royal wedding since the day she could walk in high heels."

"From the look of things, she's turned it into a happily-ever-after," Sherilyn observed.

"You gotta love that," Fee commented.

Audrey watched her friend beam at them until she almost couldn't stand the glare of it and had to look away. Carly almost looked like an excited first-time bride!

Audrey recalled the giddy phone call she'd received the night before Devon shipped out for his last assignment to the Middle East.

"Guess what!" Carly had bubbled. "We got married!"

She could hardly believe it. Carly had been chasing the fairy tale with steel-like focus on the trip down the aisle and the big white dress, for as long as they'd known one another.

"Caroline! What about the big wedding?"

"I can't let him go away again without pledging him everything I am, Aud. Really, as long as I have the husband," Carly had said with a sigh, "the wedding can wait until later."

And wait it had! Carly had channeled all of her energies into planning the festivities. Rather than thinking about where Devon was and what he might be facing, she thought about preparing a home to which he could return, and about living out the dream of the dress, the cake, the flowers, and the guests. It was really the only way she could face the knowledge of him on another extended trip into harm's way. And now it was time for the happy ending Carly had been dreaming about since the first grade.

Audrey tried not to wonder if there might be a happily-ever-after of her own out there somewhere, reminding herself to just be happy for her friend's success, but Audrey had turned thirty years old on her last birthday. Aside from a couple of relationships that survived longer than a few months but never more than a year, she had very little to show for her pursuit of romantic happiness.

Not that she'd been actually pursuing it so much as just hoping it might stumble upon her while she cemented her design career. Carly, on the other hand, had brushed professional ambition aside ever since college in deference to an organized plan to find Prince Charming. After years of speed dating, online matchmaker sites, basketball games and gym memberships, who knew she would find him sitting next to her at the dentist's office? It was almost simple enough to laugh about.

"Now we need to find someone for Audrey," Carly remarked, drawing Audrey back into their conversation.

"How about J. R.?" Sherilyn suggested. "You guys should have seen the way he was checking her out at lunch."

"Oh, no you don't!" Audrey warned them. "Don't go dragging me into this macabre bridal cult you've got going here."

"Oh, come on," Fee said seriously, staring at her over the top of her glasses, raising one arched eyebrow under short ebony bangs. "Join us. You know you want to."

Audrey raised both hands, making a cross out of her index fingers. "Get back, I warn you. I have garlic and a *Single & Loving It* T-shirt, and I'm not afraid to use them."

"Join us, join us, join us." Fee led them into a sort of chant, and they all followed, slowly closing the circle around her.

Audrey covered her head with both arms and shrank away from them, cackling at the absurdity of it all.

"Join us, join us, join us."

"So how is it, being back home on American soil?"

"Better than I have words to tell you," Devon replied. "Hand me the slip-joint pliers."

J. R. grabbed the tool from the rusty red box on the counter and extended it toward Devon, who lay sprawled under the sink.

"I appreciate you hanging with me today, J. R. I just want to make sure I get all of these piddly little things done before the wedding. We've got four days afterward for a honeymoon, and then I'm off to Albany while Carly stays here."

"What's in Albany?"

"Logistics Base."

"No more deployment?" J. R. asked, trying to disguise his hopefulness.

"Not for a while. Just me and six hundred other Marines working to repair ground combat equipment." Devon emerged from beneath the sink and shot J. R. a smile. "Nice and boring, I hope."

"I guess you could do with some boredom for a while."

"You have no idea," he replied, hauling himself to his feet.

Devon pulled two long-necked bottles from the refrigerator and handed one over to his brother.

"Red Rock Ginger Ale," J. R. sang as he inspected the label. "I haven't had a bottle of this stuff since I don't know when."

"Well, that's because you've been off flitting around the country. They don't make this stuff anywhere but good old *Hotlanta!*"

"First of all," J. R. said seriously, "I do not flit."

Devon chuckled and threw back half the bottle before setting it down on the counter.

"Second of all, it's what I do. Just like you soldier up and go where the Marines send you, I go where bike dollars take me."

Devon tilted into a shrug. "How's business anyway?"

"Russell set me up with a guy in L.A. Restored Harley-Davidsons are big business for the guy. I've sold twelve bikes to him, with another six on the horizon."

Devon nodded as he considered it. "I guess you're rolling in the dough then. Good for you, big bro."

"Not rolling in it," he corrected. "Still, I'm not complaining."

As Devon began replacing the tools on the counter into the box, J. R. spun one of the chrome chairs around backwards and sat down. The taste of ginger blended with pure cane sugar packed a spicy punch as he chugged back several swallows from the icy cold bottle.

"So tell me about this shindig tomorrow night," he said as Devon clamped shut the toolbox. "Carly says everyone has to go in costume. What's up with that?"

"Yeah, but not you."

"Why not me?"

"Look atcha!" Devon exclaimed. "Faded out jeans, black T-shirt, and a leather jacket—that shaggy hair of yours and a couple days' growth of beard. You already look like a character straight outta *Easy Rider*, man. You *live* the costume."

J. R. brushed him off with the wave of his hand before drinking down the rest of the ginger ale.

"It's fine for a night of burgers, bowling, and sock-hopping," Devon continued, "but afterward maybe you wanna think about a shave and a haircut. My treat."

"What, you want me to look like you, Marine?"

"You should be so lucky."

"Ha!" J. R. popped with laughter.

"Hey, I'm a stud, Dennis Hopper. Ask anybody. I'm adorable."

"You? *Adorable?* Please. That crew cut doesn't make you adorable, Dev. It makes you a soldier."

Devon got up and smacked J. R.'s shoulder as he passed him. "Carly's got my truck today so I can change the oil in her car. Gimme a hand?"

"Yeah, all right."

J. R. stayed planted for another couple of beats, thinking about how great it felt to exchange barbs with his little brother again. He'd spent a lot of months worrying—and praying, truth be told—wishing for an afternoon just like this one.

"C'mon, old man. Get it in gear!"

He chuckled and pushed off from the chair. "Yeah, yeah. On my way. Man, the Marines sure have made you bossy."

"Well, yeah. They're the Marines!"

J. R. smacked the doorjamb with a laugh as he headed for the garage. "Semper fi."

"You know it. Salute when you say that, bro."

Audrey stepped out of the bathroom and closed the door behind her. Carly had moved into this house the very next day after the city hall wedding, and she'd converted it into a real family home for her and Devon since then.

Both walls of the wide hallway displayed framed photographs arranged in a synchronized pattern. On one side were childhood memories and family photos, Devon's interspersed with Carly's. Several black and white photographs matted in identical brushed nickel frames chronicled the many Barbie and Ken weddings the twosome had coordinated over the years; one of them in particular stopped Audrey in her tracks as she locked into the smiling eyes of her grandmother, standing over a small two-layer wedding cake with paper doll bride and groom as the topper.

"She was so beautiful," Carly said softly as she slipped her arm around Audrey's shoulders. "It seems like just yesterday, doesn't it?"

"No," she replied in a whisper. "A million years ago to me."

Carly squeezed her closer and kissed Audrey's cheek.

With their arms locked, they strolled the length of the hall, pausing at each grouping of photographs.

"When do your folks arrive?" Audrey asked when they stopped in front of the family photo of Carly and her parents.

"Dad arrives the afternoon of the wedding, and he leaves the very next morning."

"And your mom?"

"She's not coming."

Audrey turned toward her and frowned. "She's not coming?"

"She and my dad have been divorced for five years, and the two of them haven't been in the same vicinity one time since."

"But her daughter's wedding? I'm sorry, Caroline."

"She doesn't see it as my real wedding anyway. You know my mom. She says this is just my big after-the-fact waste of money and energy."

"Has she met you?"

Carly chuckled, and they inched down the hall a bit farther to another grouping of photographs. "Devon's so handsome in his dress blues, isn't he? He's going to wear them at the wedding. Did I tell you that?"

"No. But that sounds like a nice idea."

"Sherilyn has been researching military weddings, and she's got things planned down to the tip of the swords."

"Swords?"

"Yeah." Carly shrugged. "It's a tradition."

"I guess I hadn't realized how 100 percent military he is," Audrey admitted.

"Oh, yeah! He's United States Marine, through and through," Carly confirmed. "But then I think every Marine is. Devon says he bleeds scarlet and gold." She paused before tilting her head to Audrey's shoulder with a sigh. "I just hope he never proves it. With the bleeding, I mean."

"Me too." Audrey ruffled Carly's hair, leaving her friend's head where it rested. "You must go out of your mind when he's over there."

"I hold my breath the minute he leaves, and I don't breathe again until he's back in my arms."

"You know," Audrey said, and Carly lifted her head and leaned against the wall, looking at her with misty eyes. "You and I talk all the time, but you never really told me how you felt when he went to Afghanistan. It must have been horrible. Why is that, Caroline? Why have we never talked about it?"

Several seconds ticked past while Carly thought it over. Finally, she said, "It's a private fear, I guess."

"It doesn't have to be."

They shared gentle, quiet smiles.

"You're always so pressed for time, Aud. Your life is non-stop. Waking up in the middle of the night in a cold sweat, shaking with fear that I'll never see the man I love again—well, that just doesn't seem like something I can ask you to drop everything for and talk me through. Especially when it happens as often as it does."

"Oh, Carly."

Audrey's heart ached as she realized how tunnel-visioned she had become since moving to New York.

"I wish you were closer."

Audrey stopped herself from telling her friend that she may just get her wish. She wasn't going to be able to afford Soho much longer unless something drastic happened.

A sudden jingle drew their attention, and the two of them locked eyes for a moment.

"What is that?" they asked each other in unison.

"It sounds like—"

"Ohh!" Audrey exclaimed, and she pulled the cell phone from the pocket of her trousers.

"Wait just a minute. *You* have a . . . *cell phone*?"

"I know. Boggles the mind, doesn't it?"

"Well, yeah. A little bit."

The green light blinked beneath the screen.

Kat calling.

"Sorry. I have to take this."

"It's okay. Step into the office if you want to. I'll finish getting dinner on the table."

Audrey leaned into the doorway and pressed the green button, pointing the phone toward her mouth. "Hey, Kat. Did you hear from Kim?"

"Hold it like a telephone, Audrey."

"What?" She examined the cell for a moment before plunking it against her ear. "Are you there?"

"I'm here."

"Did you hear from Kim?"

The silence that followed screamed.

"Oh, no."

"I'm sorry, Audrey. She doesn't feel like you heard her. She says the sketches don't reflect her personality at all."

Audrey groaned slightly and closed her eyes, leaning back against the doorjamb.

"She did say she'd be willing to meet with you one more time, but I told her you were at your friend's wedding in Atlanta."

Audrey's heart throbbed in her chest. The sensation felt almost painful.

"She said she wanted to see more of your work, and I showed her some photos of last year's show." Kat laughed as she added, "I mentioned what a beautiful job you did on Carly's dress, and she asked to see it. I showed her the sketches and photos, and even though she loved the classic concept, she said it wasn't *three-dimensional* enough."

"Great."

"She actually offered to fly there to see it in person. Can you believe that? Uninvited, to a total stranger's wedding, just to get an eyeful of her gown?"

Audrey perked. "She did?"

"Audrey, no. Do not let Kim Renfroe interfere with your time there. Anyway, I said you'd be back in three days, but she doesn't want to—"

"I'll need you here too, Kat."

"What? You want me to come to Atlanta?"

"Yes. I want you to take the first plane out tomorrow, and make sure Kim doesn't come in until the morning of the wedding. That way, we can brainstorm, and you can free me up to do some sketches. I can be really prepared to wow her this time. You said she responded to the classic concept? She didn't communicate that to me at all, but—"

"Audrey, you do realize that there's probably a snowball's chance in a sauna that anyone is going to live up to the expectations this girl has, right? It's not even possible to please her!"

"She has a twenty thousand dollar-budget for her dress, Kat. She's got every media network in the country lining up to get photographs of her wedding day. The exposure alone could . . . Kat, it's the perfect storm for my circumstances. Dressing Kim Renfroe on her wedding day could solve all of my immediate problems."

"Audrey. I don't know."

"Call her and tell her to book a flight. I'll make hotel reservations at The Tanglewood for both of you. Get here as early as you can tomorrow, and have her come in the day after."

"You're sure?"

"Look, Kat. I'm hanging by a thread here. I have to take this one last shot. I haven't wanted to say this to you, but—"

"Audrey, I know."

She gulped around the lump in her throat. "You do?"

"I handle every piece of business on your plate. You think I haven't noticed that you're overextended?" Audrey nibbled the corner of her bottom lip without reply. "What about Carly?"

"Leave Carly to me. You just get Kim on that plane." She started to end the call, then caught herself. "Oh! Wait. And bring something fifties for us each to wear, will you?"

"Fifties?"

"Yeah, you know. Pink ladies and sock hops. We have to go to a fifties diner place tomorrow night for Carly and Devon. Everyone wears a costume, and I didn't pack anything for it."

"Fun!" Kat exclaimed, but Audrey just groaned and folded the cell phone shut.

She'd barely disconnected the call when she noticed J. R. standing at the end of the hall, and she jumped. "Oh, good grief. You scared me half to death."

"Sorry," he said, nervously tugging at the cuff of his long-sleeved T-shirt bearing a Harley-Davidson logo. "I didn't want to interrupt. Is everything all right?"

"No, actually," she admitted as she tucked the cell phone back into her pocket. "But I'm hoping for a reprieve."

"Anything I can do?"

"Afraid not, unless you have some influence over Kim Renfroe."

"The hotel magnate's daughter?"

The way he narrowed his eyes and looked at her as if she'd lost her mind made Audrey wonder for a moment if she actually had.

"Yes. Never mind. Anyway, I didn't know you would be here tonight."

"I'm staying here at the house with my brother while you and Carly play up the bride-to-be angle over at The Tanglewood."

"Oh." Why hadn't she thought about that? "Of course."

"Carly has dinner just about ready."

"Okay. I'll be out in a minute."

He was doing it again. Just standing there, looking at her.

Audrey sighed. "Didn't your mother ever teach you not to do that?" she asked him spontaneously.

"Do what?"

"Gawk at a woman like you've never seen one before. It's quite unnerving."

"I don't think I was gawking exactly."

"Well, your thinking is all wrong then. Because you are. You did it at lunch, and now you're standing there doing it again. Cut it out."

J. R. shook his head slightly, and the corner of his mouth twitched as if flexing hard to hold back laughter. And he didn't move a muscle to get out of her way, or to stop the gawking either.

"Do you mind?"

And with that, he simply raised a hand in surrender, heaved a sigh, and turned away. At the end of the hall, he turned back toward her for a moment.

"I'll be there in just a minute," she snapped.

"Fine."

"Fine."

"Okay."

"Okay.

"Aud?"

Audrey glanced up from her sketch pad to find Carly standing in the middle of the arched doorway leading to the bedroom of the hotel suite.

"What are you doing? Can't you sleep?"

"No. I had a surge of adrenaline shoot through me, and I had to come out here and try to get some of my thoughts down on paper."

Carly padded across the thick carpet toward her. She looked like that eight-year-old Audrey used to know with her hair twisted into a messy ponytail at the top of her head and wearing pink cotton pajamas with large red strawberries all over them.

"Is that for her?" she asked, peering over her shoulder at the sketch pad. "For Kim Renfroe?"

"I'm trying to give her some more options," she replied, dotting the skirt of the gown on the page before her. "She told Kat she likes the classic style of your dress, but she made it clear from the beginning that she insists on a lot of bling."

"Contradict much?"

Audrey chuckled. "Listen, I'm really sorry about cutting dinner so short earlier."

"No worries. But you know . . . I still can't believe Kim Renfroe is coming to my wedding. Isn't that weird?"

"Well, she doesn't have to come to the wedding, Carly. She just wants to see you in your gown. We can do that before you walk down the aisle."

"I don't mind if she comes to the wedding. It's kind of funny, that's all."

Audrey continued to put the finishing touches on the sketch, her eyes burning with the desire for sleep.

"Come on back to bed."

Carly extended her hand toward Audrey and just stood there until she took it. She led her friend across the sitting room and into the bedroom, releasing her hand and crawling across the length of the king-sized bed, collapsing into the pile of fluffy bright-white pillows on her side of it.

"C'mon," she said, patting the mattress beside her. "I'll tell you a story like I used to when we were kids. Remember that?"

Audrey nodded and climbed up into the bed. "You would walk me through Barbie and Ken's upcoming wedding in minute detail, from the fabric draping to the candles and flowers." Yawning, she added, "You've always had such a great sense of style, Caroline. Very imaginative."

"That's what makes me a perfect kindergarten teacher, right?"

She nodded sleepily. "Mm-hm."

"One of my students is just like I was at that age. Her name is Courtney, and she makes stages out of cardboard boxes, covering them in fabric or contact paper. She draws little designs on them and uses her dolls to act out these really involved little plays for the kids in the class—"

And as Carly chattered on, the sound of her voice sang Audrey into a lyrical sort of peace. Her words began to swirl and run into one another until nothing but blessed silence emerged, ushering Audrey downward to full-on sleep as Carly smoothed her hair and talked softly.

"I'd forgotten how you never sleep," her friend half-whispered. And those were the last words Audrey heard.

When she awoke, the other side of the massive bed sat empty. A bright ray of sunshine poked through the window like stretched-out fingers, pointing out a spot in the middle of the bedroom floor. Audrey surveyed her surroundings as a chorus of birds tweeted out a happy morning greeting from beyond the glass. The blue Atlanta sky grinned at her, slow-moving cottonball clouds shifting across it, and the fragrance of brewing coffee perked up her nostrils and drew her to her feet and into the living room.

"Good morning!"

She rubbed her eyes. "Kat?"

"Yes, Kat. Gee, how soon they forget."

"What time is it?"

"Ten-thirty," she replied. "Whatever Atlanta has in the water to get you to sleep longer than five hours, we need to bottle some and take it home with us."

"How long have you been here?" she asked, accepting the mug of creamed coffee her assistant offered.

"Not long. My flight arrived at 8:50, and Carly answered your cell when I called. Oh, and she told me to tell you not to worry about the spa thing this morning. She's going, and you should stay here so we can work. But—" Kat squinted her eyes as she recalled Carly's exact words. "—don't think you're getting out of the Jack-and-Jill because you're not."

Audrey chuckled.

"What's a Jack-and-Jill?"

"I guess it's a party or something. Like half bachelor and half bachelorette."

"Oh. Right."

"You're invited, by the way. Did I tell you that?"

"Yes. Wait until you see the dress I brought—"

"I'm sure it will be a barrel of laughs, but let's get down to business. When does Kim arrive?"

"Tomorrow afternoon at 1:45."

Still in her pajamas at 2:15 that afternoon, Audrey finally came up for air. Thankful for the sudden burst of inspiration, she'd tweaked the sketch from the night before and created two more possibilities.

"I have my emergency kit with me," she told Kat, mid-stretch. "I can use a few beads from that and—"

"You know what's an even better idea?" Kat interrupted. "If you get a shower and I order some food."

Audrey cringed. "Room service is so expensive."

"Then I'll go out and pick something up. You need to shower and get dressed before your friend comes back."

"Oh. Carly. I forgot."

"Your best friend. Her wedding. The reason you're here in Atlanta."

"I guess."

"Now, come on." Kat took her by the arm and dragged Audrey to her feet. "Do I have to start the water running too?"

"No, no," she growled. "I'm going."

"Good. I'll find a place nearby and bring sustenance."

Audrey glanced back at the loose sketches scattered on the table. "But let me just toss this last one," she said, heading straight for it. "It's not good enough."

"You'll shower, get dressed, have something to eat, and then you'll come back to it and decide," Kat instructed, nudging her back to her path toward the bedroom. "Now, go on."

Once again, no argument. Kat was right, as usual.

Audrey hated when that happened.

Top Three Trends in Today's Celebrity Weddings

1. The Destination Wedding

Celebrities just love tying the knot in a faraway, exotic locale. But for the non-celebrity, a destination wedding can be a glamorous and economical compromise. Fewer guests means less outlay of cash for wedding staples such as flowers and food.

2. The Glam Squad

No celebrity bride shows her face down the aisle without first surrendering to the skills of a top-notch team of make-up artists, hairstylists, and mani/pedi specialists. Brides everywhere have jumped on the bandwagon, often setting aside several hours before the wedding for a complete makeover.

3. The Green Wedding

Every good celebrity adopts a "green" way of thinking; if not to save the planet then certainly as a PR statement! Items such as invitations on recycled paper, proceeds geared toward their favorite earth-friendly charity included on the bridal registry, and even organic centerpieces make an effective "Goin' Green!" statement on behalf of every bride and groom.

3

Carly squealed when Kat walked into the hotel room. "You look magnificent!"

Kat struck a pose in the doorway. She wore shiny black flats and a black and white checkered dress with a pale pink satin sash, tied into a large bow at the front. A pink rhinestone bow shimmered on her shoulder, and a thick satin headband pushed her dark curls away from her face. Kat looked like someone straight out of *American Grafitti.*

"Where did you ever get that skirt?" Carly asked Audrey, running a finger around the top of the black sequin poodle appliqued to her violet skirt. "It's fabulous."

"Audrey's all about the vintage shops," Kat told her. "She actually had that whole outfit in her closet already! I just packed it up and brought it along for her."

Audrey fussed with the layered petticoat under the skirt and straightened the pink angora sweater with the pretty rhinestone buttons while Kat wrapped a thick purple ribbon around her bouncy ponytail.

"This is going to be so much fun!" Carly announced to them. "I can't wait for the boys to get here."

Right on cue came a *rat-a-tat* knock at the door.

Devon's soldier haircut fit right in with his plaid short-sleeved shirt and straight-leg jeans, rolled up at the ankles to reveal white socks worn with leather loafers.

"My little fifties nerd," Carly said with a giggle, and Devon yanked up the waist of his jeans with a snort. "Where's J. R.?"

"He's meeting us there." Devon paused for a moment before adding, "He's bringing Russell."

Carly's face contorted. "When did he blow into town?"

"Couple hours ago."

She frowned at Audrey. "You'll get to meet the infamous Russell Walker."

Kat launched out of her chair like a rocket. "What? What did you say?"

"Devon's brother is best buddies with Russell Walker," Carly informed her dryly. "So we get him by default."

"He's not one of Carly's favorite people," Devon explained.

"I think he's dreamy," Kat replied. Looking to Audrey for agreement, she added, "Isn't he dreamy, Audrey?"

"I've only seen one of his movies, and I don't really get it."

"How could you not get it? He's dreamy!"

"All right."

Audrey lifted one shoulder into half a shrug as she refocused her attention on applying a thin layer of Scarlet Kiss to her lips with a small brush.

"You chicks look like the cat's meow," Devon told them. "Let's scram."

Audrey glanced at Carly and Kat, apparently charmed by Devon's foray into fifties characterization. She wondered what was next, but she hoped it included a root beer float.

When they reached the lobby doors, Devon turned to Carly and beamed.

"What, sweetie?"

"I've got a surprise for you," he told her, leading her outside.

By the time Audrey followed the others through the door, Carly was already squealing, hopping from one foot to the other, her saddle shoes thumping on the concrete. Devon rushed forward and swung open the passenger door of a vintage convertible in the most terrible shade of aqua.

"It's a 1958 Chevy Impala," he announced as he rounded the car, leaving Audrey and Kat standing there. With a smile, he flipped up the seat behind the steering wheel and waved his hand. "C'mon, ladies. Your ride awaits!"

Kat blew past her and climbed into the car. "Audrey. Come on!"

Once she joined them, Devon slid in and turned the key. Dion crooned "Runaround Sue" from an oldies station on the radio. Devon had thought of everything to make the night special for his wife . . . *err, fiancée* . . . and the grin of sheer bliss on Carly's face told Audrey that he'd succeeded.

Pink and blue neon tube lighting welcomed them to Happy Days, promising *Burgers, Shakes & Pins*, and a valet in a bow tie and white paper hat appeared delighted to take the Chevy off their hands.

"Your friends are so fun!" Kat exclaimed as she skated across the gleaming wood floor behind Carly.

Emma gave Audrey a hug while Carly made the immediate introductions by pointing a finger frosted in pink at each person. "Emma, Jackson, Sherilyn, Andy, Fee, Sean, Audrey, Kat." And with that, Devon yanked her away toward the dance floor to join half a dozen other couples jitterbugging to "Rock Around the Clock."

Sherilyn suddenly shrieked and broke away from them, straight out the front door of the diner, leaving her husband standing behind her, shaking his head.

"What's going on?" Audrey asked.

"It's got to be Russell," Andy replied with a laugh. "Heaven knows none of us mortals elicit that response out of her."

Sure enough, Audrey saw Sherilyn jump into the arms of actor Russell Walker, the picture of a fifties beatnik with his shaggy blond hair pulled into a tight ponytail, wearing a black turtleneck and faded black jeans. Beyond the reunited friends, she spotted J. R. conversing with the valet, motioning with the hand gripping his helmet toward the two large motorcycles parked on the other side of the valet desk.

He looked almost the same as he had at dinner the night prior, except for the Fonzarelli 'do he sported. Leather jacket over black T-shirt, form-fitting Levis and slightly scuffed boots; a perfect fit for a theme party like this one, she supposed. So why did her pulse begin to race when he headed through the front door?

"Everybody!" Sherilyn exclaimed as she followed him, arm-in-arm with Russell Walker. "Look who's here!"

"Crikey!" he remarked in his trademark Austrailian accent. "The gang's all here, hey?" He greeted all of Sherilyn's friends before turning to Audrey and Kat. "Ah, fresh faces," he said, extending his hand toward Kat. "Russell Walker."

"Katarina Ivanov," she managed, if somewhat breathless.

"Ivanov. Great Aussie name, isn't it?"

Kat giggled, and Audrey turned toward her slowly. Kat was . . . *giggling?*

"Gwen Stefani, I presume," he stated, taking Audrey off guard.

"Pardon?"

"J. R. said you looked a bit like Gwen Stefani."

"He did?"

At just that moment, J. R. walked up behind them, and she narrowed her eyes at him.

"You think I look like Gwen Stefani?"

He and Russell shared a lingering scowl, and J. R. tapped his friend in the gut. "That's a new record, Walker. Dragging me into the mud in, what, forty seconds?"

"My work here is done," Russell cracked before turning back to Kat. "Katarina, will you join me in The Stroll?"

"P-pardon?"

He nodded toward the dance floor where the couples formed two lines and tapped their feet at the opening of the Mary Wells song, "My Guy."

"Really?"

"Ever so."

"Well . . . Heck, yeah!" she cried, taking him by the hand and dragging him off behind her.

Audrey watched them for a minute, grinning, and J. R. stepped up beside her.

"She used to be shy and retiring, right?" he commented.

"Not exactly. But Russell Walker seems to bring out the giddy schoolgirl in her." Audrey glanced at Sherilyn and chuckled. "And in Sherilyn."

J. R. blurted out one hard laugh. "You said it, sister. Russell says she gets him. She's the sister he never had."

"Speaking of sisters," she said, still focused on Kat out there on the dance floor, "I hope you know how blessed you are to get Caroline. Again."

"Anyone who inspires my brother the way she does is a blessing in my book."

Devon and Carly were next down the center of the two lines on the dance floor, and Audrey shook her head.

"You mean, inspires him to dress like a nerd?"

"There's that." After a chuckle, J. R. turned serious. "But also to have such joy waiting for him when he comes back from a place like Afghanistan."

Audrey looked up into J. R.'s steel-blue eyes and nodded. "She doesn't talk about it much, but I think she's all about creating a safe, inviting home for him to return to. It's really important to her."

"God bless her then."

Audrey swallowed around the lump in her throat. "And him."

"Amen."

They shared a smile, and Audrey sighed. "Do you suppose they have root beer floats in this place?"

"What kind of fifties joint doesn't have a root beer float on the menu?" he teased. "And if they have it with a burger and fries, I'm right there with you. Let's go find a booth."

Kat's eyes sparkled like perfect round diamonds over Russell's shoulder as Audrey passed the dance floor with J. R. The music had changed, and Russell took her into his arms for a slow dance to "I Only Have Eyes for You."

"There's one!" J. R. exclaimed, and he snatched up her hand and led her through the clusters of partygoers.

He stood back and let her slip into the red vinyl booth ahead of him. The chrome and laminate tabletop held squeeze bottles of ketchup and mustard, and copper-topped salt and pepper shakers. Miniature jukeboxes displayed the menu in plastic pages that turned inside.

"There you go!" J. R. told her. "Root beer floats. D-32." He pressed the buttons on the jukebox to place the order. "Cheeseburger and fries?"

"Perfect."

"B-8," he said as he pushed the correct order buttons. "This place is really unique."

"Just like Carly," she remarked.

"Did you see the cake she and Emma designed?"

"No. Where is it?"

J. R. pointed out the chrome counter at the front of the diner. A massive jukebox cake looked more like art than confection, and the top layer displayed the moves of two sock-hop dancers in dark silhouette.

"Good grief!" she exclaimed.

"I know," he said, shaking his head. "Emma is some kind of cake genius, isn't she? And she's diabetic to boot! Can you imagine?"

"Not at all."

The two of them shared a brief chuckle before Audrey turned serious and looked into J. R.'s eyes.

"Listen," she started, then flicked the edge of the laminate table with her fingernail several times. "About my behavior last night . . . you know, in the hallway before dinner."

"Oh. Yeah." He teetered on the edge of a smile, never quite giving in completely.

"I was rude."

"Ha! Yeah, you were."

Suddenly defensive, she countered, "Well, you really shouldn't hover that way and surprise a person, you know. And the way you just gawked at me—"

J. R. reached across the table and touched the top of her hand. Audrey went immediately silent.

"I can see that I bring out the worst in you, for some reason," he observed.

"Oh, no, it's not that—"

"No use denying it, Audrey. A man senses these things. But the fact is you haven't gotten to know me yet, or given me a chance to show you that I'm not really rude. The fact is I only gawk when I'm overwhelmed by unbelievable beauty. And you, my friend, are . . ." He shook his head from side to side as he withdrew his hand. ". . . breathtaking."

"Oh. Well, I . . ." His smile finally uncurled and spread across his face like a sudden sunrise. ". . . I don't really know what to say to that."

"You could try thanking me."

"Thank you."

"You're welcome."

She nodded, returning her attention to the tabletop as he slipped out of his jacket and tossed it to the booth next to him. She hadn't seen his bare arms before, and her whole body tensed up like a clenched fist at the suntanned and chiseled muscular arms before her. One of them sported a colorful masterpiece of a tattoo depicting a Harley-Davidson, a desert horizon, and a cross standing tall at the top of a hill.

"And now," he continued, "you could say something reciprocal back to me," he suggested.

Audrey couldn't stop the grin that blossomed. "Like . . . ?" she began. "Oh, I know. How about this: *Grease is the word!*"

He casually ran his hand along the side of his head, not actually touching the slicked-back pompadour, and Audrey laughed. "Or maybe I could say, 'Nice ink you're sporting there on your arm.'"

He shot a glance down at his right arm and the corner of his mouth twitched slightly.

"Or how about, 'Cool pack o' Lucky Strikes rolled up in the sleeve of your T-shirt'?"

"You could say that," he said, considering it carefully. "Except that they're candy cigarettes because I don't smoke."

Audrey chuckled. "In that case, chuck 'em out on the table, Fonzie. Let's share a smoke then."

J. R. kind of took her breath away when he grinned at her. "Maybe later." With a nod toward the waitress heading their way, he added, "Here comes our burgers."

"Two root beer floats," the girl said as she unloaded the tray. "Two deluxe cheeseburgers and fries. Anything else?"

"That should do it," he answered.

J. R. felt certain he'd never met a woman as competitive as Audrey the wedding dress designer.

"Last frame," she announced, hovering over his chair behind the score table. "You and Russell both need strikes, or Kat and I wipe the floor with you."

"Promise?" Russell interjected, and Kat encouraged him with laughter.

Grabbing Kat by the hand, Audrey forced an over-the-top jitterbug to the Coasters tune crooning at them from the overhead speakers.

"Speaking of *yakety-yak*," J. R. tossed at her, referencing the song and punctuating it with yak-yak mimes between his fingers.

She pulled away from her dance with Kat and stood over him, her hand on her shapely hip. "All right, smar—"

"Smarty pants!" Kat dove in and finished for her as she sank down next to Russell on the bench. "That's what she was going to call you. Smarty pants."

"Sure it was."

"Just get up there and throw your gutter ball," Audrey taunted, "so we can call this a victory for The Pink Ladies."

Kat and Russell sat side by side, Russell's arm around her shoulders, and Kat's hands folded neatly in her lap. When he noticed J. R. glancing at them, Russell nodded toward the alley. "Go on then. Show 'er how it's done, mate."

J. R. stood up, and Kat leaned forward and looked up at him. "Try to ignore her," she said, nose wrinkled. "She's stressed."

"So that's her excuse," he remarked, and he picked up the dark green bowling ball from the rack.

Audrey followed him, standing so close that he could smell faint traces of her perfume.

"You wanna back off a little here, Jesse James?" he pointedly asked. "Give me some room to slaughter you?"

"In your dreams."

He raised the ball to his chest and held it there, glaring at her until she took two large steps backward.

"Thank you."

Just as he extended the ball and started to pull it back for a roll, Audrey shouted, "You're so welcome!"

J. R. lowered the bowling ball and stared hard at her for a moment. "What is with you? Compete much?"

Russell and Kat snickered, and Audrey raised her hands in surrender and joined them on the planked wooden bench. "Go ahead," she told him. "The alley's all yours. Do your stuff."

J. R. cracked his neck and stretched it out. What an annoying little delicacy this one had turned out to be.

"Go on, J. R." Russell encouraged. "Take it home, buddy."

Clenching his teeth, he took careful aim . . . stepped forward—one, two, three—and he sent the bowling ball sailing down the alley. He held his breath as it rolled, releasing it with a shout when the ball exploded against the pins and knocked every one of them over.

When he finally turned around, she made quite a picture with her face all pinched up that way. He unabashedly broke into laughter.

"What's the matter, Jesse? Nothing to say now?"

She seemed to think it over for a long moment before perking up. "Well, Russell still has to make a strike. And that's not very likely." With an apologetic glance at Russell, she added, "No offense, Russell."

"None taken, love."

"Get up there and show her how it's done," J. R. told him.

Russell unfolded from the bench and stood there looking at them for a long and frozen moment before he turned to Kat and reached for her hand. When she took it and started to follow him around the bench and away from the alley, J. R. shouted, "What are you doing?"

"You can't walk away now!" Audrey countered. "You have one more frame."

"Russell," J. R. called after him. "What are you doing?"

When Russell turned back, his face was deadpan serious. "Saving you two from yourselves," he stated. Grinning at Kat, he added, "Karaoke, my pet?"

She nodded. "Sounds good. What will you sing?"

Audrey appeared at J. R.'s side, both of them with their hands on their hips and elbows touching as they watched Russell and Kat scoot away.

"I don't believe he just did that."

"I never liked him," Audrey added.

"Yeah, me neither."

"We would like to thank all of our family and friends for being with us tonight," Devon said into the handheld microphone from the karaoke stage. "You've all supported our relationship in some way, or you wouldn't be here, and we want each of you to know how much you mean to us."

Leaning across Devon to talk into the microphone in his hand, Carly said, "I'd like to introduce everyone to a very special person in this room. At least I know for certain she is beloved and treasured by my husband."

"Sorry, honey," Devon cracked, and Carly kissed his cheek.

"Emma Rae, can you come up here, please?"

Emma looked around in shock before her fiancé, Jackson, stood up and let her out of the booth. Audrey could see how uncomfortable the attention made her.

"When my wedding planner, Sherilyn, introduced me to Emma Rae Travis, it was to talk about our wedding cake," Carly announced, with her hand affectionately placed on Emma's shoulder. "It's going to be fantastic, by the way. But while we were talking about what she could do for us, I told Emma about tonight's party, and she dreamed up the design for this fantastic jukebox cake right over there."

Audrey noticed that the cake had been wheeled into the room, parked next to the stage.

"When I told her that Devon's best childhood memory was the marble layer cake his mom used to make on special occasions, she baked two different versions, and Sherilyn had us all over for a tasting."

"You can see where this is going," Devon interjected, and the crowd rumbled with laughter.

"So I am pleased to tell you all that you are going to experience the ecstasy Devon and I were allowed to experience that night at Sherilyn and Andy's house. So, Emma, on behalf of this entire room of, what, about thirty of our friends and family members, we thank you."

"Now, honey?" Devon asked pathetically, and Carly nodded. "Yes! The wife says, 'Let us all eat cake!' Thank you, Emma, from the bottom of our hungry, cake-loving hearts."

Applause filled the karaoke room, and Emma escaped the stage as quickly as she could. When she slid back into the booth beside Jackson, Audrey caught her eye, and Emma shook her head and grinned.

A photographer snapped away as Carly and Devon made the first cuts, and Audrey thought one more time that she'd seldom seen her friend as happy as she seemed to be with Devon. Her heart squeezed a little as she watched them, playfully sharing a slice of cake, pausing for a loving kiss.

Forcing herself to look away, she landed on Sherilyn and Andy, but the way they looked into one another's eyes at just that moment did nothing to dilute the regret pulsing through Audrey.

Wait a minute.

Happy couples were everywhere, in fact. Fee and Sean, as unlikely a pairing as Audrey could think of, their heads tipped close together and chatting as if no one else existed in the room; Jackson, delivering a cup of tea to the table and setting it down in front of Emma, and he kissed her hand as he slid in next to her; even Kat and Russell Walker had paired off. Audrey looked around eagerly, almost desperate to find one other single in the room. But they were all squared off neatly, the whole room of them, as if cordoned into two-by-two segments by some invisible coupling tape.

What is this place? Freakin' Noah's Ark?

And then her eyes landed on J. R. Hunt.

Watching her again, of course. He smiled one of those smoldering, casual smiles at her from the other side of the room.

Oh, for crying out loud. Quit your gawking.

There had to be someone else uncoupled in the place, and Audrey set out to find them. Her gaze moved to and fro, from table to table to table, until she found one, two—*no, three!*—apparently unattached singles in the immediate vicinity.

Not one of them looked even remotely interesting, however, and she noticed that her disappointment sort of sucked the air out of the room. She grabbed her bag and wove her way between the tables until she finally reached the front door and pushed through it. Standing outside in the cool night air felt good as she inhaled deeply. She closed her eyes and leaned back against the concrete wall of the building.

When she opened them again, Audrey jumped to find J. R. standing next to her.

"Smoke?" he asked, extending an open package of candy cigarettes in her direction.

Her first inclination had been to swat him for scaring her, but he looked almost adorable, so she shrugged and took one of them from the pack and held it loosely between her lips.

"Well?" she said with one eyebrow arched.

"Well, what?"

"Got a light?"

J. R. Hunt unexpectedly charmed her with a wave of laughter that sounded as sweet as church bells on a distant hill. And Audrey didn't have the good sense to listen to the other bells—*the alarm bells*—sounding off in her head.

"How about you take me for a ride on that motorcycle of yours," she suggested.

And five minutes later, Audrey lifted her petticoat, tossed one leg over the bike and hiked herself up to the back of the seat. With her cotton poodle bag pressed into his back and her arms tucked beneath J. R.'s warm leather jacket, Audrey held on tight as they flew over the hill and rode straight out of Sandy Springs.

"It's one of my favorites," J. R. said from atop the picnic table where he and Audrey had parked near the mill in Roswell. "I bought this bike and restored her with the intent of resale, but I just couldn't bring myself to let her go."

"Her?" Audrey repeated. "I sense a bit of a love affair going on here."

"You could say that."

"Does she have a name?" she teased. "Tell the truth. You've given her a name, haven't you?"

He waved her off at first. How could he admit to her that he really had dubbed his bike with the moniker of his all-time favorite female? Then, on a spontaneous whim, he shrugged and confessed.

"Tillie."

"Tillie!" she echoed with a laugh. "Tillie Harley-Davidson Hunt. I like it." After a moment, she coyly asked, "So? Out with it. Who's Tillie?"

"My family's cocker spaniel when Dev and I were growing up. I have very fond memories of my summers with Tillie."

Audrey's laughter twirled around him like a lasso, and it snagged him by the heart suddenly, tightening until he could hardly breathe.

"She's a '57 Sportster," he managed, shoving through to another subject beyond the living doll seated below him on the bench of the picnic table. "That was the year Harley-Davidson introduced the Sportster. I guess I've put six grand into restoring her, but she's a fine bike now."

Audrey pulled the candy cigarette he'd given her from the zippered compartment of her bag and lifted it toward him. "Well. Here's to Tillie," she said in a sort of a toast before she took a bite out of it and fed him the other half.

The moon hung low in the midnight blue Georgia sky, casting a silverish glow over Audrey that made her look a little like a porcelain doll in her petticoat and angora sweater. Her platinum hair turned to pewter in the moonlight as she stared out into the sky. Then, without so much as a glance in his direction, she sighed.

"You're doing it again, aren't you?"

"What?" But he knew what. And yes, he was staring at her again. He couldn't seem to help himself.

"You're watching me."

"Yeah," he admitted softly. "I am. How do you know?"

Audrey turned around and narrowed her brown-gold eyes. "I can feel it."

"Can you?" he asked, and he reached forward and sifted his fingers into the hair at the base of her ponytail.

She stunned him a little when she moved into his touch, and she closed her eyes for a moment as he tightened his grip on the back of her head. Vowing not to let a moment like this one pass, he dropped from the tabletop down to the bench beside her in one quick swoop, his fingers tangling into her hair until he pulled the ribbon and the cloth band clean out of it. Digging both hands into her loose silky hair, he pulled her face gently toward him and pressed his lips to hers.

They were soft and pliable, and she tasted like frosting. Wondering if she would let him, J. R. deepened the kiss. Slowly, cautiously. It was a little like stepping into a caldron of warm, simmering water, and J. R. could think about nothing more than the pleasure of plunging completely into it for a swim.

With no forewarning whatsoever, Audrey inhaled sharply. And then she gave him the biggest surprise of his adult life when she slid her arms around his neck and pulled him toward her enthusiastically.

J. R. thought he heard the distant sound of . . . *angel's harps?*

"She's a nightmare. As Kat often reminds me, there's absolutely no chance of actually pleasing her. And yet I continue to try because . . . well, because I need her."

"Look, you're a talented girl," J. R. commented as he stood over the sketches scattered across the table before them.

"Certainly, there's another client that can offer you what Kim Renfroe can, minus all the drama."

"Sure there is," Audrey replied, sinking into the chair beside him. "Angelina could ask me to design a wedding gown, and then make the covers of every magazine in the known world wearing it."

J. R. caressed the side of her face with his thumb, tenderly holding her chin in the palm of his hand. As Audrey looked up into his light eyes, a surge of electricity shot through her.

What was it about this one guy that just melted her down into a walking cylinder of warm liquid mush? Audrey had never been the type to kiss someone she barely knew. But one touch of his hand to her face, one crooked smile, and she had fallen to pieces! No man had ever had this kind of effect on her before, and it had a strange impact. She felt part powerless and part empowered.

Get ahold of yourself, Audrey. He's just a boy.

"There's no gray area for you, is there?"

"I'm sorry. What?"

"There's black, and there's white. No in-betweens."

She shrugged slightly, trying to smile, but it didn't seem to reach the surface.

"I suppose you're right," she replied, leaning forward with her chin in her hands, elbows propped on the edge of the table. "I'm sure there are lots of other opportunities out there for a designer trying to make her mark. But none of them came across my path. Kim Renfroe walked right up to my door and knocked. It was like some sort of . . . miracle."

J. R. pressed his hand on her shoulder, then he took hold of it and guided her to her feet. As she stood there facing him, hoping with all her strength that he might kiss her again—but knowing she shouldn't let him—Audrey swooned slightly. She tilted toward him, completely against her conscious will, and his arms engulfed her as she did.

They fit together so perfectly, and she nuzzled her face into the curve of his neck where it fell as naturally as one glove resting in the palm of another. He stroked her hair and leaned his head down toward her, his warm breath tickling her ear as he whispered her name.

Even as she moaned softly, Audrey thought, *This is very bad. What am I doing?*

And yet she raised her face toward him just the same. Closing her eyes, she allowed J. R. to kiss her. Before she knew it, her thoughts had descended into completely unfamiliar places; and if he'd have asked her, she would have gone anywhere with him. Absolutely anywhere, doing absolutely anything.

"Audrey," he repeated. "I have to go."

A diamond-tipped needle screeched across the record of the night, and Audrey looked up at him.

Go? You have to GO?

"This is a very dangerous attraction we've got going here," he told her. "Despite my basest instincts, I'm a smart enough guy to know that there's a fork in the road right now. And I'm going to choose the high one."

Yes. Take the high road, Audrey thought. *Thank you. Good boy. I hate the high road.*

"And you need to get some sleep before Kim arrives in the morning."

"Yes." It was all she could muster.

"Tomorrow is going to be a very big day for you, angel."

She nodded. "Yes."

"I'm betting on you."

Audrey managed to push a smile up to her tingling lips.

J. R. grabbed his jacket from the arm of one of the chairs in the sitting room and headed straight for the door. When he opened it and turned back toward her, Audrey imagined herself flying across the room and leaping into his arms. Instead, however, she remained firmly planted.

"See you tomorrow?"

She nodded. Again.

Just hang on. He's almost gone. Don't do anything stupid. Just stay strong and don't make a fool of yourself. He's—

When J. R. smiled and extended his arms toward her, Audrey instantly stalked across the room and fell into them. She slipped her arms around his neck and pressed his head toward hers until their lips met. When they parted, she felt breathless and faint, and she almost heard the audible *click!* as their eyes locked together.

"Well, isn't this a fine how-do-you-do?"

They both reeled toward the corridor where Russell and Kat stood there staring at them.

"Audrey, I was worried sick!" Kat exclaimed. "You just disappeared without a word."

"I-I'm sorry. J. R. took me for a ride on his motorcycle, and we kind of . . . lost track."

"Well, thank goodness you're all right. Why didn't you answer your phone? I didn't know what to think."

"But now we do," Russell cracked, shooting J. R. a boys' club kind of grin.

"No, you don't," J. R. snapped. "Let's go. These ladies need to get some sleep."

Russell leaned down and pecked Kat's lips. "Had a real bonzer bash getting to know you, Kit-Kat," he told her. "See you tomorrow?"

"Absolutely."

Russell looked at Audrey and winked. "Glad you're safe. Relatively."

Before she could answer, J. R. snagged Russell's arm and dragged him down the hall.

The door had barely latched before Kat moved in on Audrey. "Spill!"

"You first," she said as she returned to the table and began pulling the sketches together into a neat pile. "You and Russell Walker. That's an interesting and unexpected pairing."

She melted down into a string of giggles. "Isn't it?"

"So tell me what happened. You two looked like dates at the senior prom."

"It felt a little like that," she said, crawling into one of the dining chairs and tucking her feet under her. "We couldn't stop talking, Audrey. After we left you at the bowling alley, we went for a walk, and he told me all about Australia and losing his family."

"He lost his family?"

"His parents and two brothers," she said, wide-eyed. "In a car crash."

Audrey sat down in the adjacent chair, reaching over and touching Kat's knee. "That's awful!"

"I know. He was only sixteen. That's when he came to America. Some photographer discovered him, and he did some modeling. But he lived in a one-bedroom apartment in New York City for two years with five roommates, and then he was homeless for almost a year."

"Homeless?"

"I know, but after that is when he got his first movie role and his career took off." Kat sighed and looked at the sketches in front of Audrey.

"Speaking of careers taking off, do you want to see what I have ready for Kim?"

"No."

Audrey blinked at her. "No?"

"No. Not until you tell me what led up to that lip-lock we walked up on."

"Oh. That."

"Yes, that. Audrey, for as long as I've known you, I've never seen that side of you."

"Well, I hope you got a good look," she said. "It was a momentary lapse of focus. It won't happen again."

I hope. That boy just . . . brings out . . . something . . . HEAT.

"That's a shame," Kat remarked.

"I don't know what came over me tonight. Maybe it's just the pressure that's been building. Maybe I just needed to let off a little steam."

"Or create some."

Audrey dropped her head into both hands. The groan that rose in her throat turned into a sort of growl, and she peered at Kat through her fingers. "It *was* kinda steamy," she admitted. "He is so hot, Kat."

"He really is."

"Oh, and he's got this unbelievable tattoo."

"Tattoo!"

"Yeah, it's all down his right arm."

"No. I mean . . . You like tattoos, Audrey?"

She hesitated. "I do on *that arm*."

The two of them snapped with laughter, then Kat's face turned instantly serious and she gasped. "I wonder if Russell has any tattoos. I'll bet I could Google him and find out."

"Or you could just wait and find out for yourself."

Kat chuckled. "It's not like I'll probably ever see him after we go back to New York though, is it?"

"You never know, *Kit-Kat*."

The way Kat grinned, Audrey almost expected her to meow. Instead, her assistant just quietly purred.

Carly's Marble Engagement Cake

Preheat oven to 350 degrees.

3 cups all-purpose flour
1 Tablespoon baking powder
¾ teaspoon salt
1 cup whole milk (not too cold)
2 teaspoons vanilla extract
1 ½ sticks softened, unsalted butter
2 cups granulated sugar
4 large eggs
4 ounces bittersweet chocolate

Mix flour, baking powder, and salt.
In a separate bowl, mix milk and vanilla.
Beat softened butter until creamy.
Add sugar and beat until fluffy.
Fold in eggs and continue to beat.
Add dry ingredients slowly, alternating with the milk mixture.

Transfer 2 cups of the batter to a small bowl and set aside.
Scrape the remaining batter into prepared cake pans.
Stir melted chocolate into the batter that was set aside.
Drop the chocolate batter over the plain batter in dollops and swirl with a butter knife.

Bake in the lower part of the oven for 40 minutes.
Let cakes cool in their pans for 15-20 minutes.
Remove from pans and transfer to cooling rack for at least an hour.

4

Oh good, you're up! Sit down, bro. Tell me about you and Audrey."

J. R. stood in the doorway to the kitchen in T-shirt and boxers, squinting his sleepy eyes as he scratched his head. He'd known that, one way or another, he would regret issuing the invitation for Russell to stay the night at Devon's; but seeing the two of them sitting at the kitchen table, a glass coffee pot and a couple of mugs between them, brought the regret floating to the surface sooner than expected.

"Are you impaired, you idiot?" he asked, smacking Russell's shoulder. "I asked you not to make a big deal out of it."

Russell could hardly respond through the laughter. "I didn't. I just casually mentioned how Kat and I happened upon you and Audrey . . . while you were . . . you know . . . sucking her face off."

Devon burst into cackling laughter, bumping fists with Russell as J. R. turned away and ignored them both, pulling a cup down from the cabinet.

"Did you leave me any coffee, at least?"

Russell picked up the near-empty carafe and waved it at him. "Sorry, mate."

J. R. snatched it from his hand and set about making a fresh pot.

"So seriously," Devon said, and J. R. groaned. "What is going on with you two? Anything?" When he didn't answer, his brother popped up from his chair and stood next to him at the counter. "I think you two are a pretty good match, bro. You think it might go anywhere?"

"What? I dunno."

"I mean, don't tell Carly I said so, but she's hot, man. You could do a lot worse."

"Yeah."

"And has!" Russell chimed in.

J. R. turned around and faced Russell seriously. "That's enough outta you."

"C'mon, mate. It's just us fellas. Take a load off and fill us in."

"Fill you in on what? Like I can even talk to you two about anything."

"Hey," Devon objected. "You didn't just say that, bro."

"You want me to repeat it?"

"J. R."

"You're all . . ." He scrunched up his face and imitated Devon. "'. . . c'mon, tell me all about it 'cause she's *hot*.'" Flipping the button on the coffee maker, he turned back toward Russell. "And you! You're the worse of both of you."

"Me?"

"Yeah, you. You couldn't even wait until I hauled my butt out of bed and opened my eyes before you gave my little brother all the sordid details?"

Devon and Russell exchanged glances before Devon asked, "Was it sordid, bro?"

J. R. slid his empty cup along the counter as he left.

"Hey, come on!" Devon called after him. "Hey! It's my wedding day."

"You're an infant."

"Your room is way better than mine."

Audrey took a deep breath. "Well, it's actually not my room. It's Carly's."

"It's still better than mine."

Kim dropped her bag and jacket on the table on her way to the large window. She stood before it, raking coral acrylic fingernails through her long black hair.

"It's the bridal suite," Audrey told the back of her head. "I think it's better than every room. I mean, I think it's *supposed* to be."

Kim turned around and narrowed her cat eyes. "I don't understand. Why are you in the bridal suite?"

"Carly invited me to stay with her until the wedding."

"Oh, that's right. You're the maid of honor, aren't you?"

Audrey nodded. "Why don't you come on over to the table and have a seat. Can I get you some coffee or—"

"Nothing. I'm on a cleanse."

"Oh. Okay. Well, let me show you what I've worked up for you."

"Let's see the dress first."

"Oh. Well, I—"

"Better yet, why don't I try it on," she said, heading straight for the bedroom. "Is it in here?"

"Uh, Kim, no. I don't really think Carly wants anyone else trying on her dress."

Kim propped a hand on her hip. "Well, I'll give it right back," she said, indignant. "It's not like I won't let her use it after."

Audrey sighed. Her mind raced with a few dozen objections, none of which were likely to deter Kim from getting what she wanted. But there was no way she was going to let her step into Carly's wedding dress without—

At just that moment, the hotel room door swung open, and Carly breezed in, followed by Kat.

"You really should have come. Anton Morelli's restaurant lays out a real spread for breakfast. I had the most . . . Oh! I'm sorry. I didn't know you had arrived," she told Kim. "I'm Carly."

"The bride," Kim noted with a wide smile. "Congratulations."

"Thanks."

"Hi, Kim," Kat greeted her. "How was your trip?"

"Oh, it was fine. But my room isn't as nice as this one."

Kat chuckled. "Well, this is the bridal suite."

"So I've been told."

"Carly, we were just talking about your dress," Audrey interrupted. "I thought you could slip into it and model for Kim so she can get a close look at it." Turning to Kim, she added, "There's nothing like seeing it on a bride, from all angles, to get a clear three-dimensional picture of a gown."

Kim thought it over, and Audrey breathed a sigh of relief when she nodded. "That seems logical. Yes. Let's do that."

"Oh, I'd love to!" Carly sang. "Just give me five minutes. Kat, do you want to help me?"

Carly grabbed Kat's hand before she had the chance to reply, then bounded into the bedroom and closed the door behind them.

"She's cute," Kim said, and Audrey thought it sounded like something a person would say when they saw a kitten but weren't really much of a cat person.

"While she's getting into it, why don't you come over and have a look at these other designs," Audrey suggested, spreading them out across the table. "I've taken everything you said to me, and later to Kat, and I've incorporated them into a few different customized alternatives that I think you're really going to like."

Kim waltzed over toward the table and grazed each sketch with half-mast attention. "Mm-hm," she muttered over the second one, a satin pleated drop-waist with pick-up skirt.

"With that one, I can do a twenty-foot train for the ceremony that can be removed for the reception for dancing."

"I do want to be free to dance," Kim said without looking up from the next gown. "But I might want to have a separate party dress that I can change into."

Audrey had suggested that very idea to Kim at their first consultation, and she'd immediately shot it down.

Kat opened the bedroom door and stepped out with a huge grin on her face. When Carly followed, Audrey's hand instinctively lifted to her heart, and she sighed. No matter how many entrances she made, Carly always took her breath away. That was definitely *her dress!*

"Oh, it's stunning," Kim said with a sigh.

"Isn't it?" Kat added. "Carly, you look exquisite."

Immediately, Kim turned to Audrey and said, "That's the dress."

"I'm sorry, what?"

"I don't want any of these others. I want that one."

"Not exactly this one, right?" Carly clarified. "I mean, this is *my dress*. One-of-a-kind. Audrey designed it just for me."

"Well, you can make another one, can't you? The same dress, maybe with a little more cleavage?"

Audrey's heart began to race, and the damp, wide-eyed expression on Carly wasn't helping it to slow down.

"Kim, I thought you wanted that same thing—to have a dress that is uniquely yours. A dress that no one else has ever worn before."

And Audrey heard the words before they ever left Kim's mouth. Kim turned to Carly, and declared, "I'll buy you another dress. I want that one."

Audrey cringed and covered her face with both hands.

"No!" Carly exclaimed. "I'm getting married in seven hours. And I'm wearing this dress."

"Audrey?"

She tilted her head and looked at Kim. Was she for real? "I'm sorry, but no. I think Kat was very clear about you coming here and seeing Carly's dress. It was just so you could see my design in person. This dress is not an option for you. I have five alternatives for you right here . . ."

"Listen," Kim interrupted as she moved toward Carly. "I'll give you twice what you paid for this dress, and I'll pay for another one to replace it. You think about it."

As she headed for the door, Audrey followed. "I have an appointment with Weston LaMont at his showroom out in Buckhead," she announced. "I'm going to see what he has in mind for me."

"You're seeing another designer while you're here?"

"If your friend will give up her dress, I'll go with you. If not, well, then I need to keep looking."

And with that, Kim left the hotel room and headed down the hall.

Audrey just stood there, her mouth as wide open as the door, her heart pounding. She tried to speak, but all that came out was a funny little grunt. Looking to Kat, she produced the same sound again.

"I know," Kat said, shaking her head.

"Well, she's horrible," Carly cried out. "Just . . . just . . . horrible!"

Kat walked around Audrey and shut the door. Taking Audrey's arm, she led her toward the sofa and nudged her down to it. A moment later, back at Audrey's side, she handed her a cold bottle of water with the cap already untwisted. Audrey could barely hold the bottle, much less drink from it, and she just sat there, her mouth still open, her heart still thudding in her chest.

"I can't believe she wanted me to choose a different dress seven hours before I get married!" Carly said. "Aud, you don't really want me to, right?"

Audrey closed her eyes and shook her head to rattle around some clear thinking in it. "Of course not."

"I mean, I know you designed it. But as a wedding gift. I mean, it's my dress, right?"

"Yes."

"It is, right?" she asked Kat.

"It is abolutely your dress, Carly. Now why don't you go on and get out of it so it's fresh for you later on."

"Okay." But Carly just stood rooted to the spot. "Aud?"

She shook her head again, and when she looked up at Carly, she saw that her friend's eyes had misted over with emotion. Audrey rose from the couch and crossed to her side.

"She's a lunatic," Audrey reassured her with a squeeze to her hand. "That dress is one hundred percent Caroline Hunt. No one is walking down any aisle in any city in any venue in that dress except you."

Carly sighed and smiled. "Thank you."

"Are you kidding? She's nutso."

"She really is," Carly replied. "But thank you."

"Do you need help getting out of the dress?"

"No. I'm good."

The minute she left the room, Audrey turned around, and her eyes locked into Kat's.

"I'm really sorry," Audrey told her.

"You're sorry? For what?"

"I thought Kim was the answer."

"I know."

"But clearly . . ."

"It's okay, Audrey," Kat reassured her, taking her hand and shaking it. "It's going to be okay."

"You really believe that?"

"I absolutely do."

"Good," she said with a nod. "Because you're fired."

"Dude," Fee sympathized. "That bites."

"It really does," Audrey said as she plucked her fourth cookie from the platter between them.

"Do you think you'll be able to bring her around to looking at your other designs again?" Emma asked, and she picked up the cookie on the napkin before her and bit off a sizeable chunk of it.

"I'm not—" Audrey stopped mid-word and gasped. "Emma! Are you eating cookies?"

"Yeah."

"Aren't you diabetic?"

Emma chuckled. "Thanks for watching out for me, but this is a sugar-free recipe I'm trying out."

"These are sugar-free?"

"Yep."

"Really," Audrey clarified. "They're delicious!"

"You think so?"

"Honestly. You are really good at this baking thing."

The corner of Emma's mouth twitched slightly as she replied, "Thanks, Audrey."

"It's important that some people succeed at their chosen craft, don't you think? Not like the rest of us who fail miserably and land on our duffs with a thud."

Emma whimpered as she rounded the table and wrapped a sympathetic arm around Audrey's shoulders and squeezed. "Sorry."

"It's okay. Really. I hate New York anyway."

"You do?" Kat asked from the doorway.

"Yeah. I do."

"Why don't I know this?"

Audrey lifted up the plate of cookies and extended it toward Kat. "Try one of these. Emma's a genius."

Kat took one and moaned at first taste. With a full mouth, she told Emma, "*Theesh are yummm.*"

"How many of them can I safely eat without puking or something?" Audrey asked.

"You may have passed that limit a couple of cookies ago," Fee stated.

"Then I'd better stop," she said, and she took another bite.

"Hey," Sherilyn interjected, and she timidly pointed at Kat before tapping her own throat. "Kat, I love the necklace."

A single strand of floating pearls, with a dangling rhinestone heart. One of Kat's originals.

"Thanks," Kat replied without revealing that she'd designed it herself.

"It's really beautiful," Sherilyn said, approaching for a closer look. "So dainty, but really eye-catching."

Audrey waited, but Kat didn't confess. So she did it for her.

"Kat dabbles in jewelry design. That's one of hers."

"You made this?"

Kat nodded, twirling a lock of hair around her finger. "Yeah."

"It's stunning! You should really get these on the market. Have you ever—"

"It's just something I mess around with. I've taken a few classes."

Sherilyn looked at Audrey, her blue eyes wide and one eyebrow arched. "Right?"

"I know," Audrey answered. "It's beautiful."

Kat plunked down on the stool beside Audrey and bumped her shoulder. "Really? You hate New York?"

"Everything about it."

"Everything?"

"Well," Audrey corrected. "Not everything. I like you. And I *love* the pizza at Maggio's."

"That's it?"

She thought it over for a moment and nodded. "Yeah. That's it."

"I guess this is stating the obvious, but what are you doing there then?" Fee asked.

"I'm a designer. It's New York."

"Oh. I guess there's that."

"The good news is I'm about to be an ex-designer. So the world is my oyster," she announced. "I can live under any bridge in any city I choose."

Emma tilted her head to Audrey's shoulder. "You can always come back to Atlanta, right?"

"Why?" she asked seriously. "Are you hiring?"

The kitchen door swung open, and an elf of a woman poked her head inside. "Emma, you need to come next door."

"Hey, Pearl. Come on in and meet Audrey and Kat. They're—"

"Good to meet you," the woman interrupted. "But really, you want to come next door now."

"What's going on?" Emma asked as she hopped off the stool.

"Your aunt is here."

"She is?"

"And she's just wandered into Anton's kitchen."

"Ohh!" Emma's face cemented over with sheer panic as she hurried out the door behind Pearl.

"C'mon," Fee said with a nod of her head. "She may need reinforcements."

Kat and Audrey exchanged glances before they followed the line of women around the corner and through the identical swinging door beside the one leading to Emma's kitchen.

"Aunt Soph, what are you doing in here?" Emma asked, gingerly taking the hand of an elegant woman in a light blue party dress draped with a large white apron.

"Oh, Emma Rae. Have you met Anton?" she asked, reaching for the wooden spoon Emma removed from her hand.

The short man in a matching apron huffed as he snatched the spoon and began to stir the steaming pot on the stove.

"Yes, I have," Emma said, nodding with animation directed at the the man. "Anton Morelli, meet Audrey Regan and Kat Ivanov. They're dress designers."

Morelli looked Audrey over like a pork chop he considered breading, and he muttered something indecipherable before moving on to Kat.

"Good to mee—," Audrey began, but he cut her off, mid-word.

"Ivanov," he repeated, focusing on Kat with slightly narrowed eyes.

"Yes."

"Russki."

"Um, yes."

The man glanced at Pearl, his waif of a sous chef, then back at Kat. He rubbed his bulbous nose with a balled fist as he asked her something in another language.

Everyone in the room turned toward Kat curiously.

"Oh, my father's family is from Chechnya."

"Da," he muttered, nodding. Then he tried out her first name as if simultaneously spitting a lint ball from his tongue. "Kat."

"Katarina," she replied, and a smile spread across his round face like a warm pat of butter.

"Ah! Katarina Ivanov."

"Yes. But I can't take credit for it. I was born in Abilene."

The man turned to Fee and looped his arm into hers, pulling her toward him. "America is indeed the melting pot of the civilized world, is it not, Fiona Bianchi?"

"We're a smorgasbord," she replied, deadpan.

"You," he said, pointing his finger at Kat's face. "You come to eat in my restaurant. I make you some borscht, a little *tabaka*. Yes?"

"That would be lovely," she answered, and Audrey knew Kat well enough to recognize the forced smile. "Thank you."

"Come on, Aunt Soph," Emma interjected. "I'm trying a new recipe, and I really need your help."

"Oh," the woman sputtered. "Well, all right. Anton, you don't mind, do you?"

Anton raised his hand and waved it, giving Sophie a hint of a smile. "Somehow, I carry on without you." After the elderly woman had passed, he shrugged at Kat.

"Chechnya," Audrey said as they rounded the corner and headed back into Emma's kitchen. "Who are you really, Katarina? I don't know a thing about you."

"And yet I know everything there is to know about you," she teased in reply. "Hmm. Quite a conundrum, isn't it?"

Before Audrey had the chance to respond, Sherilyn Drummond flew past her, nearly knocking her over as she tore into the kitchen and landed on Emma's heels.

"What's up with you?" Emma asked as she recovered.

"I'm so late!" Sherilyn cried.

"Then why are you stopping to tell me about it?" her friend countered. "Where do you need to be?"

"No!" Sherilyn exclaimed, looking around at the group of women gathered at the stainless steel table in the middle of the room. "I'm *LATE!*" she shouted.

"I heard you," Emma answered, taking a bite of a cookie and handing another to her aunt. "So why—"

"Emma Rae!"

"What?"

Fee stepped over to Emma and slipped her arm around her shoulder. "Dude. She's telling you that she's late." Emma thought it over for a moment, still not making it to the same page.

"I think I'm pregnant!" Sherilyn bellowed. With her hand on her hip, she shook her head and added, "Sheesh, are you on a sugar high, or what? . . . And what are you doing eating *cookies*?!"

Kat and Audrey made their way across the lobby, and suddenly Russell appeared from around the corner. His chiseled face brightened at the sight of Kat.

"Just the kitty-kat I was hunting," he said, taking her hand between both of his.

Audrey suppressed the inward groan. *Not now!* she wanted to shout at him. Instead, she just kept on walking toward the elevator.

"What are you doing here?" she heard Kat ask him.

"Getting out of the boys' hair for a bit. Me thinks J. R.'s had a snocker full of me, so I brought my suit and headed over early. How's about a spot of lunch?"

Audrey pressed the call button and waited, hushed tones of their conversation wafting here and there, and she wondered if J. R.'s day had already been wrung out too. The elevator doors opened, and she stepped onboard. She pushed her floor button and leaned back against the glass. Just before the doors closed, Kat slipped between them and stood next to her, grinning like a ridiculous schoolgirl.

"None of that," Audrey said, facing forward.

"Pardon?"

"No happiness today."

"Oh, all right."

"Thank you."

Kat remained silent for a moment, then asked, "No one?"

"No one, what?"

"No one is happy today?"

"No one."

"What about Carly?"

Audrey groaned. "Right. A wedding. Yay."

"So just to be clear. Carly can be happy, but she's the only one."

"Yes."

"Got it."

As she opened the door to the bridal suite, an invisible burst of unmistakable "happy" puffed right out at her. She hadn't even laid eyes on Carly yet, but she could feel it, all of that unbridled joy on the other side of the doors.

"I'm so glad you're back," Carly bubbled, fiddling with the thin purple rollers knotted all over her head. "Can you help me with my hair? Oh, and I had your dress steamed and pressed. It's hanging on the armoire. The bouquets should arrive in about thirty minutes, so I thought Kat could wait for them while we're in the bedroom figuring out my hair. You know, I forgot to ask you. Did you bring shoes?"

Audrey sighed, smiling at her friend as she nattered on. Every thought that crossed her mind seemed to take an instant conveyor belt right out of her mouth. Carly's enthusiam had boarded an express train, and Audrey no longer had the heart to slow it down.

Go ahead, Caroline. This is your day.

"Are you still thinking of wearing your hair up?" Audrey asked, casting a quick glance at Kat before they moved into the bedroom.

"I'm not sure. What do you think?"

"I could go either way, but I thought you looked really lovely before when you tried on the dress and the veil, and your hair was loose."

"Yeah, Devon likes my hair down."

"There you have it. Problem solved."

Audrey sat down on the bed while Carly stood in front of the mirror, holding up varied amounts of hair.

"I wish she could be here," Carly stated, and Audrey looked up to see her friend gazing back at her through the mirror's reflection.

"Who?"

"Your granny."

"Oh." A warm breeze of nostalgia blew by her, and Audrey smiled. "She would be so happy for you, Caroline. She really loved you."

"There was no one like her, Aud. And I miss her."

Me too.

"I'm sorry about Kim Renfroe."

This time, she said it out loud. "Me too."

"Do you think it would have gone differently if you'd given her my dress?"

"Honestly, I have no idea. She's a bit of a loose cannon."

Carly plopped to the bed beside her and rubbed Audrey's arm. "It's hard to hitch your wagon to a loose cannon, I guess."

"You have no idea."

"You have so much talent. You're gifted, you really are."

Audrey waved her off and turned away.

"I mean it. And she doesn't know what she missed by not giving you more of an opportunity to prove it to her."

"Thanks."

"You're going to get your break."

Audrey wanted so much to believe Carly, but she couldn't muster it up just then.

"You are. Kim Renfroe is a stupidhead."

Audrey pushed out a laugh. They had been using the term since childhood, but she hadn't heard it for years.

"Yeah, she is." She squeezed Carly's hand and smiled.

"I love you."

"Love you too, Caroline. Now let's start on your hair."

Wedding Traditions
When the Groom Is in the Marine Corps

- The Marine Corps groom wears dress blues.
- A boutonniere is never worn with a military uniform.
- The arch of swords—where six or eight Marines (or men in uniform) raise swords overhead as the newly-married couple leaves the altar.
  No one else may pass beneath the arch.
- The last sword-bearer forming the arch will often tap the bride lightly with his sword, saying, “Welcome to the United States Marine Corps, Ma’am.”
- If the groom is in uniform, it is customary for him to stand ahead of the bride in the receiving line.
- The official Marine Corps song is often played as the bride and groom enter the reception hall for the first time as husband and wife.
- A noncommissioned officer’s sword is often used to cut the wedding cake.

5

"I'm so glad we did this, man."

J. R. nodded at his brother and took a swig from the Coke in front of him.

"Carly never lets me eat like this. Today's my only chance."

"I'm all for the splurge," J. R. said with a chuckle. "But you better take it easy there. That's about your fifth or sixth Krystal burger, bro."

"Eighth."

"You get the trots on your wedding night, and who do you think she's gonna blame?"

Devon cracked up. "My stomach's made outta steel. You oughta see the stuff we eat in the desert."

"Still."

Devon stuffed the last tiny cheeseburger into his mouth. "You worry too much."

"And you don't worry nearly enough." J. R. thought about it a minute before he asked, "Speaking of which, how are your nerves about getting hitched? Again."

"Good," Devon replied over a mouthful. "I mean, I'm already Carly's husband in every way that matters. This is all just for her benefit, to let her have her dream, you know?"

"I'm just making sure you're ready, that's all."

"I was born ready," Devon quipped, his eyes sparkling as he grinned at him. "Carly's the one, man. Nuff said."

J. R. nodded, and any reply he might have made was pushed away from his thoughts as his cell phone pulsed.

"Russell," he told Devon before answering. "What's up?"

"I just saw your chickadee, mate. Got her britches in a wad. Thought you might want to pop over."

"Audrey?" he asked. "None of your Aussie nonsense. Talk English, bro. You're in America now. What happened?"

"Morning meeting left her eating dust," Russell cracked. "Kit-Kat says she's in a really harsh way."

J. R. groaned. "She was meeting up with some blueblood this morning. I guess it didn't go well."

"Not from the looks of it, mate. Thought you'd wanna know."

"Thanks, Russell. Where are you?"

"Tanglewood," he answered. "Gonna take my new sweetie to eat in a bit. Got my duds handy too, so I'll meet you boys here a little later, rightie?"

"Yep. Later."

J. R. folded his phone shut and tucked it into his pocket. A poke in his gut made him wonder why Audrey's bad news felt so personal.

"Something happen?" Devon asked.

"Yeah." Then, "Nah. Not really. You ready to go?"

"I was—"

"Born ready. I know."

As they climbed into Devon's bright red truck, J. R.'s gut lurched a bit. Audrey had been hanging her future on that morning meeting, and it just about killed him to know she'd been disappointed. He reached forward and cranked down the stereo.

"I'm just going to make a quick call," he said, and Devon nodded, still mouthing the words to the Keith Urban song whispering in the background.

"Honeymoon suite, please."

When the operator at The Tanglewood connected the call, Kat picked up on the second ring.

"Hey, Kat. It's J. R. Hunt. Is Audrey there?"

"She can't really come to the phone right now," she told him. "Can I have her call you?"

"Oh, man. Is she all right? Russell told me about the meeting."

"Yeah. It was brutal. But she's healing the wounds by diving into the whole maid of honor deal. She's painting Carly's toenails at the moment."

J. R. grimaced, trying to picture it. "Well, I guess that's a good thing."

"With Audrey, it's hard to tell."

He chuckled. "I hear that. Listen, can you give me her cell number so I can put it into my phone?"

"You mean . . . to call her?"

"Well, not right now. But later, maybe."

Kat giggled. "That's very optimistic of you. Yes, I'll give it to you. But don't take it personally if she doesn't answer. She's still working on embracing the advancements of today's world."

J. R. repeated the number three times before saying a quick good-bye, still repeating the number. He quickly tapped it into the address book on his phone as Devon cranked up the stereo again.

"Ah, Blake Shelton," he commented. "Love this dude."

Devon sang along, something about a deer head over somebody's bed. Had he heard that right? At the stoplight, Devon turned to J. R. and shouted the colorful chorus in full rock star animation.

"Settle down, bro," he said with a chuckle.

"Nah!" he blurted. "It's my weddin' day! And I'm marrying the most—" He poked his head out the window like a hound and shouted. "—beautiful girl in Atlanta!"

J. R. wondered if he'd ever find his match the way Devon had. He didn't figure any woman would put up with his lifestyle for long. Oh, he had a permanent place in Santa Fe to call home, but he sure didn't spend much time there. Four rooms with a couch, a bed, a stereo and some tools sat perched atop his real home, a large garage. He spent twice as much time on the road as he did in Santa Fe, and it had been such a long time since he'd even considered making room for the possibility of a regular someone; the saddest part was that he hadn't even noticed anything missing from his life until it reflected back at him in the mirror of his brother's life.

And until he'd spotted a platinum blonde pin-up girl who instantly tossed off a few sparks and ignited something J. R. wasn't even sure he'd *ever* felt before. Or if he had, he sure didn't remember it like this.

Devon's thoughts about Carly were more about a long-range future, a bunch of kids, a dog in the back of the truck, and a country song soundtrack than J. R.'s would ever be. Audrey Regan sure didn't have *that* in her! Not that he cared, of course. But still . . . he'd thought of little else in the last eighteen hours beyond the softness of her lips and the way she'd grabbed him by the neck and pulled him into another kiss.

J. R. rolled the window all the way down and leaned into the cool breeze, reminding himself of a wedding on the horizon. And after that wedding, she would go back to New York City, and he'd set out for Austin to meet up with another corporate raider type in a thousand-dollar suit with a broken-down Harley in his garage and a lingering dream in his head: a leather vest, torn-up old jeans, and the roar of their bikes as he jammed through the desert with his buddies who bore no real resemblance to Dennis Hopper and Peter Fonda anywhere except in his imagination.

"You're thinking about Audrey, aren't you?"

J. R.'s eyes popped open and he jerked toward Devon so quickly that his neck cracked. "What?"

"You can admit it, man. I can see that she got to you."

"What are you talking about?" he objected. "I'm thinking about my trip to Austin, you dolt."

"Sure you are."

The pompous, knowing smile on his brother's face made J. R. toy with the idea of slugging him.

"Hey, check it out. I haven't been to this bakery in years. Let's stop in for a couple brownies."

"Dev, are you joking, man? You just had eight Krystal burgers, fries, two Cokes and a lemon pie. Now you want a brownie?"

"C'mon," he said as he reeled around the corner into the parking lot. "These brownies will blow your mind."

Devon was right about the brownies at the Backstreet Bakery. They were great. But it was a little unappetizing to watch him shove three of them down in the space of about ten minutes. To make matters worse, he belched all the way back to the house, stinking up the cab until J. R. rolled down the window again in an effort to save himself.

"Man, you reek. You better gargle with Windex or something before you try to kiss your bride later."

"Yeah," Devon replied halfheartedly. "I guess I overdid it. I'll try some Pepto when we get home."

"I hope you have the industrial stuff because you're getting married in just a couple of hours."

Devon groaned. The minute he threw the truck out of gear, he pushed the door open and lost his lunch. Literally. All over the driveway.

"I can't believe this," he strained, bent in half, partway out of the truck and partway still in. "I can eat anything without it getting to me."

"All evidence to the contrary," J. R. replied, tossing his head back against the seat.

The next round began with more of a scream than a heave, and J. R. threw himself out of the truck in search of fresh air that didn't stink of fast food grease and curdled chocolate.

"Ah, man, Carly's gonna kill *meeeeeee.*" And it started again.

"Not if I do it first."

Kat laced up the back of Audrey's champagne satin gown, and Audrey used her fingernail to turn a few wayward purple crystals that had strayed from the pattern on the front of the sweetheart strapless. She placed the lavender silk scarf around her neck and passed the ends back to Kat to fasten into place as she slipped the lavender satin gloves over her forearms and nudged them smooth. Pushing a wave of hair back, she secured it with a rhinestone hydrangea clip and paused to check her frosted lips.

Kat leaned over the slope of Audrey's shoulder and grinned at her in the mirror. "You look like Grace Kelly or something. You're so beautiful."

"Aud?" Carly called out from the other side of the bedroom door. "You have company."

Kat shrugged, and Audrey stepped into champagne Paris pumps with lavender and pink jeweled embellishments.

"Those are really cute!" Kat remarked. "Where did you find them?"

"I had them."

"Of course you did." She giggled before adding, "Well, they match the fabric of that dress perfectly."

Audrey opened the bedroom door to find the bride standing next to the wrong groom. But J. R. looked delicious in his black tuxedo and champagne brocade vest.

Two-button notch, she took note. *Single breasted. Satin lapels.*

She fought off a swoon as Carly pinned a single lavender rose to J. R.'s lapel. When he looked up and his eyes met Audrey's, he jumped slightly.

"Hold still," Carly reprimanded. "There. That looks just right."

He blew out a breath noisily and shook his head before grinning at Audrey. "You look like a Grace Kelly movie."

"I know, right?" Kat chimed in from the doorway. "I just told her that."

"Aud, you really do look stunning."

It struck her as almost funny, coming from the most beautiful bride she'd seen in her life. Carly embodied every Happily Ever After fantasy they'd ever conjured up; and there had certainly been no shortage of those over the years.

"Uh, listen," J. R. said, railroading her eyes back to him. "Could I, uh, talk to you in private for a minute?"

"I have to put on my jewelry anyway," Carly said. "Kat, maybe you could help me?"

"Of course."

The two of them disappeared in a flash, latching the etched glass door shut between them.

"Actually, I need you to go for a little walk with me, Audrey."

"I can't leave—"

"Really. I wouldn't ask if it wasn't really important."

"Is everything all right?"

"Not exactly," he replied, and the way he narrowed his blue eyes at her sent her heart to pounding.

"I'll be right back," she called out to Carly without breaking away from J. R.'s eyes.

"What? Where are you going?" Carly asked as she pulled open the door.

"J. R. says Sherilyn needs to see me about the flowers. I'll be right back."

The moment they made it to the hallway and closed the door behind them, Audrey turned to J. R. with a glare. "Do not tell me that brother of yours—"

"Are you joking?" he interrupted. "Devon would marry her in a bus station every other week if that's what she wanted. That's not it."

"Then what is it?"

"Come with me," he said, and he pulled her by the wrist toward the elevator.

"J. R."

"Just come."

In the elevator, Audrey summoned up the courage to say what had been ricocheting around in her head. "Listen, J.R. . . . About last night . . ."

"Yeah?"

"I kind of lost my head with you."

"You wore it well."

The sly smile didn't help her resolve. She trudged through the temptation to kiss him again, and she took a deep bracing breath.

"The thing is . . . I'm not interested in starting anything with you. I hope that doesn't put a dent in your ego or anything, but I've got a lot going on, and—"

The elevator doors slid open and J. R. walked out without so much as a glance back at her.

"Okay," she said to the empty car. "Glad we could have that little talk."

They came upon Emma in the lobby just as Audrey caught up to J. R.

Emma gasped. "Audrey! You look amazing."

"Thanks," she managed. "See you in a bit."

J. R. muttered something that sounded like, "Yeah, later then. Okay," and never broke stride.

"Slow down, would you? These are five-inch heels."

"Sorry," he mumbled, but he stalked on at the same speed until coming to an abrupt halt in front of a closed door. "In there."

Curious, she reached out for the door handle, then hesitated.

"Go on. You'll see."

With a deep breath to brace her, Audrey pushed open the door and peered inside. Before she saw Devon, she heard him, roaring unceremoniously as he vomited into the trash can he clutched with both arms.

"Devon? What's—"

The noisy heaving broke her sentiment right in two, and she hurried inside and shut the door behind her.

"Hey," J. R. said, letting himself in and closing the door again.

"Devon, are you all right?"

"Uh-uh," he managed before whimpering. "No."

Audrey's eyes darted toward J. R. "What's going on? Do you know?"

"He sort of porked out today. We had lunch at Krystal, then made a stop at this bakery—"

"Ohhhh," Devon reacted to the reminder.

"When you say 'porked out,'" she began.

"Half a dozen of those little cheeseburgers . . ."

"Six of them?"

"Well, maybe more like eight."

"Eight!"

"Fries."

"Fries?"

"Lemon pie."

"Oh, come on," she answered with a moan.

"Coke and brownies."

"Is that it?"

"I think so."

"How could you let him do that?"

"*Have you met my brother?* I don't have any control over what he eats, or anything else, Audrey."

"I've eaten twelve of them before," Devon offered, peering up over the rim of the trash can. "I don't know what happ—" He paused to stifle a belch. "Happened."

"Oh, crud," she moaned. "What should we do?"

J. R. looked up to find her eyes on him, and he reacted. "What? Me? I have no idea! That's why I came to get you."

"Well, we're going to have to call off the ceremony."

"No!" Devon objected. "We can't call it off. She'll never forgive me." He pushed himself upright for a moment, then folded in half again. "You know better than anyone else how long she's been planning this day, Audrey. I just need somewhere to get cleaned up, and maybe something to settle my stomach."

At just that moment, the door opened, and Audrey reeled around on her heels to find Jackson Drake and Sherilyn Drummond standing in the open doorway.

"Wow, Audrey. You look gorgeous," Sherilyn remarked. "What are you guys doing?"

"Is everything all right in here?" Jackson asked them.

"Well, not really," Audrey replied. "The groom isn't feeling very well. Is there somewhere he can go, maybe to lie down for half an hour to pull himself together?"

"And maybe you've got something for an upset stomach?" J. R. asked Sherilyn hopefully.

"Andy should be here in a few minutes," she told him. Looking to Audrey, she added, "He's a doctor."

"Isn't he an orthodontist?" Audrey mentioned.

"Orthopedist," Sherilyn corrected. "But he has emergency medical training. He'll know what to do. Jackson, can you take our boy upstairs to an empty room?"

"Absolutely."

"And J. R., you come with me to my office. I have a stash of things for the nervous groom there. I'll send you down with it while I check on Andy's ETA . . ."

Audrey wanted to laugh out loud as Sherilyn kicked into full red alert wedding planner mode. Taking Devon by the arm, she helped him to his feet. "Go with Jackson, Devon." When he started toward the door with the trash can wrapped in one arm, she tried to take it from him. "Maybe you should leave th—"

"No!" Devon exclaimed. "I might need it."

"Okay. Maybe you're right. Go on now. Jackson will take good care of you."

Devon paused in front of Audrey, raising his eyes and looking a little pathetic.

"What?" she asked him.

"You do look pretty amazing," he managed, then effectively ruined the compliment by gagging.

"Yeah. Thanks, Devon. Now get out of here."

The moment they left, Sherilyn turned to Audrey. "Does the bride know?"

"No clue."

"Excellent. Let's keep it that way for the time being. You go help her finish getting ready. Don't tell her a thing, and we'll meet you two in the ballroom at I Do time."

Sherilyn linked her arm into J. R.'s and smiled. "You clean up like a movie star, J.R," she said with a grin, and she tugged him away with her. Just as they reached the center of the lobby, she called back to Audrey. "Bring Emma into the loop," she said, pointing out Emma, crossing toward them.

"Talk to Audrey," Sherilyn declared, and she and J. R. were gone from sight in another moment.

"She really is a wedding planner, isn't she?" Audrey said as Emma reached her.

"In every area of life," she replied dryly. "What's going on?"

"Can you walk with me? I need to head back up to the bridal suite."

"Okay, bro. Marines are in place, guests are seated. You need to go stand up there and wait while I walk Audrey up the aisle toward you. Can you do it? Can you hold it together?"

"Where's that doctor they said was coming?" Devon asked, his pale face misted with perspiration.

"Sherilyn's husband. He's on his way."

"Oh. Good."

J. R. doubted his brother's ability to stand at the altar on his own, but he had no choice. He nudged his shoulder. "Just go stand there. You know where to stand?"

"In the front."

"Right. Go on now."

"Ooo-kay."

J. R. watched Devon as he swiped his face with both hands and gave his head a swift shake.

"Dev?"

"I'm all right," he answered, waving his hand. "I can do this."

J. R. prayed that was true.

Once Devon took his place at the front of the room, J. R. looked around for Audrey. He glanced down at his watch for no real reason, then scanned the hallway in both directions, releasing the breath he hadn't noticed he'd been holding when she appeared around the corner, followed by Carly and her father.

Audrey hurried to reach him before the others, fiddling with two bouquets of flowers as she whispered, "Where is he?"

"Up front and ready to get married," he replied softly.

"Good work."

He repeated her words in his mind. *Good work.* Deadly serious, as if he'd just reported back after an important overseas mission.

Audrey turned to Carly and handed her the larger of the two bouquets, and she gave her friend a tender kiss on the cheek.

"I love you," she said sweetly.

"You too."

With a quick squeeze to Carly's father's arm, she hurried up beside J. R. and looped her arm through his. Hot tingling electricity moved through him as the music started and she nudged him.

She's not looking to start anything, he reminded himself. *Well, maybe I'm not either. Ever think of that? No, of course not.*

As they walked up the aisle, arm in arm, J. R. put the kibosh on his active inner dialogue centering around the irritating, stunning blondes of the world who kissed one minute and recanted in the next, and he focused on Devon.

He appeared to be fine, smiling and alert as he stood there in his dress blues. J. R. noticed Russell and Kat seated on the aisle, and he gave them a nod. But when he looked back at Devon, he realized that, the closer he got, the more peaked his brother appeared.

J. R. parted from Audrey without so much as a glance, and he stepped up next to his brother.

"You okay?" he whispered.

"Nope," he replied through clenched teeth and a broad, toothy smile. But one look at his bride as she and her father came into view, and he rescinded. "I'm good now."

Carly radiated as she glided down the aisle on the arm of her father. J. R. recalled that Devon had to really work to gain the trust of the man, but the two of them had bonded over a shared respect for the American flag and the Atlanta Braves. The man appeared at ease about turning over his only daughter into the hands of her chosen husband. For the second time.

It choked him up a bit to watch his brother accept Carly's hand, kissing it tenderly before he led her to the altar.

"What's wrong?" Carly asked softly, and J. R.'s pulse began to thump. "You don't look right." She darted her eyes toward J. R. "What's wrong with him, J. R.?"

"Baby, I'm fine. What are you doing?" Devon assured her. "Let's get married, huh?"

Carly glanced over her shoulder at Audrey, who nodded her toward her waiting husband. After a moment's thought, she sighed. "Sorry," she told the minister. "Go ahead."

As the ceremony got underway, J. R. couldn't help but look at Audrey.

Man, but she takes my breath away.

For a moment, he let himself imagine they were standing there for a different purpose, without another couple in a tuxedo and wedding dress placed between them. Her porcelain skin glistened, and just the casual way she held the purple flowers in front of her made him envy the lucky bouquet.

Devon managed his vows and "I do" like a champ. In fact, the Marines took their place in the back of the room, forming an arch over the end of the aisle with their drawn swords, and J. R. figured they were home free when the minister pronounced them "Husband and Wife, Take Two."

But as they moved in for the kiss, Devon wobbled slightly.

"Dev?" Carly said.

Devon muttered, "Sorry, swee—" And he collapsed to the floor.

Activity swirled around them as J. R. knelt next to his unconscious brother. He gave his face a gentle tap, but Devon didn't flinch. He felt the heat at the same moment that Carly sensed it, and both of them pressed their hands to Devon's cheeks.

"He's burning up!" she cried. "Devon?"

J. R. craned to search the room for Sherilyn. When he found her, he asked, "Where's Andy?"

"He just arrived," she said as she moved into the swarm. "Could we just have everyone stand back and give Devon some air, please?"

As they complied, Devon opened his eyes slightly and the corner of his mouth twitched as he looked at J. R. "Am I married?"

"Yeah, bro. You're married."

"Oh. Good."

And with that, he rolled to his side and proceeded to vomit all over the skirt of his new wife's elaborate gown.

J. R. thought the blood-curdling scream that followed came from Carly . . . until Audrey threw herself to the floor beside her.

"Not on the dress! . . . *Noooooo!!*"

Safe Cleaning and Preservation of Wedding Gowns

- Whether you're going to save your gown for posterity or sell it so that someone else can benefit from its use, your first action will be to have the dress professionally cleaned.

- Dry cleaning, although it does address soil and stains, does little to prevent discoloration over time. Professional cleaning and preservation involves more; preserving and protecting the fabric includes special treatment under special lights where soil and stains are cleaned by hand.

- It is recommended that a gown be preserved within three months of the wedding. Until that time, the dress can safely be stored in a clean, dry place protected by a cotton sheet or bolt of fabric.

- Never store a preserved wedding dress in a basement or attic.
Preferred locations for storage include a guest room or hall closet so that the temperature is consistent and levels of humidity are controlled.

- Inspect the gown every year or two in order to assure its safety.

6

J. R. went with Devon to the hospital while Audrey helped Carly out of her soiled wedding dress. Carly tossed on some jeans and an oversized chambray shirt, and Audrey quickly changed into a short cotton dress with triple spaghetti straps.

"Come on, come on," Carly whimpered as she waited at the door of the hotel room. "I have to get to him, Aud."

"I'm ready," she said, grabbing her denim jacket as she flew past the coat rack. "Let's go."

Kat and Emma waited in an SUV outside the front door, and Emma drove them to North Fulton Hospital. Squealing to a stop in front of the emergency room doors, she told them, "Go! I'll park and be right in."

Audrey didn't stand a chance of keeping up with Carly, so she let her fly ahead of her.

"Thank you so much," she said to Emma, leaning through the open back door.

"No problem," she said. "Go ahead."

Kat stayed in the front seat, and Emma pulled away from the curb the moment Audrey shut the door. Carly was nowhere in sight, but Russell nodded to her as he rose from a chair in the corner of the crowded waiting room.

"J. R. is with him, and now Carly."

"Should I go in?"

"Prolly not," he replied in his thick Australian accent. "Too crowded back there. J. R. will pop out and tell us when he knows something."

"You're probably right," she said, and Audrey dropped into a chair beside him.

"Kit-Kat with you?"

"Yes. She and Emma are parking."

"You be all right if I go find her?"

"Of course. Go ahead."

A little girl around four years old tottered up to her and smiled, batting long golden eyelashes. "I got pink boots," she said boldly. "You ever wear pink boots?"

Audrey glanced down at her own almost-to-the-knee taupe boots with a braided belt and buckle at the ankle. "Nope," she replied. "I'll bet they're pretty though."

"They are. They're prettier than yours." And with that, the miniature fashion police girl wobbled away to continue walking her beat around the waiting area.

Thanks for sharing.

The large glass door slid open and Emma walked in. "Kat found a place that will clean the dress, and she's on the phone with them now," she announced before taking the empty seat beside her. "Any news yet?"

"Not yet."

"Have you ever been to a wedding like that one?" Emma asked.

Audrey glanced over at her, and Emma's amused smile ignited a laugh from deep down inside. "No," she said between chuckles. "I never have."

"I've seen a lot of weddings," Emma told her. "And I can tell you I've never seen a groom puke on his bride before. That's a new one."

They both hopped to their feet as J. R. appeared and headed toward them. He carried the jacket of his tuxedo over his arm, his shirt sleeves rolled to the elbow, vest unbuttoned, and the bow tie hung loose around his collar. Just looking at him gave Audrey a little quiver.

"He's going to be okay," he told them as he approached. "It's his appendix."

"What?"

"Yeah. His appendix burst just as the ceremony concluded. They're taking him into surgery now."

"You're sure he's going to be all right?" Audrey asked him.

"The doctor seemed very confident. I guess they do this surgery all the time."

Audrey noted the glimmer of doubt in his eyes, and she ran her hand along his arm. "Then I'm sure he'll be fine."

"I know."

"Listen, Sherilyn texted and said they went ahead with the reception for all the guests. She and Carly's dad are keeping it all together. I'm going back to see if they need help," Emma said. "Do you want a ride, or are you staying here?"

Audrey glanced at J. R. before answering. "I'm going to stay here in case Carly needs me."

"When her heart starts beating again, tell her I'll put the cake into the freezer and we'll figure it all out later, but they'll still have a celebration when he's up to it."

"Thank you."

"Sure." She grinned at J. R., and he nodded. "You take care. Call if you need anything at all."

Once Emma had gone, Audrey let out a heavy sigh and deflated into an uncomfortable upholstered chair. A few seconds later, J. R. did the same thing, and the two of them sat there, wilted and glazed, staring straight ahead.

Finally, Audrey broke the silence. "So. Your brother's appendix bursts, and you blame it on fast food hamburgers."

"If you'd seen what he ate, you would have blamed that too."

"I've never really seen someone get that sick from a food binge."

J. R. turned sideways in his chair, but just before he spoke, the little blonde girl appeared between them.

"Yes?" J. R. prompted, but the girl just stood there staring at them. "Do you have something to say, young lady?"

"She probably wants to tell you that my boots aren't as pretty as her pink ones."

J. R. leaned forward, propping his elbow on his knee, and asked, "Is that it? You want to discuss high fashion with me?"

She giggled. "Nooo."

"Then what can we do for you?"

"I wanted to ask you something," she admitted.

"Yes. This, I figured out. What would you like to know?"

"Did you just get married?"

J. R. smiled and cast a glance at Audrey before replying, "You mean because of my tuxedo?"

"Yeah. Except for that on your arm—" She tapped a finger on J. R.'s tattoo. "—you look like Ken. 'Cept you need a haircut."

"Who's Ken?"

The little girl huffed and placed her hand on her hip.

"That's Barbie's boyfriend," Audrey informed him.

"You know Barbie?" the child asked.

"Oh, yeah. Barbie and I go way, way back. I've designed a lot of wedding dresses for her."

"You have?"

"Yep. And dozens of red carpet gowns."

"Wow."

"Wow indeed."

Finally. She'd surpassed the stigma of un-pink boots.

"What's your name?"

"Roslyn."

"Roslyn," she repeated with a nod. "That's a very pretty, grown-up name."

"What's yours?"

"Audrey."

She considered it. "Yeah, that's okay, I guess."

"And this is J. R."

"That's not a name," she told him. "Those are letters. They can only stand for something; they can't be a whole name."

He leaned closer to her and whispered, "They do stand for something. Do you want to know what?" She nodded. When he looked at Audrey, she nodded too. "John Robert."

"Those are good names. Why do you hide them?"

"I don't know," he answered with a chuckle. "I've been called J. R. since I was your age, and I guess it just stuck with me, Roslyn."

The little blonde looked up at Audrey with a serious expression. "You better call him John from now on so he doesn't forget."

"Maybe I'll do that."

Roslyn's mother called her over. "Don't bother the people."

"I'm not botherin' them," she said, rushing to her mother's side. "That lady makes wedding dresses for Barbie, Mommy."

Audrey's attention snapped in half as Carly came around the corner and stepped into view.

"Caroline. Over here."

She dropped into the chair next to Audrey and groaned. Audrey expected her to say something about a ruined wedding or never making it to the first dance. Instead, Carly rubbed her temples with her index fingers and said, "He nearly died, Aud."

"I know," she said, touching Carly's arm. "But he's going to be okay now."

Carly nodded, and she sighed as the realization set in. "Look," she suggested, "you two don't have to stick around."

"Of course we're staying."

"No, really. Go back to the hotel. I'm staying here with Devon tonight."

"Not exactly the ideal wedding night, is it?" J. R. asked her.

"Any night with Devon is a good night," she answered, and her eyes misted over with tears.

Audrey could almost read her friend's thoughts of Afghanistan and Devon's frequent absences. In that light, she supposed spending the night in the hospital together was a pretty good alternative.

"Why don't you go on back with Russell and Kat," J. R. suggested to Audrey. "I want to stick around until he's out of surgery."

"I'll stay too," she said, taking Carly's hand and clasping it between both of hers. "We can take off once he's all settled in his room."

Carly crumpled suddenly, tearful and trembling, and she leaned into Audrey's embrace. "Thank you," she whimpered. "Thank you both so much."

The taxi dropped her in front of The Tanglewood just after 12:30 the next morning. Devon's surgery had successfully relieved him of his appendix, but infection had threatened further complication, which came to fruition through a high fever spike. Carly hadn't left his side except for a quick run to the ladies room at midnight and, although the nurse had arranged for a cot to be placed in the hospital room, Carly remained planted in the vinyl chair she'd dragged alongside Devon's bed. J. R. had decided to sack out in the waiting room for the night, but he'd summoned a taxi and tucked Audrey into it before he did.

The hotel lobby echoed with an unusual lack of traffic, and the guy behind the front desk greeted her in a somewhat hushed tone.

"I was in the bridal suite," she told him. "I think I was moved to another room during the wedding?"

"Ah, yes, Ms. Regan," he replied, and he handed her a card key. "You're on the second floor in two-ten."

"Thank you."

"I heard about the groom's appendix," he stated. "How's he doing?"

"Bad news travels," she remarked with the twitch of a smile. "He's recovering nicely."

"Very good." He nodded. "Russell Walker was in the lounge earlier, and—"

"No need," she said, turning away from the desk. "That says it all. Goodnight."

"Goodnight, Ms. Regan."

The hum of the elevator seemed to accelerate Audrey's desire to close her eyes, and she tilted her head back against the glass. When the doors slipped open, she sighed, pushing herself forward.

Room 210 held all the charm of the bridal suite, on a much smaller scale of course. The tall queen-sized bed looked comfortable and inviting, and Audrey tossed the card key to the table and began shedding her clothes on her way toward it. In bra and panties, she yanked back the linens and dove in, tugging off one boot and tossing it at the chair before sliding her leg under the blanket. The second one came off, crashing against the leg of the chair at the same time that she flipped the switch and bathed the room in blessed darkness.

She moaned as she squirmed down into place and dropped her head into a cloud of pillows. "Longest day in history," she said out loud, and she punctuated it with a sigh as the distant tinkling of harp music lulled her to sleep.

In the next instant, or what seemed like it anyway, Audrey awoke to the clamor of Kat shaking her. The overhead light bore down on her like an interrogator's lamp, and she groaned as she pushed Kat away.

"Stop it! You're fired, okay? You don't work for me any more. Now, go bother a different person."

"Wake up, Audrey. You'll thank me tomorrow, I promise."

"I won't," she objected. "*I promise.*"

"Kim has been trying to reach you for an hour," she said, dragging her to an upright position. "She wants you to go downtown to some club where she is."

"What time is it?" Audrey whimpered.

"Almost two."

And with that, Audrey folded over and plopped face down into the pillow.

"She wants to talk about her wedding gown, Audrey."

She moaned. "Now?"

"Right now."

"I'm too tired to know for sure. Do I care?"

"I'm almost certain that you do."

Audrey groaned again. "Ah, *maaan.*"

"I know. But do you want to blow her off tonight and then kick yourself tomorrow?"

"It is tomorrow."

"I can turn off the light and go away." Kat offered, albeit insincerely.

"Okay."

"Really?"

Reluctantly: "No."

Twenty minutes later, Kat and Audrey raced through the lobby for the second time in less than twenty-four hours and pushed through the front doors. Russell revved the engine of an SUV and grinned at them.

"I feel like the getaway driver," he joked as Audrey climbed into the back seat. "Want we should knock over a convenience store on the way?"

"Don't even joke like that," Audrey warned him. "Whose car is this?"

"Russell borrowed it from the wedding planner," Kat said from the front passenger seat.

"Sherilyn?"

"She's a real cobber," he told them.

"Do you know where you're going?" Audrey asked, buckling her seatbelt.

"Oh, yeah," he assured her.

A moment later, Kat leaned over toward Russell. "Is that true?"

"Nah."

Audrey moaned as Kat plucked her cell phone from her bag and began pressing buttons. Another instant, and Kat spoke into the phone. "Find Opera Nightclub, Atlanta."

A computerized voice piped up. "Merge. Georgia four hundred. South."

Audrey knew, but she asked anyway. "Who is that?"

"It's Ramona," Kat replied. "My GPS."

"She has a name?"

"She never fails me. Always gets me where I'm going."

"She sounds right tasty," Russell threw in, and Audrey fell back against the seat and sighed.

"Really? You're evaluating the wiles of the GPS?"

Kat giggled, and Audrey imagined Russell had pulled some sort of face about her but felt too tired to care. Her eyes burned and she closed them, against better judgment. As anticipated, she drifted off. In what felt like the next minute, Kat called her name, and they all hopped out of Sherilyn the wedding planner's Ford Explorer.

Opera had all the noise and flair of a New York nightclub. Audrey felt the throbbing bass of the very loud music in the center of her chest as they bobbed through throngs of attractive, well-dressed people. She couldn't hear what Russell said to the large muscular man ahead of them, but the guy nudged them inside, and Audrey followed.

"She's in a private room," Kat mouthed back at her, and Audrey nodded as Kat gently grabbed her wrist and led her along behind Russell.

The thump of the bass kicked down a couple of notches once they reached the exclusive VIP area. They passed myriad groupings on their way past the opera boxes, and Audrey couldn't help naming them as she moved by.

Diddy and his crew.

Paris Hilton and her BFFs.

Charlie Sheen and the goddesses.

At the end of the row, surrounded by half a dozen people, sat Kim Renfroe. She flicked her long dark hair over her shoulder when she saw Audrey, and said something softly indecipherible to the woman to her left.

"Russell?" Kim cried when she saw him. "What are you doing here?"

"Hey, Kimmy," he said, scooting into the booth before the girl on the end had a chance to give him room.

"You know Audrey?" she asked, somewhat shrill.

The confused glances as she tried to put it together made Audrey feel oddly vindicated.

"Oh, yeah. When Kit-Kat told me they were coming over to see you, I had to throw myself in. Who're all your mates here?"

Audrey wanted to laugh out loud at the way Russell looked from one to the other, that big innocent grin on his handsome face, only partially masking the mischief in his eyes.

"Oh. Well." Kim looked around, then tilted her head slightly. "This is Maddie and Joe, Carrie Anne Russo. And this is Weston LaMont."

Audrey bristled. Had she heard that right?

"I'm sorry," she said, stepping up to the table. "Did you say Weston LaMont? The designer?"

"I did tell you I'd be meeting with him while I'm here." Kim flashed a very white smile that didn't quite reach her dark eyes. "Wes, this is Audrey Regan, her assistant Kat, and I guess you recognize Russell Walker."

LaMont's spiked black hair shimmered bluish as he tipped his head and grinned. "Audrey Regan," he repeated, and he tapped the leather seat next to him in the booth. "Come sit down."

"Well, actually, Kim asked me to come and meet with her—" She chuckled at the realization and added, "I'm not entirely sure why, now that I see you here too."

"Kimmy," Russell chided. "Are you playing a game of musical designers? Not too cool, hey?"

"Looks more like Designer Fight Club," LaMont cracked. "Is that it? You want to put us in the ring and see who's the last one standing?"

"*It is* my wedding dress, Wes," Kim replied in a strange form of baby talk. "I have to make sure it's perfection, don't I?"

"And you determine that by pitting them against each other at two in the morning?" Kat exclaimed.

"Kat," Audrey said softly.

"No!" And with that, Audrey's calm, level-headed assistant lost it. Her head, that is. "Are you kidding me with this? How many hoops do you want her to jump through for you, Kim? You told me on the phone—"

"Kat."

"—that you'd had a change of heart, that you wanted to talk it over with Audrey."

"Well, that's not entirely untrue," Kim defended. "But it took you so long to call me back that, while I was waiting, I called Wes. He was here at Opera, and so I hopped in a cab and—"

Audrey caught Russell's eye, and she locked in on him for a moment. "Are you going to drive me back to The Tanglewood?"

"You bet," he answered, and he hopped to his feet. "Let's bounce, Kit-Kat."

With one arm looped through Audrey's and the other through Kat's, Russell led them away from the table.

"Audrey, come on," Kim sang from behind them, and it set Audrey's teeth to grinding.

"I'm sorry, Ms. Regan, but your credit card was declined."

Audrey felt something heavy drop through her until it thudded at the bottom of her stomach. "Okay," she said, producing another one and sliding it toward him. "Try this one?"

He did, and the expression on his face ignited a churning, warbling panic within her.

"That one too?" she asked him, and the clerk nodded. "I . . . don't know how that's . . . possible. I . . ." Humiliated, she dropped her warm face. "All right. I . . . I'm . . . sorry."

"Sorry for what?"

Audrey spun around to find Emma standing behind her at the desk. She didn't have a clue what to say, and her heart began to race so fast that the hum of it filled her ears.

"Is there a problem here?" Emma asked.

The man behind the desk looked to Audrey for clarification.

"Carly asked me to stay a few more days, but—"

"Oh, right. Sherilyn mentioned a small party to cut the wedding cake since they missed out on their reception."

"Right."

"That's so great that you can stick around. I know it will mean the world to Carly."

"Well," Audrey began, and she looked away with a sigh. "I'm sort of short on funds these days, and . . . well . . ."

Emma looked at the man behind the desk, and he nodded at the credit card in his hand.

". . . I'm afraid I just don't have the funds available to do it."

"Ohh." Emma was silent for a moment before reaching over and squeezing Audrey's hand. "Listen, this is an unexpected expense. I get that. Don't worry about a thing. Roger, will you comp the rest of Ms. Regan's stay, please?"

He didn't even hesitate. "Of course," he replied, and he set Audrey's credit card on the glossy counter with a click.

"Emma, no, I can't ask you—"

"You didn't. I offered."

"But what about Jackson?"

"I have some pull with the owner of the hotel," she said with a grin. "It's not a problem."

Audrey heaved a ragged sigh. "Thank you. I'll repay it as soon as I can."

"You know what you can do to repay it, Audrey? Come somewhere with me and Sherilyn. Kat's coming. You join us too, okay?"

"Join you where?"

Emma smiled. "Just change into some comfy clothes—something you can move around in—and meet me here in the lobby in about half an hour. Are you in?"

How could she refuse? Audrey nodded.

"Oh, and Emma? Could we keep this between us?"

"Absolutely. I'll see you in a bit?"

"Yes."

After Emma had gone, Audrey returned her worthless credit cards to her wallet and thanked the clerk behind the desk. Wondering what Emma had in mind, she headed back upstairs to change clothes.

Less than an hour later: "Are you kidding me with this?"

"What do you mean?" Sherilyn asked. "I'm telling you, you'll feel so much better after a really strong workout."

"Have we met?" Audrey muttered.

"I know, I know. The first time Emma dragged me to her kickboxing class, I thought the same thing. But before you could say *Kick butt and take names!*, I was really into it."

Sherilyn, Emma, and Kat stood before a line of punching bags, feet apart, gloved hands raised, while Fee sat sprawled on a sofa angled into the corner of the room. Working on a ragged fingernail with a torn emery board, she paid little attention to them until Emma smacked her gloves together and exclaimed, "Fiona. A little punching music, if you please?"

Fee flicked the switch on the boom box propped beside the couch, and the room swelled with music she'd never heard before. The chorus seemed to repeat something again and again, and Audrey strained to make it out.

"Bryan Duncan?" Kat asked Emma. "I love him."

"Yep." Emma turned to Audrey and smiled. "The song is called 'Yes I Will.' And it restores the will to fight like nothing else can."

Kat laughed, but Audrey remained glazed by the scene before her.

Sherilyn tightened the gloves on Audrey's hands and smacked them with her own. "Just watch Emma and me," she told Audrey, and she nodded at Kat. "Dive in whenever you're ready."

Emma and Sherilyn raised their gloves. Sherilyn stretched her head down to one shoulder and then the other, and on the same note of music they stepped into a sort of practiced choreography.

Punch-jab-kick, punch-jab-kick.

By the second verse of the song, Kat stepped right into line and joined them, leaving Audrey standing on the edge of the activity like a lost cat. She glanced at Fee, who stared at her over the bridge of dark angular glasses.

"Dude," she said over the music. "You may as well just surrender to the wave. It's a twelve-footer."

Audrey considered it for a moment before Kat chimed in. "C'mon, Audrey! It's fun. You'll feel better, you really will."

"That's what you said about whole grains," she replied. Looking back to Fee, she added, "It's all fun and games until that third day."

Fee popped with laughter, tossing her head back against the sofa cushion.

"Well, you can't discount the importance of fiber in your diet," Kat defended, and she jabbed at the bag in front of her twice before landing a flying kick against it.

"Okay, okay," Audrey said with a laugh. "I surrender."

Stepping into line with the others, she began to throw half-hearted punches into the air between her and the bag.

But despite her best efforts to remain uninvolved, ten minutes later, to the tune of Aretha Franklin's "Respect," Audrey wailed on the bag before her, punching and kicking the stuffing out of every one of the problems she'd been carrying on the other side of the gym door a short time earlier.

Kim Renfroe and the dangling carrot of the wedding gown that could have saved her suffering design career. Punch-jab-kick.

Weston LaMont, gawking at her from Kim's private table at Opera, all pompous and successful in the glare of her beaming failure as a designer. Punch-jab-kick.

Kat. Poor Kat. The soon-to-be unemployed light of her professional life. Punch-jab-kick.

And J. R.

She jabbed and punched at his ridiculous crooked smile and glistening blue eyes . . . those muscular tattooed arms . . . his thick waves of shaggy hair . . . and that sometimes-shadow of a beard . . .

With one hard kick that knocked her straight to the floor on her behind, Audrey dented the fender of his infuriating, lingering kiss; the one that still felt hot on her lips, even now; the one that, without his own restraint, might nearly have done her in.

"Are you all right?" Sherilyn asked, standing over her. "Audrey?"

"I'm fine," she lied. "Just great. Let's go again."

Top Five Fabrics For Your Bridal Gown

1. **Silk** is the most sought-after and beloved fabric for a bridal gown; it is also the most expensive. There are various textures of silk, such as raw, Gazar and Mikado.

2. **Chiffon** is sheer and delicate, often with a soft sheen to it. Because of its transparent appearance, chiffon is often used for skirt overlays and sheer sleeves.

3. **Crepe** is a lightweight fabric, not unlike silk; however, it is usually slightly crinkled.

4. **Organza** resembles a blend of the delicate texture of chiffon and the stiffer appearance of tulle. It is ideal for full skirts, fitted bodices, and overlays.

5. **Tulle** is known as the stuff ballerinas are made of. A fine netting made of silk or rayon, tulle makes a beautiful skirt overlay or bridal veil.

7

Carly leaned over Devon and kissed his forehead before tugging on the blanket and pulling it up to his chin. J. R. couldn't help thinking that, if her care for getting Devon settled at home was any indication, the woman was going to be a great mother one day.

"What can I get you?" she asked her tired husband. "Water? Juice? How about some hot tea?"

"Yoo-hoo?" he teased.

"Okay," she replied, and she turned immediately toward the door.

"Wait a minute. We have Yoo-hoo in the house?"

"I got some just in case you asked."

Devon shook his head as Carly hurried from the bedroom, and J. R. plopped to the edge of the bed.

"Am I the luckiest guy you've ever met?" Devon said with a chuckle. "I have no idea what I ever did to deserve someone like her."

"Me neither."

"Hey!" his brother laughed, smacking J. R. on the arm, then moaning from the pull of it.

"Sit back and relax or you'll be back at the hospital before you can finish your Yoo-hoo."

Devon leaned back against the wall of pillows behind him and sighed.

"So when do you report to Albany, in light of this new development?" J. R. asked.

"Well, that's in question. Things are a little dicey in the Middle East right now."

"No."

"Yeah, 'fraid so. I'll be recovering here for another two weeks, and then it looks like I may be redeployed instead of staying stateside."

"Have you told Carly?"

"Not yet. I want to hold off until I know for sure in a couple of days."

J. R.'s heart began to beat against his Adam's apple. He hadn't realized the degree to which he'd taken comfort in knowing Devon would be assigned to the cushy safety of Albany, Georgia, for a while. But now—

"Don't let on, bro. Okay?"

J. R. shook his head. "Nah. Course not."

Carly stepped into the room and handed them each a frosty cold bottle before she set a paper towel and four chocolate chip cookies on the nightstand.

Three parts Perfect Wife, and one part Nurturing Mother.

Just what Devon never knew he needed.

J. R.'s cell phone buzzed, and he pulled it out of the pocket of his dark brown shirt and glanced at the screen.

"What's up, Russell?"

"Hey, mate. Just happened on news about the place to be tonight. You in?"

"Depends."

"Birthday party for The Man."

"Jackson?"

"Yeah. It's at his sister's digs. Everyone who's anyone will be there."

"You mean Kat's going to be there," he deduced. "Are we invited? Or are you just planning one of your social coups?"

"Nah, I got me some manners, you bloke. Sherilyn texted me an invite for the both of us. You in or out?"

"In. What time?"

"Meet up with you around seven."

"Good."

"Oh, and it's a surprise, so don't blow it."

"Gotcha."

The moment he disconnected the call, Devon asked him, "What am I missing out on?"

"Birthday deal."

"Oh, that's right," Carly said as she entered with a folded blanket in her arms. "Jackson's surprise party."

"Are we going?" Devon asked with a grin, and the glare from Carly set him back. "Are you going?"

"I have my hands full here," she said as she laid the blanket across the corner of the bed. "I'll have to miss it. Besides, Sherilyn is my Tanglewood connection. I don't really know Emma and Jackson much at all."

"Emma and Sherilyn are like you and Audrey," J. R. observed.

"Still," she replied with a smile. "I have a better offer here at home."

"Him?" J. R. teased. "A better offer? Marriage has stripped you of your good judgment."

"Don't be hateful," she returned, and she dropped to the bed beside Devon. "This is all the party I need."

"A drugged-up Marine with a hole in his gut," Devon summarized.

"MY drugged-up Marine," she reminded him, placing a peck on his cheek before she told J. R., "Give Jackson our best."

"Will do," he said.

"And if Audrey is there—"

"Audrey?"

Settle down, you idiot. It's just a name.

"Yes, I thought she might be there."

"Oh. Yeah?"

Trying too hard.

"Maybe. If she is, ask her to call me later? I've been trying to reach her about the reception."

"What reception?" Devon asked first.

"Well," she sighed. "Emma saved the wedding cake, and we're going to plan something really small and simple once you're feeling up to it. I asked Audrey to stick around for a few days to see if she can be there."

"A few days?" J. R. interjected. "Do you think you'll be out of bed that soon?"

"Dunno. Enough to eat some cake? Maybe."

Audrey's staying in town a little longer.

"I'll talk to her. Ask her to call you."

"Good, thanks. And have fun tonight."

J. R. grabbed his helmet and keys from the table by the front door, mid-stride.

The ride over to The Tanglewood was fraught with traffic, but his own thoughts were considerably louder than the rev of motors and the honk of horns. Despite the recurrences of Audrey on the fringe of his thoughts, he kept coming back to what Devon had confided about possibly heading back to the Middle East, and it wrenched his gut each time the realization crashed again. If the idea hit him in such a profound way, he wondered how Carly would take the news.

"Hey, you!" Sherilyn greeted him with a hug when she saw him crossing the lobby. "What are you doing here? How's Devon?"

Shrugging back the truth, he pushed a smile to his face. "He's got some healing to do. But Carly's on the case."

"They're a great couple."

"Yep, they are."

"So what are you doing at The Tanglewood?"

"I want to give them some privacy. I was hoping I could get a good rate and crash here for a couple of days."

"I think I can help with that."

Sherilyn grinned at him and linked her arm through his, closing the gap between them and the front desk.

"Hey, Rog," she said to the guy behind the desk. "Do we have availability for tonight?"

Roger nodded and tapped at the computer, examining the screen.

"How about we give Mr. Hunt a discounted rate, if there's one available." She poked his side with her elbow. "He's the brother of the groom who ended up in the emergency room. He's going to hang around for a few days to help them out."

"Three nights?" Roger asked him. "Four?"

"Why don't we start with three. It could be more. I just don't know yet."

"Yes, sir."

Sherilyn propped one elbow on the counter as Roger firmed up the details of the reservation. "So, J. R."

The hair on the back of his neck shimmied. "So, Sherilyn."

"You and Audrey."

"What about us?" He casually took his card from the clerk and tucked it into his wallet.

"Is there a love connection going on there?" She tossed her red hair and grinned at him like a gorgeous Cheshire cat.

"Why do you ask?"

"I've heard some scuttlebutt," she told him. "Just wondering if there's any truth to it. You know. Inquiring minds and all that."

"She's a beautiful girl," he stated carefully.

"Yes. She is."

"And she seems very sweet."

"Very."

J. R. tapped her arm several times before turning away.

"Hey," she said. "Are you coming to Jackson's party tonight?"

"Possibly."

"Possibly? Russell said absolutely."

"Then why did you ask?"

Before another word was exchanged, J. R. accepted the card key from the clerk, turned around, and walked away.

"See you tonight," she called after him, and J. R. lifted his arm and shot her a backwards wave. "Do you know where to go?"

He couldn't help himself, and J. R. laughed out loud. He felt fairly certain that, if anyone could adeptly tell him *where to go*, it was Sherilyn.

Audrey raked the hairbrush through her platinum hair before using the large-barrelled curling iron to add a few waves. Kat stepped into the doorway behind her, waiting until their eyes met before asking, "Am I underdressed?"

She skimmed the outfit: short blue gingham dress beneath a light blue cardigan with pearl buttons, bare suntanned legs and cute little white sneakers with blue laces. A simple crystal cross dangled from the braided ribbon choker around her neck. As always, Kat looked like a commercial for sunshine. Or a new fruity lip gloss.

Audrey gazed over her own reflection. Pleated crepe trousers, dark mustard with a high waistband; a white silk tank and a short black bolero jacket with scrollwork on one shoulder; strappy wedged sandals; dark eyeliner and mocha frosted lips.

"Am I *over*dressed?" she countered.

"Oh, hush. You always look like you stepped off a runway or through a movie screen."

"Wait. Is that good? Or bad?"

"It's good, silly. Are you ready to go?"

On their way toward the door, Audrey asked, "Did you get Jackson anything?"

"Espresso machine for his office."

"Are you kidding?"

"No. Well, it's from Russell and me both. Why? What did you get?"

Audrey dug through her handbag for a moment before producing a roll of breath mints. "Minty fresh breath?"

Kat giggled as they closed the door behind them. "We'll add your name to the card."

"So how are you getting there?" she asked in the elevator.

"With Russell."

"Oh." Audrey paused for a moment. "Motorcycle?"

"He rented a car so we four can all go over together."

"Oh, Kat, will J. R.—"

Before she could complete the thought, the elevator doors slipped open.

"There's my Kit-Kat," Russell greeted them, his arms open wide. Kat stepped into his embrace, and J. R. stood behind them like the match to Audrey's uncomfortable bookend.

Russell gave the cross around Kat's neck a tender caress.

"Love this. One of yours?" Kat nodded and smiled happily.

Audrey and J. R. didn't exchange a word as they stepped into line, side by side, and followed behind Russell and Kat.

"Hey," J. R. tossed at her.

"Hey," she returned.

"Can we add Audrey's name to Jackson's gift?" Kat asked Russell.

"Sure."

"Oh, a gift," J. R. grumbled. "Can I get in on that? Will you add mine too?"

"You two ever attended a birthday party before?" Russell teased. "It's customary to pick up a little something for the birthday boy."

Audrey glanced at J. R., and he shrugged.

"Wait until you guys see Jackson's birthday cake. Emma used the recipe for his favorite brownies, and she used them to build—"

"Spoiling the surprise, Kit-Kat."

"Whoopsie. Sorry."

"Is that Jackson and Emma?"

"I think so."

"Well, you can't pull up and park," Kat urged. "The party is a surprise."

Russell countered. "But there are twenty cars on the street in front of the house, Ducks. I think he probably has it figured out."

"Well, go around the block! Just in case."

J. R. caught a glimpse of the amusement in Audrey's pretty amber eyes and he snickered, darting his gaze away from her and out the opposite window.

On the third circle around the block, Emma and Jackson still stood there in the same spot,

"Russell!" Kat reprimanded, but Russell slowed the car, and Emma waved him down and jogged over to them.

Audrey lowered her window and Emma poked her head inside. "Are you guys here for Jackson's birthday party?" she asked as her fiancé stepped up beside her.

"Shhh," Kat urged, nodding toward him.

"Oh, Jackson knows. He knows every year."

Audrey grimaced, and Jackson added, "They give me a surprise party at the same sister's house each and every year, and then spend the whole night congratulating themselves for keeping the secret and pulling off the surprise."

"The only real surprise for him from one year to the next is the theme."

"The theme." Audrey repeated. "There's a theme?"

"Jackson's family is very southern, and every party is an extravaganza. Last year, the theme was Cirque de Soleil. They had acrobats on the back lawn."

J. R. laughed at the visual Emma conjured up.

"But three years ago—that one holds the record for Most Likely Thrown by Someone Who Has Never Met Me," Jackson cackled. "Oscar night."

"As in the Academy Awards?" Audrey clarified, and Russell belted out rolling laughter.

"A red carpet and everything," Emma told them. "I'm so sorry I missed that one."

"Sure she is," Jackson cracked.

"And every year, they think you're surprised," J. R. recapped.

"You never told them that you know?" Kat asked him.

"He doesn't want to ruin their fun," Emma said with a chuckle. "So go on and park the car, and go on inside. Tell them you saw us arrive, so they can get ready to yell surprise."

"So what's the theme this year, by the way?" Jackson asked, and Emma began to hum as she stared idly at the clouds. "Oh, come on." But she only hummed louder.

J. R. offered Audrey his hand as she followed him out of the back seat and, when she accepted it, a current of warm electricity jiggled up his arm. He wondered if she felt it too, and the way her eyes locked into his for several beats told him that she did.

From the entryway, J. R. could see that the large adjoining room teemed with people there to celebrate Jackson's birthday. The guests ran the gamut from very young to very, very old.

"Russell Walker?" one of the women said in a thick Southern drawl. "What a pleasure to have you join us!"

"It's a pleasure to be had," he said. Then, hamming it up like only Russell could, he added, "Hey, everyone! The guest of honor is coming up the driveway right now."

"I'm Jackson's sister, Norma," the woman half-whispered to their small group before urgently rounding up the guests. "Did you hear that? Jackson's on his way inside right now. Does everyone have a horn?"

A horn? J. R. thought, just an instant before Audrey turned to him and whispered, "A horn?"

He chuckled as party horns that looked like small megaphones were jammed into their hands amid a chorus of shushes.

"Anybody home?" Emma sang from the foyer.

"George?" Jackson called out. "Georgiann, are you here?"

"In here, *sugah*," an older version of Norma replied. "Come on *ee-in*."

J. R. stepped back, and the moment Emma and Jackson rounded the corner, the guests roared in unison: "*Suh-priiise!*"

Emma feigned astonishment far more convincingly than Jackson, with her brown eyes big and round, her hand to her heart for only an instant before she burst out laughing. Jackson looked down at her and loudly asked, "Did you know about this?"

"I did," she told the room with a grin wide enough to be shared by everyone. "I knew! Madeline, Norma, and I cooked it up together, and Georgiann offered her home."

J. R. watched the hostess as she beamed. "Happy birthday, little *bruthah*!"

"Thanks, everyone," Jackson told them as he moved from guest to guest, shaking hands, kissing cheeks, and smacking backs. "J. R., good to see you." Then, leaning in closer, he added, "Be sure and get some of my sister's crab cakes before they're gone. They're killer."

"Will do," he replied with a chuckle. "Thanks for the tip."

He wondered how Jackson knew there would be crab cakes when he didn't know the theme, but Emma answered the musing as she passed behind her fiancé.

"Norma's crab cakes are Jackson's favorites. They make the menu every year. Except *not this time*." She gave him the impression that she had a delicious secret burning a hole in her resolve to keep it. "But he's right. They're awesome!"

J. R. recognized a few people in the room, but not many of them. When his eyes landed on Sherilyn and her husband, Andy nodded at him and began to make his way toward him.

"Diverse group, huh?" Andy said with a sideways grin.

"Very."

Andy produced a cigar from the pocket of his jacket and handed it to J. R. "We're pregnant," he announced. "Have a cigar."

J. R. took it and smacked Andy's back. "That's awesome, buddy."

"Thanks," he said, tucking one of them, still wrapped in cellophane, into the corner of his mouth. "We're really excited. You can't smoke it here. No smoking at Georgiann's house, not even outside. Can't stop me from chomping on it though." After a short pause, Andy leaned in close and added, "Truth is I don't smoke 'em. But it's tradition for a new pops, right?"

J. R. laughed. "Well, congratulations, man."

"Thanks. Hey, wait til you see what Emma's pulled off for this party, man. You like football?"

"Sure."

"Well, Jackson and Emma are die-hard Falcons fans. He's going to *wet himself*." With a nod toward an open veranda, he asked, "Get you a drink?"

"Nah, I'm good for a while."

"I'm gonna grab one. See you later."

Emma floated toward him, tugging Audrey behind her by the arm. She pressed her hand to J. R.'s back and urged him to come along. "Let me introduce you guys around."

The next fifteen minutes were comprised of a sea of faces and names that J. R. knew he'd never quite remember. But both he and Audrey nodded and smiled, shook a few hands, and made polite conversation with a couple of Jackson's football cronies and their wives, Emma's parents Gavin and Avery, Jackson's assistant Susannah Something, a pastor named Miguel, and an elflike woman who only lit long enough to ask if Emma had seen Anton.

When Fee and Sean appeared from the other side of the crowd, J. R. guessed that Emma felt safe abandoning him and Audrey into their safe hands.

"Good to see you again, Sean!" J. R. said as he shook Sean's enormous hand. "Audrey, have you met Fee's intended?"

"Sort of. But not really, at the Jack-and-Jill," she replied, grinning at him. "Sean, it's great to see you."

"You as well."

"Audrey is a dress designer from New York who did the dress for the wedding where the groom's appendix burst," Fee filled him in. Turning to Audrey, she stated, "Sean was Russell's bodyguard after he fell out of the sky into Sherilyn's lap, and before J. R. arrived to mop up the mess."

J. R. laughed. He liked Fee. "Thanks for the recap," he told her.

"It's like that game," Audrey observed. "The one with Kevin Bacon."

"Yeah, but it's the Six Degrees of The Tanglewood Inn," Fee joked.

Looking around him, J. R. remarked, "Now there's a game that could keep on going into next year."

"At least," Fee said, leaning against Sean who looked like a large, well-dressed wall next to her. The two of them were oddly well-matched. Despite the obvious differences—she with ultra-pale white skin, and he a dark African American; Fee's tattoos and piercings, and Sean's clean-shaven face and bald head—still, they were a perfect fit somehow.

"Do I smell hot dogs?" Audrey asked softly.

"Have you seen the spread?" Fee asked them.

"Not yet," she replied.

"Dude. You have to go see."

Audrey looked up at J. R. with a curious smile and a semi-arched eyebrow. "Shall we?"

"I think we must."

He followed Audrey toward the wall of glass that had been pushed to one side, allowing wide, easy access to an enormous stone veranda. To one side, huge barbecue grills sizzled with hamburgers, hot dogs, and chicken, and long rectangular tables flanked the perimeter. A dozen or more picnic tables dotted the grounds, and bright white paint measured out the back lawn in yards, like a football field, with huge goalposts on either end.

A loud shout drew their attention, and J. R. laughed as Jackson and his friends reacted to the arrival of several very large black men in Falcons jerseys. Jackson grabbed Emma and twirled her off the ground.

"Is this the best fiancée a man could have?" he bellowed. "To turn my birthday into a tailgating party with Falcons players? Are you kidding me with this?"

Emma beamed as he looked her in the eye for a long moment. "You did all of this, didn't you?" he asked her softly. She shrugged, and he pulled her into a deep kiss.

The players passed thick black markers from one to the other as they signed a jersey spread out on Jackson's back.

"I know just enough about Jackson," J. R. told Audrey, "to know that this is some kind of dream-come-true for the guy."

"Are you into football too?" she asked him.

"Sure," he replied with a shrug. "I mean, I watch it sometimes. I don't schedule my Monday nights by it or anything. I prefer NASCAR myself."

"That's car racing, right?"

He nearly snapped his neck, but she met him with an amused grin.

"Yanking my chain," he surmised. "Okay. I see how you are."

"I couldn't resist." Her smile dazzled, and J. R. felt a little diminished in its light. "You know what else I can't resist?"

He could only wish he knew the answer.

"Hot dogs."

He chuckled. "Hot dogs?"

"I know. Kat tells me all the time how disgusting they are, and Carly always wants to tell me what's really in them because, apparently if I knew, I would never eat one again. Although that's doubtful. I mean, is there really anything like a couple of dogs with mustard, ketchup, and relish?"

"Mustard *and* ketchup?" He grimaced at the thought.

"You can't have one without the other," she replied. "Are you telling me I'm going to have to educate you on the crafting of the perfect dog?"

"Why don't we grab a couple of plates," he suggested. "You dog it up, and I'll make a play for the burgers."

"No dog?" she asked, seemingly appalled. "Whatever floats your bun, I guess."

J. R. followed Audrey to the buffet tables where they loaded up plates with potato salad, baked beans, and cole slaw. Audrey came more alive at every serving tray.

"Carb heaven," she commented as she dropped a spoonful of macaroni salad to her plate. "Wouldn't this party just drive Carly right up the wall?"

"Would it?" he asked, smearing mayonnaise on both sides of a hamburger bun.

"Haven't you ever noticed how she is about food? Every meal has to have all the right colors."

"Colors." He thought back, trying to remember that quirky detail about Devon's bride.

"Yes. A dinner plate cannot just be green or brown. It has to have other colors too. It's the color chart of nutrition."

"Well, your plate looks very colorful," J. R. observed. "I would think she'd be quite proud." Audrey's laugh was lyrical. "The ketchup is red, the mustard is yellow, and the relish—"

"Green," she finished for him. "I guess you're right. I'm far more Bob Harper than I thought."

"Who's Bob Harper?"

"Oh, he's the hot trainer on *The Biggest Loser* who goes around yelling at people for not eating right."

He didn't mention that the clarification didn't help. J. R. just nodded tentatively and reached for a few rings of Bermuda onions. Then with a second thought about eating onions, he changed course and grabbed a couple of thick, red tomato slices instead.

J. R. snagged two bottles of root beer from a large tub of ice and followed Audrey along a flagstone path toward an unoccupied picnic table on the lawn. Once seated, and just as they started to dig into their feasts, Audrey's attention pushed right over J. R.'s shoulder. The golden flecks in her brown eyes shimmered, and she blinked one time slowly.

"Is that Ben Colson over there, talking to Russell?"

J. R. turned around. "It looks like him."

"I have every CD he's ever recorded. He's amazing."

"Yeah, he's all right," he commented, but just as he lifted his burger to his open mouth, Audrey smacked the table and he paused.

"I can live with the denial of the hot dog, but Ben Colson isn't just all right, young man. That's like . . . like saying your Harley is just a *ride*!"

He glared at her playfully. "I'll forgive you for that once. Don't say it again."

Audrey grinned. "Do you think he's going to perform?"

"If I know Russell . . . and I do . . . he'll have company."

She giggled as she took her first bite from the hot dog extravaganza she'd concocted.

"Ohhhhh," she groaned. "This is so good!"

J. R. watched her closely for a minute as she devoured her prey. "You do enjoy your frankfurters," he observed, and Audrey laughed.

"When I was a kid, my granny let me pick any meal I wanted on my birthday. Every year, it was a comfort food carbfest. Hot dogs, baked beans, macaroni and cheese, and fried onion rings."

"Really." He found it hard to believe she looked as good as she did, eating like that.

"Oh, yeah. I should have weighed two hundred pounds by the twelfth grade, right? Me and food," she said, pressing two fingers together, "we're *likethis*. Which probably explains why I'm such a fan of *The Biggest Loser*, right?"

Again, the reference dropped to the ground.

"But Granny was smart, and she trained me well. Everything in moderation and all that. Not that I liked it or anything. I'd rather eat hot dogs and junk food every day for every meal, but that wasn't going to happen in my granny's house. Oh, and she used to watch this TV show where some lady sat in a chair doing exercises for old people, and Granny would make me do them with her." Audrey shook her head at the memory and brushed a wave of ice-blonde hair away from her face. "She was such a trip, my granny. She—" Stopping herself, a blush of embarrassment stained her face. "And why am I telling you all of this?"

"Because I'm interested?" he asked with a smile.

Before he could say another word to encourage her, an elderly woman appeared out of nowhere and sat down next to him. She wore a cherubic smile and a mint green party dress with wrist-length gloves that looked like something straight out of a southern cotillion.

After a moment, Audrey greeted her tentatively. "Hello."

"Hello, dear."

The woman smoothed her gloves before pressing the full skirt of her dress and smiling at J. R. "Is this your beau?" she asked Audrey.

"Um, no. He's just a friend."

"Whatever you say, dear."

"J. R. Hunt," he introduced himself. "And this is Audrey Regan."

"It's an honor to meet you both," she told them sincerely.

J. R. shifted. "Are you one of Jackson's sisters?"

"No, this is Emma's aunt," Audrey pointed out, and the woman tilted her head as she looked at her.

"Have we met?"

"At the hotel."

"Oh." After a moment's thought, she gazed at J. R. "Jackson is my nephew. He married my darling Emma Rae."

Married. They're not married.

"It was a beautiful ceremony," she expounded. "Her father walked her down the aisle, and Jackson looked so handsome in top hat and tails. Emma Rae wore my Parisian lace veil, and the air was thick with the scent of magnolias. There were doves in golden cages, and afterward we all dined on cornish game."

J. R. and Audrey exchanged flickering smiles.

Live birds in cages and dead ones on their plates. It sounds dreadful.

"Waiters in tuxedos served the most delightful sweet tea in crystal glasses," she continued. "I wonder if they have any of that here today."

"Why don't we go and find out?" J. R. suggested.

"Could we?"

"Of course," he said, and he pushed up to his feet and offered her his arm.

When the sound of a harp drew their attention, Audrey shrugged and pulled her cell phone from the outside compartment of her purse.

"I'll be back," J. R. told her as she answered it. Then he smiled at the woman on his arm and asked her, "Ready?"

She nodded sweetly, and he escorted her up the path and toward the veranda.

"I see you've met Aunt Sophie," Emma exclaimed as she crossed before them, and she planted a kiss on the woman's cheek.

"She's quite charming," he told her with a smile.

"Look who you're telling," Emma said with a chuckle. "I'm her biggest fan."

"Do you know J. R., Emma Rae?"

"I do, Aunt Soph. He's become a friend to all of us at The Tanglewood."

"Your aunt has been telling me about your wedding," J. R. disclosed.

"Oh." Emma chuckled. "The one on the beach in Savannah? Or the one where Jackson wore a top hat?"

"The latter."

"Oh, it was such a lovely day, wasn't it, Emma Rae?"

"Indeed," she replied, tossing J. R. a toothy grin.

Jackson's Favorite Fudge Cashew Brownies

Preheat oven to 350 degrees

2 sticks butter
2 cups granulated sugar
1 cup cocoa powder
4 eggs
1 teaspoon vanilla extract
1 ¼ cups all-purpose flour
1 teaspoon salt
1 teaspoon baking powder
½ cup halved cashews, plus additional for garnish

Melt butter and pour into large bowl.
Add sugar and cocoa, mixing with wooden spoon or rubber spatula.
Add eggs and vanilla, continuing to stir.
In separate bowl, sift flour, salt, and baking powder together; then add dry ingredients to butter-sugar-cocoa mixture; stir in ½ cup cashews.
Mix well, and pour mixture into a greased 9"x 13" baking pan.

Bake for approximately 30 minutes.

After cooling, cut into small squares.
Layer two squares and fill with cocoa or chocolate icing, then frost top and garnish with additional cashew halves.

8

"How did you get this number?"

"Kim Renfroe gave it to me. I hope you don't mind."

Audrey didn't know how to respond to that. Why on earth would Weston LaMont want her number anyway?

"I was hoping we might take a meeting, if you're interested," he told her, and Audrey squinted at the torn label on her bottle of root beer for a long moment.

"About what, exactly?"

"I felt badly about the way things went with Kim. I think she pitted us against one another, and I—"

"Oh, you know, there's no need, really. I appreciate your call, but it's just business. I get that."

"That's very gracious. I hope you'll harbor no hard feelings."

His words dispelled any residual mystery about whether Kim had made a final decision yet. Audrey clearly heard the dregs of her design career as they tumbled to the ground.

"You are a brilliant designer," she told him, her eyes closed, rubbing her temple. "I'm honored to have been considered alongside you."

"Well, now you're just twisting the knife," he said with a chuckle. "At the very least, I think you should slam the phone down on me right this minute."

Don't tempt me.

"Don't be silly," she said instead. "The business of design is very personal. And for a bride, it's that much more so. She has to weed through us until she finds just the right fit. I just wasn't it for Kim. I wish you both the best, Mr. LaMont."

"Wes."

"Wes," she repeated. "Thank you so much for calling."

As she disconnected the call, Audrey was torn between her excitement that a designer with the reputation of Weston LaMont had just casually requested that she call him Wes . . . and the utter despair of reality. She'd gone into her association with Kim Renfroe knowing full well that her financial life depended on it. She'd been at the end of her rope, and now Audrey felt the whoosh of the air passing by as the frayed rope released her and she plumeted to the ground.

"It's over." She hadn't meant to say it aloud.

I'm sunk.

She felt a little dazed as she pushed to her feet and picked up her purse. With her free hand, she grabbed the soiled plates and bottles from the table. She carried them across the lawn to the veranda, deposited them in a tall trash can, and kept on walking, right into the house.

"The powder room?" she asked a random party guest, and the woman pointed at a hallway. She proceeded toward it without breaking stride. "Thank you."

The locked door told her that the bathroom was occupied, so she leaned against the wall across from it. Staring straight ahead, she controlled her breathing into steady ins and outs.

In with the good air, out with the—

The door across from her opened, and Audrey forced a smile to her face.

The woman gave her a good-natured grin in return and teased, "Next?"

"Thank you. That would be me."

Audrey stepped inside, closed the door behind her, and flicked the lock. Crossing quickly to the toilet, she pushed down the lid and descended into a full-on cry before she even had time to sit down. She placed her hands over her face and sobbed into them, careful to choke back the audio that threatened to let everyone beyond the door know that some lunatic from the party had locked herself in the bathroom so she could get her hysteria on.

A few minutes later, a light knock on the door jolted her. She sat erect, her lips parted and her eyes wide.

"Yes," she finally managed. "I'll be right out."

"Take your time," an unfamiliar voice replied.

Audrey hopped up and crossed to the mirror.

"Ohhhh, maaaan," she whispered when she saw her own reflection.

Swollen eyes leaked streams of black eyeliner, and a red knob gleamed at the center of her face where her nose should have been. She tugged a glob of tissue from the roll and dabbed at the mess underneath her eyes, then blew her nose into it. When she finished, she lifted the lid to the toilet, dropped the tissue into the bowl and flushed.

"Just one more minute," she promised the person on the other side of the door as she ran cold water over her hands. With the tip of her finger, she tidied up her smeared lips and eyes, dried her hands, and approached the door.

With her hand on the knob, Audrey closed her eyes and drew in a deep breath, releasing it slowly before opening the door. As she did, the harp in her handbag sounded, and she grabbed for it as she passed the woman waiting on the other side.

The screen announced the caller as Carly, and Audrey peered into a nearby room that looked like an office before she depressed the green button.

"Hey, Caroline. How's Dev?"

She left the door slightly ajar behind her and sat down on a floral settee by the window as Carly caught her up on details such as his growing appetite and the various levels of his pain since his return from the hospital.

"We were talking about the reception, and I think we're going to plan it for Tuesday night."

Audrey counted down the days until Tuesday. Thank goodness Emma had offered to comp a room for her and Kat . . . although she would probably let Kat go back to New York to begin the conversion process from design business to living space . . . and perhaps she could place the ad for—

"Aud? Are you listening to me?"

"I'm listening," she fibbed. "Go on."

"I asked J. R. to have you call me. Did he give you the message?"

"No."

"Of course not. Well, can you tell Sherilyn I need to talk to her about the party?"

"I'll find her before I leave and tell her to give you a jingle."

"Audrey, is everything all right?"

"Yes. Fine."

"Don't lie to me. What aren't you telling me? Do you want to come over after Jackson's party?"

"Oh, no. I'm really beat. I'll come over tomorrow, if that's okay."

"Of course it's okay. But I really wish you'd tell me what's going on. I've known you since time began. There's no fooling me."

"I know," she admitted, and Audrey grinned and shook her head. "I know. We'll talk tomorrow. I promise."

"Okay then. Call me when you wake up in the morning."

Audrey disconnected the call and tucked the phone into her bag. She thought about finding Kat and pulling her aside, then discounted the idea. Kat would be somewhere hanging on Russell Walker's every word, and Audrey wanted her to enjoy it while she could. Reality would dawn soon enough. No need to push it along.

She gazed out the window behind her. Jackson's party had been confined to the view from some other window. She was thankful that this view looked out over a small sloped hill. Green velvety grass carpeted the way to a colorful garden bordered on all sides by a short knee-high wall of stacked stones.

Audrey wondered what it must be like to live this way. To throw a party like this one, every single year, without ever wondering how to also keep the lights on. She leaned back against the arm of the settee and sighed. Before the breath had been fully expelled, emotion crested again and tears spilled down her face in streams.

No, she told herself. *Do not lose it, Audrey. Buck up and be strong.*

She sat upright and braced herself on the edge of the couch, her teeth clenched and her expression chiseled into one of strength. She dried the tears with the back of her hand and drew in a sharp breath as she reminded herself that this was no time to falter. A hundred virtual strangers did not need to see her break down, and Jackson's festivies needn't be dampened by the sudden collapse of someone's life. There would be plenty of time for tears later. Back in New York. But not here, not now.

"There you are!"

She jumped to her feet as J. R. pushed the door open and occupied the doorway.

"You've got to see Jackson's birthday cake. It's a football field of brownies!"

"Really," she managed, pushing the embers of a smile to her face. "Brownies?"

"Hey," he said softly as he closed the gap between them. Taking her hand, he asked, "Are you all right?"

Without losing the smile, she shook her head and admitted, "Not really."

He led her to the settee and told her to sit down, and he joined her there, tenderly rubbing the back of her shoulder. "Do you want to talk about it?"

"Not so much," she replied.

"Okay. Then we'll just sit here and be quiet for a minute. Will that help?"

"Probably not."

"No. Can I do anything?"

"Uh-uh."

"Do you want me to leave you alone?"

She sighed. "No."

A few long, silent seconds ticked past before he told her, "Then you just tell me. What do you want to do?"

Leave.

Run away.

Go for a ride on that motorcycle of yours.

Her thoughts squealed back to that night when he'd whisked her away from Carly and Devon's party. They'd stopped at a park, and . . .

Audrey turned and looked into J. R.'s steely blue eyes. He arched an eyebrow as he held her gaze. "What?" he finally asked.

Shifting from his eyes to his mouth, Audrey felt her lips begin to tingle.

"Are you all right?" he asked. "Did you think of something that—"

Without another moment's thought, she lurched forward, slipped her arms around his neck, and kissed him.

"Thank you so much for bringing me up here," Audrey said as she gazed out over the landscape before them. "It's just beautiful."

"Devon and I used to fish in that stream down there when we were kids," he told her.

"It's funny that we both grew up in the area," she commented. "You know, and then we both left. And we come back and . . . Sorry. I'm rambling. Anyway, I've never been up here before. It's beautiful."

"It seemed like a good spot to unwind."

"It is. Very relaxing."

Russell had surrendered the keys to his rental, they'd wrapped up two huge brownies in napkins emblazoned with Falcons logos, grabbed a couple more bottles of root beer, and they'd escaped the party for a while. As much for a change of scenery as for the opportunity to put a little space between him and those kisses of hers. Even the firmest resolve to do the right and gentlemanly thing could be shattered with enough of *that!*

"So you were telling me about the designer who called you," he said, pausing to bite off a corner of the large brownie in his hand. "Oh, man, these are great."

"I know, right!?" she exclaimed, and she took another bite out of hers. "Weston LaMont. He stormed the bridal market about two years ago. He's a genius with draping, and he's sort of famous for creating these unbelievable body-hugging silhouettes."

"And that's good."

"That's very good. He's based here in Atlanta, so when Kim made her plans to come here to see Carly's dress, I guess she had the revelation to meet with LaMont too. Well. Wes. He told me to call him Wes," she added with a downward turn to her luscious red lips.

She chomped down on the brownie like an angry dog with a long-awaited bone. "I don't know," she said after a long silence. "I don't know."

"This opportunity with Kim Renfroe," J. R. surmised. "That was pretty important."

"It was all I had left. I've been at this for so long," she said with a sigh. "I'm out of options."

The pain of the admission was unmistakable, and he reached out and caressed her face. "No. There's always another option. Sometimes it takes looking for it at a different angle, but it's always there."

He could plainly see that she wasn't buying it.

"You have no idea how broke I am," she told him in a raspy, weary voice. "How long I've been at this, how hard I've worked to . . ."

And the girl crumbled right before his very eyes.

J. R. slid next to her and took Audrey into his arms. To his surprise, she acquiesced, melting into his embrace with complete surrender. Her entire body trembled as she sobbed, and the vibration of her cries burned his chest where her head stayed buried. Ten minutes must have passed, maybe longer, before she slowly withdrew, wiping her cheeks dry with both hands and pushing her platinum hair straight back from her tear-streaked face.

She looked up at him and smiled. It was a pure smile, untainted by her usual perfect black-lined eyes and impeccable scarlet lips. It was the smile of resignation; the aftermath of her meltdown, the unmistakable remnant of war.

And she looked exquisite.

He ran his thumb along the line of her jaw and gazed into her amber eyes.

"Thank you," she whispered.

"For what?"

"I needed a soft and safe place to fall. You gave it to me."

So many thoughts raced through his mind, so many crazy notions about what should or could come next. Instead of surrendering to the appeal of any one of them, J. R. inhaled deeply.

"Any time," he promised.

"Audrey, I don't want to go back yet."

Kat stood before her with those big chocolate doe eyes even more wide and round than usual, the corners of them misted with emotion as she stared at Audrey, playing with her necklace, an eye-catching double strand of floating, multi-colored gems.

"You don't need to stay, Kat. I'll just be here long enough for Carly and Devon's party, and I'll be right behind you."

"No, I want to stay. I mean, am I not invited to stay?"

Audrey didn't understand this reaction.

Until she did.

Realization dawned like a fast-moving thunderstorm on the horizon. "Ohhh. It's Russell," she said, nodding. "You don't want to leave Russell."

"I know it sounds crazy, but I've really fallen for him, Audrey. I can't bear the thought of leaving while he's still here. I mean, it's not like I'll probably ever hear from him again. I know that. But—"

"No, no," Audrey said, waving her hand. "I get it. As long as you don't mind working that much harder and faster when we get back to New York . . . and of course you'll have to share this hotel room with me because I can't afford to put you up in another one . . . you can stay. We'll go back to New York together."

Kat surprised her with a spontaneous hug. "Thank you. I just want to get as much time with him as I can before we go back to the real world. That's crazy, right?"

A knock sounded at the door before she could reply, and Kat grinned. "That will be Fee. I told her you would help with alterations to her dress, and I'm going to show her how to create finger waves."

"And you were going to mention this to me . . ."

"Right now," she said, yanking open the door.

"Thank you so much, you guys," Fee said by way of greeting. "I haven't been nervous this whole time, and now we're a few hours away, and I'm a bundle of shaking Chihuahuas. I'll go put it on."

Clutching a bulge of ivory lace, she sped past them, and the bathroom door clanked shut behind her.

"She's getting married *today?*" Audrey asked as she grabbed a bottle of water and unscrewed the cap.

"Yes. Right here." Kat pointed at the hotel room door.

"Here in the hotel?" she clarified.

"Here, outside this room."

Audrey sat down on the edge of the bed and crossed her legs. "Our room?"

"Yes. Isn't it romantic?" Kat glanced toward the bathroom before sinking down next to her. "This is the room Russell was in when he stayed here before. And Sean was kind of a bodyguard. Well, he was posted outside the door like a sentry. Less of a protector for Russell than protecting everyone else *from Russell* I think."

Audrey chuckled at the distinction. It seemed apt.

"Anyway, right outside this room. That's where they first laid eyes on one another. Fee said the moment she saw him, her life changed forever."

Audrey melted just a little, and her hand moved to her heart. "That really *is* romantic."

"Isn't it?"

Fee pulled open the door and took a few steps outside of the bathroom—then froze. With a tentative stab at a smile, she faced them with her head cocked, fidgeting with her glasses and twirling them in one hand.

"It's awful, isn't it?" she asked them. "Like I'm trying to be someone else?"

Audrey sighed and shook her head. It was an understated dress. Ivory lace with cap sleeves, drop waist, and scalloped tea-length hem. She looked very 1930s, like she should be photographed in black and white.

"Fee. You look beautiful."

She snickered. "Right."

"Really, Fiona," Kat said, and she hurried to her side and gripped Fee's hand. "You look unbelievable. Sean is going to drop his teeth."

Fee thought it over before replying. "Let's hope not."

Kat and Audrey chuckled.

"What. He has really nice teeth."

Audrey grabbed her travel kit. "It needs to come in slightly at the shoulders," she said as she wrapped the elastic band of her pin cushion around her wrist. "If you put it on inside out, I can pin it and have it done in twenty minutes."

"Dude. Thank you."

"Then I'll show you what I had in mind for your hair," Kat told her. She turned to Audrey as she added, "Finger waves."

"Ooh, that will look so great with the dress. Do you have a veil?"

"I'm not exactly the veil type of chick."

"If you wave your hair with a side part, you could place one flower here . . ." She picked up the side of Fee's hair and tucked it back above her ear. "Very understated. Retro chic."

Fee looked at Audrey so hard that it almost took the form of a glare. With a quick glance at Kat, and a darting look back to Audrey, her face crumpled slightly.

"Fee. Are you going to cry?"

And with that, she pulled it back together in a millisecond. "I don't cry," she stated. "I'll go turn the dress inside out and we can get started."

Kat shot Audrey a flicker of a grin before Fee turned back toward them from the doorway. "Guys?" she said. "Thanks a lot."

"Ah, we love a good wedding," Audrey replied, waving her hand. "It's as much for us as it is for you."

As Fee turned away, Audrey caught the beginning embers of a full-on smile.

"Who's the Denzel?"

"That's Sean's brother, Tyrone."

"Cute."

"Isn't he?"

J. R. pulled a face at Jackson, and Russell poked a small flower behind his ear before collapsing to the bed behind them.

"She looks stunning," Audrey whispered as she peered through the peephole. "I don't think she has any clue how amazing she looks."

"Oh, she doesn't," Sherilyn said, pushing her way between Audrey and Kat for her turn at a peek out into the corridor. In a hushed tone, she added, "And did you get to see Emma's dress?"

"She looks so pretty," Kat answered, nudging Sherilyn away from the peephole so that she could take a look.

"Ooh, here come the vows!"

The three of them pressed their ears to the door.

"Why don't you—"

Jackson's words were sliced cleanly in half as they shushed him in three-part harmony. He raised his hands in surrender and fell silent, shaking his head.

"You don't know better than to try to part a woman from a wedding on the other side of the door, mate?" Russell inquired quietly.

"You'd think I would."

"Jackson," Sherilyn reprimanded. "Shhh."

Jackson saluted her and turned the invisible key in the lock of his mouth.

"Why are they having the ceremony in the hall?" J. R. asked in a whisper. "It seems to me it would make for much easier spying if they had it in the courtyard downstairs. Then all three of them could climb a tree and get a bird's eye view."

"Fee doesn't like to be looked at," Kat answered softly.

"So why don't you stop looking then?" Jackson suggested.

All three women turned slowly and glared at him. It was too much for J. R., and he burst into laughter that was immediately met with another chorus of shushes.

"They met in that hallway out there," Russell whispered, looking slightly ridiculous with the flower still tucked into his hair.

"And they wanted something completely private," Jackson added. "Just them and their witnesses."

"And the spies who love them," J. R. added, nodding toward the threesome of women pressed against the door.

A moment later, with her hand to her heart, Audrey crossed to the chair by the window and melted into it. "That was beautiful."

"Heart-wrenching," Sherilyn added, shaking her head.

"Fairy tale," Kat chimed in, sinking down next to Russell.

"Four people and a minister," J. R. summed up. "Saying their vows in a hallway."

"*The* hallway," Kat corrected. "The hallway where they first met."

A soft rap at the door set Sherilyn into motion. She pushed a basket filled with flower petals at J. R. and told him to take some of them. "Hurry. Hurry!"

When everyone in the room had a fistful of flowers, she urged them to their feet before giving Kat the go-ahead to open the door. But it was Emma who received the full benefit of the flowers being tossed at her, and one petal remained on her cheek where it landed. Fee and Sean entered behind her, and Kat hurriedly refilled her supply before tossing petals at them as well.

"Sean," Sherilyn called out, raising a digital camera. "Kiss your bride."

As he obliged, Sherilyn snapped several pictures, and Fee pulled out of the kiss with a blotchy red face and neck.

"C'mon," she said. "Enough."

"I'll call down for the cake," Emma told them as she reached for the phone. "Fiona, make the introductions?"

Miguel the minister and Sean's brother pushed into the room, and Kat closed the door behind them. J. R. felt a bit like one of the sardines waiting for the can to be sealed.

"Everyone," Fee said, somewhat deadpan as she pointed them out. "This is Sean's brother, Ty; this is Pastor Miguel; that's Russell and Kat; Sherilyn; Audrey; J. R.; Jackson and Emma. And this . . ." She paused emotionally as she gazed at Sean and smiled. ". . . is *my husband*."

J. R. wasn't sure he'd ever encountered a more unlikely couple than Fee and Sean. But as they leaned into one another and kissed, he supposed no real purpose would be served by his understanding anyway. Two people had managed against all the odds to find each other, and somehow it just worked.

In fact, the room teemed with couples matching that description. Emma and Jackson, still unmarried but working, times two hundred. Even though Andy hadn't been able to attend, Sherilyn reminded him of their ideal blend. And as he glanced over at them, the playful new relationship between Russell and Kat further evidenced an unlikely but perfect match.

He'd known Russell for years, and a steady parade of nameless beauties had marched through his friend's radar. But never once had J. R. seen the kind of impact that Kat's appearance had made. He'd long equated Russell to that one crazy gorilla at the zoo, the one that people gathered to watch, never able to look away for fear of missing whatever surprising thing he might do next; a volatile mix of spontaneity, dangerous curiosity, and unbridled zeal. But Kat had somehow tamed him. J. R. wondered if she even knew what she'd done.

Audrey unwittingly drew his gaze toward her with the gravitational pull of a magnet to steel. Smiling at the happy couple, completely unaware of his scrutiny, she stopped time for J. R. The perfect wave of platinum blonde hair folded atop her shoulder, light eyes like creamed cocoa, glistening in lyrical rhthym with the lilt of her soft laughter.

It suddenly occurred to him that The Tanglewood Inn might just be the Bermuda Triangle of singleness. A poor, defenseless guy just happened to wander through, and the next thing he knew, fate had stepped in like some sort of hidden drug, a roofie compelling him to couple with some other unsuspecting wanderer. He and Audrey should probably run, not walk, as fast as they could before—

"Hey," she whispered as she leaned toward him, and his eyes locked onto her velvety scarlet lips. "After the cake, would you be up for a ride?"

"Uh, yeah."

And there you had it, right on cue. Drug-induced behavior leading to coupledom.

"Just a ride," she clarified softly.

Maybe it's something in the cake, he thought as Emma handed him an irresistible slice of her crème brûlée specialty.

"What?" Emma asked as he stared at the cake on the plate.

"Sometime you'll have to tell me what's in this," he stated.

"I could," she replied with a charming smile. "But it's a secret, so—"

"If you told me, you might have to kill me?"

"Don't be silly. I'm no killer."

But somehow…

It's just as I suspected. It's the cake that does it. The stuff is lethal.

When they'd all decided to head over to Sherilyn and Andy's house to continue the wedding celebration, something had dropped inside of Audrey. It felt a little like disappointment. She'd planted her hopes on some wind in her hair.

"Why don't we take that ride on the Harley," J. R. had suggested to her. "Then we'll head over afterward."

Her heart began to beat again.

"Yes," she said, nodding eagerly. "That sounds perfect."

Now, on the back of J. R.'s motorcycle, her arms clenched tightly around his mid-section and her helmet-shielded face nuzzled against his back, Audrey congratulated herself for her boldness. She'd come right out and asked him to take her for a ride, and the night air around her provided just the right amount of happy diversion that she'd been hoping for.

Hot guy, fast bike, wind at my back. All the right ingredients.

But even as she reassured herself with a nostalgic look backward at a more carefree Audrey from years ago, she knew full well that an appealing diversion couldn't erase the current realities of her life. When the engine fell silent and J. R. climbed off his Harley, when she removed the helmet and shook loose the pile of blonde hair tucked undereath it, Audrey's failed career and rapidly collapsing life would still be waiting for her.

So I'll think about it later, she decided. *Right now, I'll just hang on and enjoy the ride.*

J. R.'s neck smelled of citrus and spice, and the fabric of his chambray shirt felt soft and somewhat soothing. As he navigated the bike around the arched curve in the road, his muscles flexed beneath her touch. Disappointment crested as Audrey realized they'd entered a neighborhood, likely Sherilyn and Andy's. Before long, J. R. steered them to a slow stop at the end of a driveway crowded with cars.

"Do we have to?" she asked him as she pulled off her helmet, and he turned the key and followed suit.

"Nope" was his reply, and he kicked the stand downward. "Not if you don't want to."

He clamped his hands over hers where they rested at his ribcage, and he squeezed them gently before he angled off the bike. With one quick turn, though, he surprised her by setting his helmet on the ground and climbing right back onboard, this time straddling the bike backwards and facing her. Audrey chuckled nervously as he gazed into her eyes, and his warm breath caressed her cheeks.

"Stay or go," he told her. "I'm just along for the ride. Wherever you want to go, whatever you want to do. What'll it be?"

She gulped down the reply pressing against her throat and groaned, letting her head fall down against the center of his chest. "Oh, I dunno."

"Then let's go inside and have some grub. If you want to leave, we'll leave."

He placed two fingers beneath her chin and raised her face toward him.

"Are you always this agreeable?" she asked him, and he smiled at her.

"No. Not at all."

"So why now?"

"Because a little agreeable goes a long way sometimes. And you, Audrey Regan, appear to need some agreeable."

"Well. You said a mouthful there," she admitted.

He raised up and hiked one leg over the bike. "Do you like dogs?"

"I'm sorry," she said, shaking her head. "What?"

"Dogs," he reiterated. "Do you like them?"

"I guess."

"Good. Because Sherilyn and Andy are dog-endowed."

"What does that mean?"

"Come meet Henry," he said, offering his hand. "You'll see what I mean."

She climbed off the bike and handed him her helmet. He carried them both, and she followed him up the sidewalk. J. R. opened the porch door and led her toward the front door of a two-story house. Before the bell let out a fraction of a chime, something large thudded into the door from the other side, accompanied by a chorus of frantic barks.

"Henry, I presume," she remarked.

"A whole lot of him."

Russell tugged open the door. "We thought you two had gone on a walkabout. What took you so long?"

"We took the scenic route," J. R. told him.

"By way of what?"

Audrey let out a little scream as the barking mass of hair jumped on its hind legs, planting its front paws on J. R.'s shoulder.

"Yeah, Henry. Nice to see you too," he said, ruffling the fur from the Old English Sheepdog's eyes.

"Henry, this is Audrey," Russell added. "Be polite. She doesn't know you like I do."

The dog hopped down and followed Russell away from the door.

J. R. gave her a nod and led Audrey into a large, open living room. Sherilyn and Emma stood at the counter in the adjoining kitchen, and the rest of the crowd occupied an enormous sofa, a couple of chairs, and a few dining chairs pulled away from the table.

"Now that J. R. and Audrey have found their way home," Russell said, and he stood up straight as if he were about to make some great announcement, "I have some news."

"No," Kat growled. "Not yet."

"Why not?"

"I haven't spoken to Audrey yet," she said through clenched teeth and a pasted smile.

"Well, let's knock two birds then," he suggested. "Everyone . . . and Audrey . . ."

"Russell, please," Kat cried. Then she added, "Audrey, I'm sorry."

"For what?"

"I want to thank Audrey Regan," Russell said.

"What, are you accepting an award?" J. R. teased.

"Better! She brought this delicious girl into my life," and he pulled Kat close beneath his extended arm.

Audrey swallowed hard. *Please don't tell me you're getting married, for crying out loud!*

"Russell," Sherilyn said from the kitchen, and she hurried into the room as she wiped her hands on a dish towel. "Are you two getting married?"

"Don't be crackers, woman," he answered. "We've only just met."

"Oh. Sorry," she replied with a laugh as she looked around at the others. "It had that grand announcement air to it. Sorry. Go on. What were you going to say?"

"I've been thinking for a while now of settling somewhere away from L.A.," he continued, "and I've sort of landed on the idea of doing it here."

"In Georgia?"

"In Roswell, actually," he told them. "I found a great place not five miles from The Tanglewood."

Audrey moved closer to Kat and touched her arm. "You're not moving in with him, right?" Kat shook her head with vehemence.

"If you all will stop your guessing," Russell announced, "I would be glad to tell you our plans."

It was Audrey's turn. "Sorry. Go ahead."

"I'm going to move in to my new digs after we close at the end of the month," Russell said, and he perched on the arm of the sofa and looked around the room. "Since Kat's loose ends are tying up in New York very soon, she's going to move here as well."

Audrey deflated. She'd only just begun to come to terms with letting Kat go from her employ. Never once had she considered saying good-bye completely.

Kat moved next to Audrey and took her hand. Jiggling it, she told her, "I'll stay on until everything is wrapped up. I won't leave one minute sooner than you're ready for me to go."

"I'll never be ready for that," she muttered.

Suddenly, Audrey felt the heat of every eye in the room directed right at her.

"Audrey, are you going somewhere too?" Sean asked her.

"Uh, no, not . . . not exactly," she stammered.

"Audrey has been thinking of making some changes to her design business in New York," Emma said casually from the kitchen. "If she does, Kat might be freed up to find something else."

"And now she can find her something else right here in Atlanta with us," Fee added, and she embraced Kat around the shoulders. "I'm so glad you'll be sticking around."

"Me too," Russell added.

The smile pasted on Audrey's face felt like drying cement. Her cheeks ached and her eyes burned.

"That's really good news," J. R. said as he shook Russell's hand and smacked him on the arm. "You actually bought a house?"

"I did, mate."

"No more drinking, a new singing career, and a house? What's next?"

Russell cracked up. "You got me! I'm winging it here."

"It's really a time for change, isn't it?" Sherilyn commented. "It seems like everyone is moving into new seasons of their lives."

"Speaking of which," Andy chimed in, "does everyone in this room know that Sherilyn and I are expecting a baby?"

There's a second story to this house, Audrey pondered. *I wonder if that's tall enough for a successful jump from the roof.*

Top Three Hairstyle Techniques for the Vintage Bride

1. Finger Waves

Ridges placed in product-saturated hair using fingers and a comb.
C- or S-shaped waves in one direction and then the other.

2. Pin Curls

Comb a segment of hair into a ribbon and shape the ribbon into a pinwheel-type circular curl, overlapping as needed. Secure with a bobby pin or clip.

3. Barrel Curls

Comb out wet segments of hair and roll loosely over fingers. Once completely wrapped, secure with a pin or clip along the underside of the curl.

9

Emma and Sherilyn had prepared an impromtu supper of pasta primavera and greens salad, and every bite satisfied. Audrey wondered if she had ever been able to spontaneously whip up anything remotely like it for even two people, let alone for a whole group!

Sherilyn sat tucked on Andy's lap, a perfect fit, and looking for all the world like she belonged there; Sean and Fee went about the business of creaming their cups of coffee, arms interlocked as they did, and stealing quick, loving glances; Jackson stood at the kitchen counter putting the final touches on a cup of tea that he delivered to the table in front of Emma before he stroked her hair fondly and sat down beside her; the soft hum of conversation between Russell and Kat wafted in from the living room where they both sat on the floor in front of the unlit fireplace, Henry's big head collapsed in Russell's lap as he stroked the dog's fur.

J. R. seemed oddly solitary on the other side of the dining room table, his chair wedged into the corner, an untouched cup of coffee sitting before him. Despite being engaged in conversation with Andy and Sherilyn, Audrey wondered if J. R. felt as singular as she did. Reminded of a *What's Missing From*

This Picture? puzzle she'd once seen in the newspaper, she grinned, and J. R. looked up just in time to catch it. The smile he returned appeared lopsided, and the amusement in his eyes delighted Audrey.

"I think it's time for me to get back to the hotel," he announced without breaking eye contact with her. "Do you want a ride back?"

She nodded and immediately got to her feet. "I'd love that. Thank you."

Audrey rounded the table and leaned down to give Fee a hug.

"Thank you for the help with my dress," Fee said as they embraced.

"Are you kidding? I had a wonderful time. I appreciate being part of your day." She pressed her hand on Sean's shoulder and smiled. "Congratulations to both of you."

The journey from table to front door was an extended one as embraces and chit-chat paved the path. When she had just about reached the door, Audrey turned back to look for J. R. and found Jackson standing behind her instead.

"Audrey. I'd like to talk to you about something privately. Can you come to my office tomorrow morning?"

The request took her completely off guard. Nodding her head, she stumbled over her reply. "Uh, y-yes. Of . . . of course."

"Around ten?"

"Um, sure thing."

He squeezed her shoulder and smiled. "I'll see you then."

Scenarios raced through her mind as J. R. handed her one of the helmets in his arms and they stepped outside.

"Thanks for coming," Sherilyn said, and she and Andy waved at them from the porch door. "Drive safe, J. R."

"You know it."

They climbed aboard the bike and slipped on their helmets. Audrey wrapped her arms around J. R., and they sped down the driveway and around the curve of Sherilyn's street. All Audrey could see or think about was Jackson's request for her to come to his office. It seemed rather obvious to her. Emma had let on like the room was going to be taken care of, but perhaps Jackson had vetoed that idea and wanted to make payment arrangements.

I hardly have anything left to my name with no prospects for the future. What kind of arrangement can I agree to?

"Want to take the long way home?" J. R. called back to her.

"I don't think so," she returned. "I'm really tired."

He nodded. Without further discussion, he steered them to the main road into Roswell. Twenty minutes later, he walked her to Room 210.

"Do you want to come in?" she asked, hoping it didn't come off as a halfhearted invitation.

"Is there anything I can do?"

She tilted her head and considered his question. "I'm sorry. What do you mean?"

"You're out of sorts tonight. Is there anything I can do to help?"

She sighed. "Not really."

"Then I'll leave you to your thoughts."

"I'm sorry, J. R."

He shook his head and ran a hand through his mane of shaggy hair. "No need. But I'm here if you change your mind."

Audrey smiled. "Did you ever feel like life had something against you?"

He inspected the tips of his boots, nodding his head. "Life can be unreasonable that way sometimes, can't it?"

"You said it."

J. R.'s smile ignited, and he opened his arms to her. "C'mere."

She stepped into his embrace and sighed. The man had awesome arms, that was for certain. Burying her head in the crook of his neck, Audrey thanked him.

He planted a kiss on her temple and rubbed her back vigorously for a moment. "Call if you need anything."

"I will, J. R. Thank you."

After she closed the door between them, Audrey wondered if she'd made a mistake in sending him away. Even if she hadn't opened up the gates and unleashed every worry, every fear, every disastrous calamity of her tangled-up life, it might have been nice just to sit quietly with J. R. and let his light flood over her for a while.

She stood there, leaning against the door, and she sighed. Kicking off her shoes on the way, she plopped down on the bed and stared at the phone. Just two numbers into dialing Carly, she glanced at the clock and thought better of it. She hung up and pulled the drawer on the nightstand open. The menu caught her attention for a moment and she grabbed it, but she wasn't the least bit hungry. A leather-bound Bible got in the way when she tried to replace the menu, so she pulled it out of the drawer. She sighed and flipped it open at random.

"Isaiah, chapter fifty-four, verse eleven," she read. Someone had underlined the passage with a bright green pencil.

O you afflicted one,
Tossed with tempest, and not comforted,

"Yep," she said aloud. "That's definitely me."

Behold, I will lay your stones with colorful gems,
And lay your foundations with sapphires.

"Starting when?" she asked no one in particular, and she closed the Bible and replaced it. "Because now would be a very good time to toss some gems my way, if anyone is so inclined."

She sat perched on the edge of the bed in silence. She kicked her bare feet for a moment, then examined her bright red toenails. Before she sensed the approach, a cloud of emotion descended upon her, and Audrey started to cry. After a few minutes of it, she growled a note of surrender, clamped her eyes shut, folded her hands, and bowed her head.

"Seriously," she prayed. "I've never been one to look for someone to rescue me, but I'm reaching the end of a very short rope at the moment. If You have any rescue left in Your bag of tricks, I'd really appreciate You tossing it my way."

"Good morning. You must be Audrey Regan. Susannah Littlefield," she offered, and Audrey shook her hand. "Jackson's executive assistant."

"Pleased to meet you."

"He's expecting you. Go ahead in."

The woman's cherubic face radiated, and it nearly helped Audrey leave her anxiety behind at the door. But as she stepped into Jackson's office, concern crested again, and her stomach lurched slightly as he looked up from his desk and smiled.

"Audrey, thank you for coming in. Why don't you close the door and have a seat."

She draped the shoulder strap of her purse over the back of the chair and sat down, fidgeting with the hem of her cropped blouse and gently rubbing her hands over the thighs of her light denim jeans.

Audrey debated about speaking up first and making some sort of offer of reimbursing The Tanglewood for her accommodations; but before she could organize her thoughts, Jackson closed the laptop in front of him and leaned back into the large leather chair.

"I'll get right to the point," he told her, and her heart began to thump in her ears. She leaned forward to hear him over its beat. "Emma told me you'd had a recent disappointment with losing a prospective client."

Audrey nodded tentatively.

"She said you're struggling a little, and we were talking about how much we wished we could help."

"Well, you've certainly done a great deal to help," she told him with a smile. "I wouldn't have been able to stick around for Carly and Devon if you and Emma hadn't been so generous."

"About that," he began, and Audrey tightened her grasp on the arms of her chair.

"Listen, Jackson, I'll try to do whatever you think is fair to pay you back—"

He raised his hand and shook his head. "You'll do nothing of the kind. If I can't comp a night or two for someone now and then," he said, "what's the use of owning a hotel?"

He chuckled, and Audrey managed to lift a partial smile in response.

"Then . . . I don't understand."

"I think it's a bit serendipitous that you're staying, really. I have a buddy whose daughter is getting married."

Audrey's eyes instinctively narrowed as she tried to figure out the direction their conversation might take.

"Just recently, he told me about her situation. So when Emma shared your ordeal with the Renfroe woman, I immediately thought about you."

She opened her mouth slightly, but there were no words handy. Narrowing her eyes even more, she shook her head, and a little indecipherible noise escaped her throat before she said, “You thought of me . . . ?”

“Well, Curtis and I play basketball together,” he told her. “And we do some volunteer work. Anyhow, his daughter—I think her name is Lisette—she’s getting married in three weeks. She’s been working with a particular designer on her wedding dress, and the woman has flaked on her. I don’t know the whole story. But anyway, she apparently has certain . . . challenges. I don’t know if you would even want to step in, but I thought since you’re a dress designer, and Curtis’ daughter needs a wedding dress . . .”

He trailed off and stared at her tentatively. When she didn’t jump right in, he sighed.

“Okay. Probably not. Anyway, I just thought maybe—”

“Oh!” Audrey exclaimed. “No. I’m just . . . processing. I’m sorry. Go on.”

“Then you might be interested in helping her out?”

“Yes. Of course.” On second thought, “You said she has some challenges. What kind of challenges do you mean?”

“Well, she’s apparently quite . . . you know . . .” Jackson made a circular motion with both hands, and a pink blotch rose on his face as he said, “She’s a big girl.”

A big girl.

“She’s a very big girl.”

Very—

“Oh! You mean she’s overweight!”

“Yes,” he said, and he sighed. “Exactly.”

“How overweight?”

“I don’t know. *Really* overweight.”

Jackson was almost adorable in his efforts not to offend.

"Would you be willing to take a meeting with her?" he asked cautiously. "Just talk to her? The poor girl is just three weeks from her wedding, and now she doesn't have a dress. Emma says, after the cake, most of the wedding is really about the dress."

"Of course." She smiled at him, trying not to laugh right out loud. "Of course I will, Jackson."

He sighed noisily. "Really? That's great. I'd really consider it a personal favor, Audrey. This whole family has been very good to Emma and me as we started things up here at the hotel. Curtis is some sort of electrical genius, and he's saved my . . . Well. I really appreciate it, Audrey. I really do."

"I'm happy to do it. Do you have a contact number, or do you want to have them call me?"

"I'll get Lisette's number and get it to you later today."

Audrey pulled a business card from her purse and scribbled her cell phone number on the back. "This is my cell. I'm headed over to Carly and Devon's straight from here, but you can call me on this number any time today."

"Audrey, I really appreciate it. I know Curtis will, too."

"I'm happy to help." Audrey grabbed her purse and crossed the office. At the doorway, she turned back and asked, "Is her wedding here at the hotel?"

"Oh. No. It's downtown somewhere."

She thought it strange that Jackson's good friend hadn't utilized his stunning hotel for his daughter's wedding, but she shrugged it off and waved at him before tugging open the office door.

Audrey could hardly contain her excitement at the prospect of an actual design job. Lisette's electrician father probably couldn't afford the kind of thing Kim Renfroe had been looking for, of course, but if the girl had been working with a designer rather than buying something from a bridal shop, at least the prospect of some money was there. Not enough to save her business, but at least enough to pay the most immediate bills until she could figure something else out.

"I'll take it!" she exclaimed right out loud as she pressed the elevator button and leaned back against the glass wall.

"I've never designed plus size before, so I'll have to do some research and make a few sketches, but I'm really excited about it."

"Audrey, this might be a whole new facet to your designs," Kat said hopefully.

She shrugged and sipped her iced tea. She didn't know about that, but it was a job at least.

"Does this mean you'll be sticking around even longer?" Carly asked as she joined them at the patio table.

"I don't really know what it means until I talk to her and see if I'm what she's looking for."

"It would be so great if you could."

Something in Carly's voice drew Audrey's focus, and she set her glass down on the table and gazed at her friend.

"Caroline?"

That was all it took, and Carly crumpled like a snowflake on the hood of a warm car. She pinched a stream of tears from her eyes and dropped her head into her hands.

"Carly? What is it?" she asked, scooting closer and wrapping her arms around her friend's shoulders.

"Devon's going back, Aud. They're sending him back."

"No."

"Where's he going?" Kat asked them.

"Middle East," Audrey mouthed to her before asking Carly, "When?"

"As soon as the doctor gives the go-ahead."

"No," Audrey whispered. "Carly, I'm so sorry."

A steel brace seemed to move into her friend, and Carly sat erect, pounding her fist on the tabletop. "Haven't we given enough?" she seethed, thick rivers of tears flowing down her cheeks. "Haven't we sacrificed enough time together, enough peace of mind, enough—"

With a throaty groan, she sliced her own words in two, and she thrust her head to Audrey's shoulder with a growl of a moan.

"I'm so angry," she sobbed.

"I know."

"I just want him home. In this country. Safe!"

"I know. I want that too."

"It's so unfair."

"It is."

Carly lifted her head. "And he's so ridiculously patriotic, which drives me out of my ever-loving mind, Aud. It's not that I don't love my country too . . . It's just that . . . Is it awful to say that I love my husband more?"

"It's not awful at all," she reassured her, stroking her hair as Carly dropped her head to Audrey's shoulder again. "But remember that Devon's moral compass, and his allegiance to the Marine Corps . . . that's part of what makes you love him so much. It's all part of what makes him the Devon that you love."

"Not this morning, it doesn't make me love him," she whimpered. "This morning, it's what makes me want to wail on him and break some bones."

Audrey and Kat both chuckled.

"Hey!" Carly said with a gasp, and she sat straight up. "They'd let him stay home longer if he had some broken bones, right?"

Audrey shoved Carly's head back to her shoulder and held it there.

"Down, girl. We're not breaking any bones here today."

Audrey's cell phone sounded from her purse and, as she reached for it, Carly asked, "I've been meaning to ask you. Is that a harp?"

"It's God calling. He asked for a direct line," she quipped in reply. "Audrey Regan."

"Audrey? My name is Lisette Gibson."

Audrey straightened, tapping on the tabletop at Kat as she answered, "Yes! My gown-challenged bride!"

Lisette laughed. "Word travels fast."

"Jackson and your father are very good friends. Jackson asked me to help if I can."

"Well, let me tell you right out front, Audrey. I've got three weeks until the wedding. I'm a size twenty-six, and I have hips that will give you nightmares. I've named my boobs North and South Carolina because they're the size of small states and, if you're actually willing to try and rescue me, you're crazier than I am."

Audrey burst into laughter. "I'm a fan of the southern states," she finally replied. "Why don't we get together and talk about how best to fly their flags."

"You sound like my kind of girl," Lisette told her. "When?"

"Can you come to The Tanglewood?"

"Any time you say."

"We're off to a good start, Lisette. Meet me at three this afternoon?"

"Absolutely."

"I'll make an appointment for tea in the courtyard and meet you there. We'll talk about what you're looking for and see if I can help."

"I can tell you that right now. I'm looking for a dress that will make me look like Jennifer Lopez. Think you can pull that off, Audrey?"

"Well, I can try. And if we can't do that, we'll shoot for *George* Lopez."

Lisette snorted. "How about *Mario* for a happy medium?"

"Done!"

"I'll see you at three."

"I'm looking forward to it."

"You know what?" Lisette asked in a soft voice. "So am I."

The instant she disconnected the call, the three of them came alive.

"I'll need to get back to the hotel to do some research."

"You can use my computer," Carly exclaimed. "I'll go get it."

As she hurried into the house, Audrey thanked her and turned immediately to Kat. "I'll need a sketch pad."

"I'll run out and get you some supplies and meet you at the hotel in an hour?"

"Good. And Kat? Thank you."

"For what?"

"Everything."

Kat grinned, tapped Audrey's shoulder as she hurried past Carly.

"It's all booted up and ready to go," she told her, setting an open white laptop on the table in front of her.

"What's going on?" Devon asked, standing in the doorway in his bathrobe, eyes squinting into the sun.

"No, no, baby, not now," Carly said, taking his arm and leading him back into the house. "Audrey has to focus. You go back to bed, and I'll bring you a sandwich."

"Any more Yoo-hoo?"

"You don't need any more. You had three of them yesterday. I'll bring you iced tea and those little cookies you like."

"The ones with the raisins or the ones with the chocolate chips?"

"Chocolate chips. Now scoot!"

The patio door clicked shut as Audrey typed **wedding plus size** into the search engine. Halfway down the page, she noticed an article about things to watch out for when styling the larger body, and she clicked on it and began to read.

A few moments later, the patio door whooshed open again, and J. R. appeared.

"Hey! I just got here and saw you out here with—"

"Uh-uh!" Carly exclaimed, cutting his words in half and dragging him back into the house by the arm. "No. She's working. Go upstairs with Devon. I'll bring you a cookie."

Audrey glanced back at him as the door closed between them, and she couldn't help but laugh as J. R. asked Carly, "What kind of cookie?"

Audrey wasn't entirely sure what she'd expected, but the young woman seated across from her wasn't it. Lisette Gibson may have been a size 26, and she was indeed more graciously endowed than any woman Audrey'd ever met in person, but that's where her challenges ended, as far as Audrey could see. Elbow-length blonde hair, crystal blue eyes, peaches-and-cream complexion, legs for days, even for someone standing tall at around 5'9".

"So I warned you," she teased. "It's not an enviable butt I'm packing here."

Audrey chuckled. "But we work with what we're given, right?"

"That's the plan."

"Why don't you tell me about your original wedding gown," she suggested as she filled both china cups with tea from the beautiful porcelain pot. Selecting a couple of cookies and squares of cake for each of their plates, she added, "What was your vision?"

"The cake is green," Lisette pointed out. "What kind of cake is green?"

"Pistachio, I think."

"Oh. Okay, I'll try some."

Audrey dropped the green cake with the chocolate ribbon running through it to Lisette's plate. "Where was I?" she asked. "Oh. Your vision."

"Well, which one do you want to hear about?" Lisette asked her with an arched brow. "My vision or the original gown? Because the two are very, very different."

Audrey nodded. "I see."

"I brought you a photo of me in the dress at the time of the first fitting."

Lisette slid the photograph across the table, and a fraction of a groan escaped Audrey's throat before she could stop it.

"So you see my dilemma."

"I'm afraid so."

The beautiful plus-sized woman across from her had been jammed into an expensive lace sausage casing. Audrey understood Lisette's distress.

"We went through three different versions of this dress before I finally gave up. She just couldn't seem to interpret what was up here," and she tapped at her forehead, "to get it down here," then tapped the photograph. "I guess maybe it wasn't her fault. I knew she hadn't designed for a bigger model before, and when she looked at me with such . . . *panic* . . . I guess I should have taken my business elsewhere right then and there. But Riley Eastwood does such beautiful work. I thought for sure she could translate that on a larger scale."

"That's who you worked with?" Audrey clarified. "Riley Eastwood?"

"Yes. She did my cousin's gown, and it was just breathtaking."

"She's amazing."

Audrey picked up the photograph and examined it more carefully, struggling to imagine someone whose designs rivaled Stella McCartney and Vera Wang designing . . . *this*.

"Isn't Riley Eastwood headquartered in Chicago?"

"Yes. And I flew back and forth four times with nothing to show for it."

Audrey gazed at the photograph again wondering how such a gifted designer could have gone so terribly, terribly wrong.

"I'm not one of those people who believes a big woman should only wear an A-line muumuu," Lisette explained. "I do have a shape under here, and I try to accentuate it when I can. But not to this degree. I think there's something between muumuu and sausage casing." Tapping her trim pink fingernail on the tabletop and working very hard to hold back the threatening emotion on her horizon, she nibbled on the corner of her lip and raised her gaze to meet Audrey's. "My fiancé really does love me, Audrey. Just the way I am, big butt and all. I want to look over-the-top beautiful for him on our wedding day. Is that too much to ask?"

"No," Audrey softly replied. "You're a gorgeous woman, Lisette. We just need to play to your strengths."

"What do you think then?"

Audrey had never been given to insecurities, at least not where her designs were involved. But Kim Renfroe had contributed the direct hit that had left a gaping wound. Further, if this bride couldn't work out satisfaction with a Riley Eastwood design, what would she think of Audrey Regan?

It's too late for second thinking now, she decided, and she lifted her portfolio from the floor where it leaned against her chair.

"I made these preliminaries before meeting you, of course," she said as she unzipped the leather case that had once housed Kim's gown sketches. "I was thinking about how you described yourself on the phone—which didn't nearly do you justice, by the way—and I thought a fit-and-flare silhouette seemed like a good bet. Meeting you, I think it might be really flattering on you." She opened to the first sketch and held it up for Lisette to view. "Fitted on the top with a thin ruffled assymetric strap over one shoulder, not too much cleavage, tighter at the waist, and only a slight flare at the bottom."

Lisette didn't utter a word, but she nodded enthusiastically.

Audrey flipped the page to the next sketch of the three she'd had time to do before their meeting.

"This one looks good on just about any body type," she said. "Strapless with a sweetheart neckline, empire waist, and then these beautiful layers of flowy chiffon for the skirt. You would look stunning in this."

"Mm-hmm."

Not much reaction to go on, so Audrey continued.

"And this third one is a beaded, blingy bodice with lace cap sleeves, and a sort of princess ball gown skirt with beaded tulle and a stiff organza petticoat. I think any one of the three would be—"

"The first one."

Audrey clamped her lips tight at the interruption.

"I adore the first one."

"Okay." She flipped back to the first page and held it up toward Lisette.

"Audrey, it's just what I had in my head."

"It is?"

"Absolutely. Not too much dress. It will show my curves without outlining them. I just would like a little more bling. Can we do some bling?"

Audrey grinned. "Bling is my specialty."

"It is?"

"Do you want to keep the strap?"

"Yes! Absolutely."

"Then since the strap is a ruffled flower of sorts, how about we add a few rhinestone petals right here," she suggested, pointing out the spot where the strap met the bodice. "And we can use a fabric with crystal beads and rhinestones, maybe in an ivy type pattern on the skirt to give you the sparkle you're looking for."

"Perfect," Lisette cooed.

"And with the shoulder being so dramatic, what do you think of this? Instead of a traditional veil, we could place a crystal band in your hair. Not a tiara, but more of a headband that—"

"Yes. With a veil at the back. Kind of like this . . ." With both hands, she demonstrated the flow of her imaginary veil, the one Audrey could see had been living in her mind since the day her fiancé had proposed. Maybe longer. "And I want a spectacular view from behind. Maybe a great train, or some sort of design that draws the eye while camouflaging the tush?"

"Okay. I have some thoughts about that," Audrey said, sketching them out. "How about—"

She looked up just in time to notice the tears in Lisette's pretty eyes.

"I'll do some final sketches this afternoon and email them to you for approval."

Lisette nodded. "And you promise it won't come out of your sketch pad and onto my body looking like *this*?" she asked, holding up the photograph she'd brought along.

"Oh, yes. I promise."

"Here's a harder one for you. What are the chances of having this dress in three weeks and one day though?"

"Well," she said, closing up the portfolio. "I'll be returning to New York in a couple of days, so—"

"I can't go to New York, Audrey. I've got wedding plans up to my eyeballs at the moment. Is there any chance you could stay in Atlanta while you work on my dress?"

Audrey hesitated, a cool chill moving through her when her bank balance breezed across her mind's eye.

"What will it take to make that happen, Audrey?"

"Well. I would need to snag some work space, and—"

"Look," she interrupted again. "Whatever it takes, I'll pay it. I need you and this dress. Whatever you need to stay through my wedding day, consider it done."

"Lisette, I don't think you realize how expensive it can be to—"

"I'll worry about the dollars. You just make that first sketch come to life for me. Okay?" When Audrey paused, she leaned toward her. "Seriously. I really feel like you understand. I need a designer who understands."

Audrey sighed. "You're going to be a very beautiful bride."

Lisette bounded from her chair and rounded the table, wrapping her arms around Audrey, and swaying her from side to side. "Thank you! Thank you so much!"

Audrey had to admit that she really looked forward to sinking her creativity into this one. And the joy of supplying something for Lisette that no one else could or would—that just made it all the more sweet.

Lisette pulled her checkbook from her purse and began writing before Audrey could even consider quoting a price. She tore out the check and extended it toward Audrey. "This should get you started with what you need. Get your ducks in a row, consider what you need to stay here in Atlanta for three weeks, and just give me the invoice."

Audrey found it hard to swallow around the lump in her throat as she stared at the check. "Five thousand dollars."

"I know. It's not nearly enough. But find out how much it will cost for your work space, the supplies, your accommodations, and I'll cut you a check for the balance. You can't believe how much I need you, Audrey."

"Back atcha," she muttered. "Thank you."

Top Five Wedding Gown Embellishments

1. **Beading**

Small pieces of glass, crystal, or gems which are glued or sewn to the fabric

2. **Seed Pearls**

Tiny versions of faux or real pearls used to create patterns

3. **Sequins**

Small iridescent disks applied to the fabric to create shimmer

4. **Bugle Beads**

Tubular glass beads sewn close together to form a line pattern, such as a vine

5. **Lace Appliqués**

Lace patterns sewn on to the dress

10

She just handed you a check for five thousand dollars. And . . . her father is an electrician? *Are you sure?*"

"I know!" she told Carly through the cell phone as Kat tapped at the laptop on the table beside her. "Okay, Kat is back, and she wants to talk fabric. I've got to go."

"But you'll be here for dinner, right?"

"Well . . ."

"Aud. You'll be here for dinner. Right?"

"Yes."

"Good. And Kat too."

"I'll tell her you asked."

"Now get to work!"

"I'm on it."

"And Audrey?"

"What?"

"I'm so proud of you."

"Thanks, Caroline. See you around six."

She hadn't even pressed the button to end their call before Kat kicked into gear from where she sat at the tiny desk in the corner of the hotel room. "I scanned them, and Sherilyn let me use her computer to send them off. I've already spoken to Lisette, and she loves them and said to tell you to 'Go forth and create.' Now, there are three possibilities downtown for quick turnaround on fabric. We can go and see the options in person, maybe take the bride with us so we don't have to bother with samples? And as far as work space goes, it may end up being easier to rent the equipment and just settle in here at the hotel. Although there won't be much space unless we get a bigger room. I'm not sure if they have bigger rooms aside from the bridal suite. Do you know? We could request the bridal suite again and both of us stay there and have some work space. What do you think?"

When she finally paused to take a breath, Audrey commented, "I have something else in mind for work space," and she curled her legs underneath her on the bed as she took the sketch pad from Kat and flipped to the one Lisette had approved. "How close together are the three fabric places?"

"I'll find out."

"I want to schedule Lisette for measurements first thing tomorrow morning. Can you set that up?"

"Yes."

"Do you want to have dinner at Carly's tonight?"

"Can't."

Audrey glanced over at Kat, taking notes from the computer screen, tapping out addresses into the GPS. She marveled at how skilled Kat could be at handling multiple tasks, everything all at once.

"Plans with Russell?"

"Mm-hmm." She tossed down the pen in her hand and smacked the desktop. "They're very close together. Do you want to go now?"

"No, let's get her measurements before we commit to fabrics. I'll also need the addresses of some embellishment shops, just in case they don't have what I need at the fabric stores. Can you—"

"On it."

"And we'll have to think about finding a plus-size dress form. Do they even make them above a size eighteen?"

"I'll find out."

Audrey wondered for the hundredth time what she would ever do without Kat to handle all her details. She reminded herself that she needn't worry about that; for at least three weeks anyway.

She examined her cell phone for several minutes before asking Kat, "How do I find the number of someone who called me?"

"See where it says Call Log on the top bar?"

"Yes."

"Click there. Scroll down."

Audrey followed the directions and scrolled until she found the number she needed. "Is there an easy way to dial it back once I find it?"

"Just hit the green button while it's showing on your screen."

She did, and Weston LaMont's voice mail picked up on the third ring.

"Wes," she said, far more casually than she felt. "It's Audrey Regan. Remember how you said you wanted to make it up to me for heartlessly stealing Kim Renfroe right out from under me?" She added a chuckle for effect. "I think I know how you can do that. Can you give me a ring back, please? Thanks. Talk to you soon."

When she disconnected the call, she looked up to find Kat grinning at her.

"Brilliant," she remarked.

"Let's hope so. How about we start gathering the numbers and put together an invoice for Lisette?"

"I've already started an Excel spreadsheet," she began.

Of course you have.

"I can make Austin in two days' ride," J. R. remarked as he inspected the map on the screen of Carly's laptop. "If I leave here on Monday morning, that will get me in late Tuesday night."

"You're leaving that soon?" she asked, standing behind him. "I thought you might stick around until Devon ships out."

"I wish I could, but I've got a pretty big job possibility in Austin."

"Oh."

Carly's disappointment clouded the room like a thick vapor.

"Come on, babe," Devon reassured her from the sofa a few feet away. "I know you'd like it to, but the world can't stop just because I'm shipping out again."

"Yes, it can."

"Yours, but not everyone else's. My bro needs to work in Austin, Audrey needs to go home to New York—"

"Oh!" she cut him off. "I didn't tell you. Audrey's in town for three more weeks!"

"She is?" J. R. interjected.

"Yeah, Jackson hooked her up with the daughter of a friend who is getting married. She had a bridal gown disaster, and he connected them. It's a good time for a windfall, and Audrey's going to work with her until the wedding."

"So she'll be here with you after I leave," Devon concluded. "That is so great. I hate leaving you alone. Bro, maybe you can swing back into town and check on my doll baby at some point."

J. R. felt a little like an intruder as Carly caved in to Devon on the sofa and buried her face in his chest. It wrenched something inside his gut to think of the two of them being separated again so soon after their vow renewal.

"You could stay a little longer if you flew to Austin instead of taking your bike," Carly unexpectedly suggested. "Couldn't you?"

"That would give you more time with Audrey," Devon jabbed.

"Shut it."

"Audrey?" Carly interjected. "Are you interested in Audrey?"

"Russell caught them sucking face the other—"

"What? Why don't I know about this?"

"—night. Oh yeah, and my bro has stars in his eyes whenever she walks into a room. Haven't you noticed?"

"Couldn't you fly to Austin then? That would give you a couple more days here. For Audrey, and for your brother."

"Don't make something out of nothing with Audrey," he replied, tilting back in the chair. "And flying would mean a huge extra expense, and renting a car too. I can't sink that much into the trip before it's a done deal."

"J. R.," she said, her eyes pleading with him.

"I never realized how rough it is, working for yourself," Devon piped up. "J. R. and Audrey both have to be so cautious while building their businesses, sweetie. That's one thing about the Corps. They pay us, whether we ask for it or not."

"Yeah," Carly mumbled. "We get those peanuts each and every month like clockwork. But still, J. R.—"

"Carly. C'mon."

That look from Devon flipped off her switch at last.

"Fine. I have to run to the market to pick up a few things for dinner."

"Just tell me what you need," J. R. offered. "I'll go."

"Really? Well, thank you. The list is on the refrigerator."

J. R. crossed to the kitchen and pulled down the list. A perfect excuse to get out of there.

"Take the truck, bro."

He nodded, grabbed Devon's keys from the counter and headed straight out.

J. R. drew in a lungful of fresh air and groaned as he released it. Like so many visits in their past, once again J. R. walked out that front door feeling like such a massive disappointment. Not so much to Devon, but definitely to Carly. She just never did understand. And Carly obviously knew nothing about whatever it was going on between him and Audrey. And now that she did know, she was sure to grill Audrey about it at first opportunity.

Ah man, she's gonna hate that.

He climbed into Devon's truck, turned over the key, pushing buttons on the radio until he landed on a rock tune. He'd had more than enough of Devon's country songs to last him. But by the time he reached the intersection, the lyrics started to poke at him, and he changed the station again.

Neil Diamond. That should be safe, right?

"Why didn't you tell me you kissed J. R.?"

Audrey just stood there, stunned, her mouth hanging open slightly as she scratched her head.

"Are you going to let me in?"

Carly stepped back, and Audrey waltzed past her into the house.

"Okay, you're in. Now I want details."

"There's nothing to tell," she replied, and she walked into the living room. "Hi, Devon. How are you feeling?"

"Hey! A little bett—"

"Oh, no you don't. You're not going to make unimportant small talk with my husband. Come into the kitchen with me."

"Unimportant?" Devon said with a chuckle. "Sweetie, she asked how I'm feeling."

"You know what I mean. He's fine. Doing better. Had a bowel movement. Now follow me!"

Audrey and Devon pulled faces at one another as Audrey obeyed Carly's command.

"Sit down and talk while I chop."

"Can I—"

"Do something to help? Yes. You can spill your guts."

Audrey sighed. "What would you like to know? It was a couple of kisses, Caroline."

"More than one?"

"Yes. Maybe . . . I don't know. Three?"

"Three kisses?" she exclaimed, and Audrey shushed her. "Three kisses, and you never thought to tell me about it?"

"Nope."

"Aud."

"Carly."

Carly stomped her foot lightly and smacked the chopping knife down on the counter. "Come on."

"It was nothing. It didn't mean anything. It's not leading anywhere. It was just a couple of isolated kisses between two people."

Carly picked up the knife again and began dicing an onion with surprising strength and speed. "You and I both know," she muttered, "there's no such thing as an isolated kiss. But if you want to carry on with that charade, and you want me to play along like—"

Audrey knew Carly could go on like that for hours. As a preemptive strike, she stepped forward and put an arm around Carly's shoulder. "It was a momentary lapse, Caroline. I was worried about what was happening with Kim and my business, and J. R. was really nice to me. That's it."

"That's it?"

"Nothing more."

"So you're not going to be my sister-in-law?"

One hard laugh popped out of Audrey. "No. I am not."

"Fine."

She began chopping again, and Audrey placed her hand over Carly's until she stopped. "What's going on?"

She looked up, and for a moment Audrey blamed the onions for the liquid standing in Carly's eyes.

"J. R. is so selfish."

"Oh," she replied, taking the knife away and leading Carly toward the table. "Sit down with me for a minute." Once they settled, she said, "Tell me."

"He's got that thing their father had."

"Which is . . . ?"

"That roaming thing, Aud. He can't light in one place. It's like he's afraid if he stops moving, the world will swallow him up or something. Just once, I'd like him to think about what it does to Devon every time he packs up his bike and heads out again. Oh, I just resent him so much right now. His brother needs him, and—"

She fell silent, mid-word. Audrey turned around to see what Carly had already seen, Devon standing in the kitchen doorway.

"I'm sorry," she offered, and the tears standing in her eyes spilled down her cheek. "I know you don't like to hear me say those things."

Devon crossed the kitchen, touching Audrey's shoulder as he approached his wife. "Is this really about me?"

Carly's confusion caught in her throat. "I don't know what you mean."

"Sweetie, I'd love it if J. R. stuck around. But it's not what he's made of. He's got a life on the road. I understand that. But I don't think you do."

She caught Audrey's eye for a quick second before looking down at the tabletop.

"Maybe having J. R. around feels a little like you have part of me staying here with you?" he suggested.

After a long moment, she answered. "A little." Devon stroked her hair as she told him, "But that's really not all of it, Dev. I worry about him. He's thirty-one years old, and he lives like some sort of nomad." Looking to Audrey, she added, "You should see where he lives in New Mexico. It's more of a bike stop than a home."

"I think that's what you said about my place in New York, isn't it?" Audrey pointed out.

"Did I?"

"Yes. You said it looked like a design studio that I flopped in for a while."

The corner of Carly's mouth tilted into half a grin. "I guess I did say that."

"Not everyone is like you, Caroline. Some of us take another road."

"Well . . . you all should just stop it."

That broke the tension and all three of them laughed.

"I just want you to be happy, Aud."

"And J. R.," Devon added.

"Yes. I want him to be happy too."

"So maybe you should let him follow his bliss?" Audrey suggested.

"On a motorcycle, on the road forty weeks every year?"

"If that's where it takes him."

The front door whooshed open, keys jingled, and J. R.'s footsteps announced his return. Devon stroked Carly's hair one last time before turning toward the doorway.

"Thanks for going, bro."

"No problem," he said as he set two bags of groceries on the table. "Hey, Audrey."

"Hi, J. R."

He looked from one of them to the other before asking, "What's going on?"

"I know we've sort of started things with dinner, but do you know what I'd like to do?" Devon piped up. "Let's get out of here, what do you say?"

"Devon, you can't."

"I can, sweetie. I feel good. We won't do anything like climb a rock wall or anything. Let's go out to Happy Days again, just the four of us."

"You can't bowl."

"So I'll eat burgers and sing karaoke."

"Oh, no," Audrey cried.

"Come on. How many times will all four of us be in one place?" Devon reminded them. "My sweetie and my bro, you two BFFs. Give me this before I ship out."

"We are not going to Happy Days, Dev."

"How about we just go out for dinner somewhere then? Somewhere low key. Just the four of us."

"What about Morelli's?" Audrey suggested. "The food is magnificent."

Okay, so it wasn't entirely about the food. Having dinner at the hotel would get her back to the room for some work time that much sooner.

Devon checked in with Carly. "Okay?"

"All right. Let me put away the vegetables."

"So we're up for it? I'll get dressed."

They exchanged glances, and J. R. groaned. "All right, but don't think you're going to pull that 'Before I ship out' card three times a day until you leave."

As he passed J. R., Devon smacked his brother's arm. "How about once a day, just because I can?"

"Move it out before we change our minds."

"I'm so sorry. We won't have a table for four until at least nine o'clock. Would you like me to put you on the list?"

Sails deflated, wind nonexistent.

"No, thank you." Carly rubbed Devon's arm. "Sorry, baby."

While the four of them stood at the entrance of the restaurant considering their options, Audrey spotted Sherilyn strolling through the lobby, and J. R. waved and caught her eye.

"Hey!" she sang as they moved toward one another. "What's up?"

"We had the colossal bad idea of coming out for dinner without making a reservation," he said on a laugh as Audrey walked up to them.

"Oooh, yeah. It's a really busy night at Morelli's."

"Any guidance on where we can go nearby?"

"As a matter of fact, I do," she replied as Carly and Devon joined them as well. "We had a cocktail party in the courtyard earlier, and they're just cleaning up. It's a gorgeous night. How about I ask Pearl to set you up with a light supper out there?"

"Really? A private party? That sounds like fun," Carly cried, and she looked around for agreements.

"Good!" Sherilyn answered. "Go on out and make yourselves at home. I'll talk to Pearl and see what she can do for you."

J. R. took the lead, and they moved out to the courtyard where several uniformed waiters removed table linens and placed glasses into plastic bins on rolling metal carts. A breeze rustled the leaves of tall trees laced with hundreds of tiny white lights, and the distant echo of music from one of the ballrooms whispered overhead.

"Here?" Carly suggested, and J. R. nodded.

"Sit down, bro," he told Devon. "You look like you might fall down."

J. R. set about dragging a couple of bistro tables closer together as Carly sat down next to Devon and took his hand. "Baby, you doing all right?"

Audrey took note of Devon's change in color and expression, and it didn't surprise her when Carly helped him to his feet. "I'm so sorry, you two. It was just too soon for Dev. We're going to head back home."

"Do you want me to drive you?" J. R. asked them.

"You and Audrey enjoy your meal. At least you won't have a long way to go home."

"I'm so sorry, guys," Devon offered.

Audrey chuckled. "Take care, Dev." She squeezed Carly's hand and added, "I'll call you in the morning."

"Love you both," Carly said, her focus already shifted to Devon as she led him through the glass doors to the lobby.

"I'll go catch up to Sherilyn and let her know it's just the two of us," J. R. told Audrey. "If you still want to have dinner, that is."

She nodded and shrugged one shoulder. "Of course. Sure."

She watched him go before taking a seat, crossing her legs and leaning back against the cool scrollwork of the chair. She caught the eye of the last waiter. He wheeled a cart and paused at her table.

"Can I have the bartender bring something out for you?" he asked. "I think there's some wine left from the party before."

"Oh, no," she replied. "But thank you."

"Sure thing. Have a good night."

"You too."

Audrey tried to imagine a hotel or restaurant in New York where someone might stop and offer a free glass of wine for no other reason than just to be courteous, but she couldn't manage it. Surely the place existed, but she hadn't run across it in Manhattan, Soho, or anywhere in between.

When the harp in her purse jingled, she expected Kat or Carly on the screen. Instead, Weston LaMont's name appeared.

"Audrey. Wes LaMont. How are you?"

"Doing very well, Wes. Thank you."

"I'm intrigued by the message you left me this afternoon."

"Oh good. That's what I was going for."

His chuckle seemed uncharacteristically good-natured, and she sighed in relief.

"So four-one-one me, my dear."

"I've come upon a design project here in Atlanta," she told him. "It's going to keep me in town for another few weeks, and I'm in the market for some work space to pull it together. I was hoping you might have some room for me at your studio. Just a corner with a machine and a cutting table, a few tools."

"I'm intrigued. What are you working on?"

"A wedding gown for a special client."

"And you'll be staying in town rather than going back to New York?"

"That's the plan."

"Who is your client?"

The question stopped time for a second. She wasn't sure she wanted to reveal any of the details, and she chastised herself for not considering that he might ask for them.

"It's a favor for a friend. Can you help me out?"

LaMont paused for a long couple of moments before he answered. "Let me check our production schedule in the morning, and I'll call you."

"I appreciate it."

"And if I can't manage it right now, I'll have my assistant make a couple of suggestions for you."

"Thank you so much."

Audrey disconnected the phone and slipped it back into her purse before noticing J. R. sitting across from her. She tucked a wave of hair behind her ear and smiled.

"Weston LaMont."

"Genius of draping," he recalled.

"You were listening."

"It's not a common name."

She grinned at him. "I'm hoping he'll rent me some work space in his design studio for this new project I'm working on."

"Carly told me. You'll be sticking around then."

"For a few weeks, anyway. You?"

"I leave for Austin on Tuesday."

A waitress approached their table, halting their exchange for the moment. "Pearl asked me to tell you that our specials tonight are our signature filet bites with creamy horseradish sauce, seared mushrooms and rum-glazed mashed sweet potatoes, or fresh Chilean sea bass with garlic smashed potatoes, sweet corn relish and grilled asparagus."

Audrey's cheeks puffed with air before she blew it out slowly. "Whoa."

"I'll have the first dish," J. R. told her. "Thank you."

"And you, ma'am?"

She paused for a moment. "I was really looking for something a little less extravagant."

"Would you like to see a menu?"

"No," she replied. "I had some wonderful macaroni and cheese the other night. Do you have any of that in the kitchen?"

"Absolutely. It's on our menu every day. Would you like a salad of greens with it?"

"Perfect."

"Dressing?"

"Balsamic."

"And can I bring either of you a cocktail?"

"Just an iced sweet tea for me," Audrey answered.

"Works for me as well."

"All right then. I'll bring your beverages momentarily."

J. R. waited for the waitress to disappear before commenting, "Pretty good for an off-the-cuff little dinner, huh?"

"The Tanglewood doesn't do anything halfway, that's for sure."

J. R. leaned back in his chair and laughed. Audrey didn't know if it was the unique acoustics in the courtyard or just the tone quality of J. R.'s smooth voice, but she felt his laughter in the deepest parts of her.

"You have a great laugh," she told him, and his smile turned slightly lopsided.

"Thanks."

"So how long will you be in Austin?"

"Pardon?"

"You said you're headed there. I just wondered."

"Oh. It's just a shot at a job. I met a guy at a show in Vegas last year. He and five of his buddies have Harleys in their garages that they want to restore so they can make like Easy Riders next summer."

Audrey grinned. "Groovy."

"I guess," he said with a sigh. "It's not that I don't love my work. I do. I love the guys who ride their Harleys every day, you know? But even though the Easy Riders bring in the bulk of my income, I have to admit that it's a little unsatisfying to spend all the time and effort restoring bikes for guys who ride them for a few weeks one summer, and then let them rust away in their garages or under a tarp in the backyard."

"Believe me, I understand," she told him. "Imagine spending months on a design that someone wears once." He nodded. "For only a few hours."

J. R. broke into a full laugh. "Okay, you win."

In stereo, they exclaimed, "Or lose!"

The waitress set two glasses and a pitcher of iced tea on the table. "Your dinner will be out in just a few minutes," she told them.

"So what would you do if you weren't a Harley man?" Audrey asked.

"I love to build things," he replied, and he gulped down some of the tea.

"What, like houses?"

"No. I'm more of a carpenter. In the off months, I shove the motorcycles to the back of my garage and pull out the wood and the sander."

"A carpenter," she said, thinking it over. "So what do you carpent?"

J. R. chuckled. "Bookshelves, cabinets, chairs. Last winter I made a dining table and chairs for one of my customers."

"Really! So you're not so different from me."

J. R. leaned back against the chair and grinned. "Wedding dresses and dining furniture."

"Well," she said with a laugh, "I mean, we start from scratch and build something from the ground up. I craft a beautiful wedding gown, and you create the table the newlyweds will move into their first home. Either way, it's starting with nothing and ending with something, right?"

"Interesting vantage point," he observed. "I suppose you're right."

"I love the rush of starting with a simple sketch, and working for weeks or months to turn that idea into reality. But even though she wears that gown on the most important day of her life, I'll never have the chance that most designers have. I won't walk down a street in Manhattan and run into some girl from the fashion district who's wearing one of my designs. That would be . . . *beyond!*"

J. R. leaned forward as he told her, "I was riding into Santa Fe about a year ago, and I saw this amazing bike up ahead of me. I gunned it to catch up and have a look because I could see the thing was cherry. When I got there, I realized it was one of mine. I'd restored it the year before in Tucson, and there it was, riding into Santa Fe."

"See, that makes me almost swoon," she admitted. "I would love to have that experience. Just turn a corner, you know? And see someone wearing an Audrey Regan original."

The waitress laid out their beautiful dinner on the table before them, and Audrey's mouth began to water at first whiff. Conversation flowed freely between them and, when the waitress returned to offer dessert and coffee, she noticed the time on the girl's watch.

"It can't be nine-thirty!" she exclaimed. "How is that possible?"

"Is Mrs. Drummond still in the hotel?" J. R. asked her.

"Yes, she'll be here late tonight. She has a vow renewal in the main ballroom. Would you like me to get a message to her?"

"Just thank her for us. Pearl too. The meal was first-rate. If you'll bring us the check—"

"Pearl said your meal is gratis," the girl explained. "But I'll give Sherilyn your message."

Audrey and J. R. exchanged surprised smiles. "Are you sure?" Audrey asked her.

"Quite sure. Have a lovely evening."

"Please at least take this for your trouble," J. R. said, offering her a folded bill. "The service was even better than the meal."

"Thank you so much."

When she'd gone, Audrey shook her head. "This place has been so good to me. I kind of never want to leave."

"I know the feeling."

After a moment, Audrey clasped her hands behind her head and stretched. "Mac and cheese. Comfort food. I actually feel like I could sleep."

J. R. smiled at her, and the twinkling lights glimmered in his eyes, melting them down to a deep steel blue. "Walk you home?" he asked, and he stood up and offered her his hand.

"Please," she said, accepting it.

They took their time strolling to the elevator, and they chatted about the night sky as they peered through the glass and ascended above the courtyard. When they reached the second floor, Audrey yawned as the doors opened. It occurred to her that she hadn't felt so relaxed in a very long time. When she turned around to share the thought with J. R., he stood close behind her.

She looked up into his eyes for a long, warm moment.

"Good night," she finally whispered, and she resisted a swoon as he smoothed her hair away from her face. She hesitated, looking down, and then back into his eyes. "I had a really nice time."

"Me too."

Those blue-gray eyes of his had her transfixed. She knew she should look away, but she just couldn't manage it.

Kiss me. Kiss me. Kiss me.

"Sleep well, Audrey."

"Okay. You too."

Traditional Macaroni and Cheese
Comfort Food from Morelli's Restaurant

Preheat oven to 375 degrees

3 cups elbow macaroni, cooked and drained
3 Tablespoons cornstarch
1½ teaspoons salt
¾ teaspoon dry mustard
½ teaspoon black pepper
12-ounce can evaporated milk
1½ cups water
3 Tablespoons butter
3½ cups shredded sharp Cheddar cheese
¼ cup grated Parmesan cheese
¼ cup crumbled bleu cheese
½ cup softened cream cheese

Mix evaporated milk, water, and butter in medium saucepan.
Add cornstarch, salt, mustard, and pepper.
Cook over medium heat, stirring constantly until mixture boils.
Allow ingredients to boil for approximately one minute, and remove from heat.
Stir in 2 cups of the Cheddar cheese and all of the other cheeses until melted.
Add macaroni and mix well.
Pour mixture into greased two-quart casserole dish.
Top with remaining Cheddar cheese and grated Parmesan.
Bake for 25 minutes until cheese is melted and top is a light golden brown.

11

An early knock at her hotel room door drew Audrey away from the window where she'd been standing for who knew how long, sifting over that moment when she'd said goodnight to J. R. She couldn't remember ever wanting a kiss so much, and even now—in the light of a new day—a cooler head had not prevailed. Her thoughts wrapped around that wish so hard that she found it a little hard to breathe.

Kat must have her hands full, she thought as she headed for the door.

But when she opened it, Sherilyn stood on the other side instead of Kat.

"Good morning!"

"Sherilyn. Hi. How are you?"

She shrugged and crinkled up her nose slightly as she admitted, "Sick as an expectant mother."

"Oh. Sorry. Would you like to come in?"

"I come bearing latte," she announced, handing Audrey one of the three paper cups in her hands. "I hope you like vanilla?"

"I do. Thank you so much."

"Listen, I know you're busy, and I won't stay long. I just wanted to talk to you about Carly and Devon."

"Oh?"

Audrey sat down on the corner of the unmade bed, and Sherilyn folded into the chair nestled in the corner of the room near the window.

"Their party is tonight, and I guess Devon ships out in another week or so?"

"Yes. On the tenth."

"That is so rough. I'm happy to hear you'll be around for a while longer to help her with the transition. I guess she's taking it kind of hard." Audrey wondered how Sherilyn knew that. Before she could ask, Sherilyn answered. "I had breakfast with J. R."

Audrey nodded and took a sip from the warm cup. "Mmm. Very good."

"Listen, some of us get together once a month for a sort of Girls' Night. I have it at my house, and we get in our jams, do facials and manicures sometimes, watch movies, or eat junk food. It's like a slumber party for grown-ups."

"Sounds fun."

"Well, we're having one on Wednesday night," she explained. "I invited Carly to join us, but she wants to spend every spare moment with Devon while she has him home."

"Understandable."

"But I was thinking you might like to come."

Audrey tilted her head slightly. "Really?"

"Yeah, you and Kat both."

"Well . . ."

"Look, I know you're busy with the new project and all . . ."

J. R. has been very chatty!

". . . but we always have such a good time. It's a great way for us to blow off steam and get some time together. Will you think about it?"

"I will."

"Good. Wednesday night. Everyone usually starts arriving around 7:30, but if you want to come later, that's fine too."

"Should I bring anything?"

"Just you and your favorite pajamas."

"Okay!"

"I hope you can make it," Sherilyn told her, and she stood up and headed for the door. "We all just love you and Kat, and it would be fun to have the chance to get to know you better while you're here."

"It's been a very long time since I've been invited to a slumber party," she admitted with a grin. "I'm actually a little intrigued."

Just as Sherilyn reached it, the door burst open and Kat stepped in.

"Oh, hey!"

"Hi, Kat. I brought you a latte," and she pointed at the desk. "And you and Audrey are invited to a slumber party after the pep rally. I'm sure she'll tell you all about it."

Kat chuckled. "O-kay."

"Awesome bracelet," she added, and she skimmed the large stretch cuff of various hues of pastel pearls that Kat wore. "Did you make that too?"

Kat nodded and held it up. "It's one of my favorites."

"Well, I'd buy it in a heartbeat," Sherilyn told her. "You really should think about doing this professionally, Kat."

"I have a profession," she replied on a giggle.

"Yes, she does," Audrey teased. "And I can't function without her!"

"Well, I'm going to go and enjoy my one caffeine product for the day before Tanglewood life takes over. Have a good one!"

"See you later," Audrey said. "And Sherilyn, thank you so much for the invitation."

"Sure. I hope you'll come."

Kat closed the door behind her. "She's so pretty, isn't she?"

"That red hair and those big turquoise eyes." Audrey shook her head. "But still, she makes it impossible to hate her for it."

"Russell says she's lost a bunch of weight too."

"That should make it easier. But—" Audrey tilted her head and stared at the ceiling for a moment. "Nope. Still can't hate her."

Kat laughed. "So I spoke to Lisette. She'll be here at noon for measuring. She also told me she has swatches of the original fabric she chose for her gown. I asked her to bring them so that you and I can hit the fabric stores this afternoon."

"Good!"

"And she has photos of the bridesmaids in their dresses so we can see them. They've all been fitted and are ready to go, but the flower girl's dress is too big. I said we could do a fitting and alter it. She'll have her cousin bring the little girl over at one o'clock."

"Excellent. Do we have any word on an alternate work space, in case I don't hear back from LaMont?"

"I haven't been able to find a thing. I'll keep trying, but let's hope—"

Right on cue, Audrey's cell phone jingled, and she snatched it up from the nightstand. "Yes, let's hope!" she said before pressing the green button. "Audrey Regan."

"Audrey Regan, this is Wes LaMont."

"Good morning."

"Speaking of morning, what are your plans?"

"Right now? I'm preparing for a fitting with my bride at noon."

"That gives you some time then. I thought I could show you the work space I have available."

"And how many millions will it cost me, Wes?"

"Don't insult me. It's a loaner. And in return, you will forgive me for the Kim Renfroe debacle."

"That seems equitable."

"She went with someone else, by the way."

"You're joking."

"I don't joke. Want to come out to Buckhead and have a look at your work space?"

Audrey opened her eyes wide and grinned at Kat as she replied, "Absolutely. What's the address?"

"This is what it looks like in my dreams," Audrey whispered to Kat as they headed up the marble staircase, caressing the clear acrylic floating banister as she went. "But I didn't think it really existed."

Kat stifled a giggle as they approached the crescent-shaped reception desk.

"Audrey Regan to see Weston LaMont."

"Yes, Ms. Regan, he's expecting you. Follow me, please?"

She resisted the urge to reach out and hold Kat's hand as their heels click-click-clicked their way down the long corridor. Enormous photographs of famous-faced models on red carpets and flower-bordered wedding aisles lined both sides of the deep burgundy walls leading to gargantuan double glass doors etched with LaMont's logo.

Beyond the doors sat a world Audrey had only imagined, never experienced: a line of glass-enclosed offices to the left and a row of small design rooms to the right. At the end of the corridor beyond the administrative offices, another set of large doors beckoned, carved mahogany doors bearing the LaMont logo engraved in brass.

"I don't think we're in Kansas anymore," Kat whispered, and Audrey shushed her with caution.

"Through those doors and to your right," the waif-like receptionist directed them.

Audrey groaned as she pushed open the heavy door. Yet another wonderland existed beyond it, and she and Kat made a right as directed. An Angelina Jolie clone with a large bluetooth angled over her ear sat before a paper-thin computer screen behind a large two-level desk. She looked up and smiled as they approached.

"Audrey Regan?" she asked.

"Yes."

She pushed a button on the telephone. "Audrey Regan is here." A millisecond later, she waved them through. "Go right in."

Audrey swallowed around the lump in her throat and drew in a sharp breath before sliding open the oak-framed glass pocket door.

"Ah, Audrey. You're right on time. Come in, come in."

"You remember my assistant, Katarina Ivanov?"

"Charmed," he said without looking at Kat. "Take a load off, both of you."

They sat down in narrow acrylic chairs, and Audrey couldn't help but gaze out the window. "That must be the best view in Atlanta."

"It should be," he replied. "Now tell me about this project you're working on. I want details."

"Well, it's a wedding gown for a bride who had been working with Riley Eastwood," she said. "They had a parting of the ways with only three weeks to the wedding, and the bride has asked me to step in."

"For Riley Eastwood."

"Yes."

"I know Riley. If this bride of yours wasn't happy with her design, I'm wondering—"

"Oh, I know. I had the same thought," she interjected. "But you know how it goes. Sometimes designer and client just don't have the same vision."

LaMont cleared his throat, leaned back in his uncomfortable-looking chair, and stared her down. Just about the time she began to resist the inclination to squirm, he blinked.

"I have a new line gearing up," he said without inflection. "The patterns staff starts on the third of next month. At that time, all of the work space will be occupied."

"We'll be out of your hair before that," she promised.

"I don't normally lend out work space to other designers, you understand."

"I know. And I'm so appreciative."

"It's just not done. But in your case, since you're a fish out of your Soho pond—" *He knows I'm in Soho?* "—and, in some distorted way, I do owe you a little something. After Kim." *The traitor.* "So you can feel free to use the space and the equipment. You'll need to order your own supplies."

"Yes. We will."

"Monique will give you a code to enter the room and lock it up when you're not here."

"All right."

"You and Ms. Ivanov will be added to the security list so you can come and go after hours, if need be."

"Thank you so much, Wes."

He depressed a button on a small black box on the corner of his desk, and it wasn't until he began to speak that Audrey realized he must be donning the smallest bluetooth headset on the planet. "Monique, show Ms. Regan to her work space and answer any questions she might have."

Before she could thank him again, the office door slid open and Monique stood just inside it. She rolled her hand impatiently, and both Audrey and Kat hopped to their feet.

"Thank you again." She offered her hand, and LaMont shook it somewhat reluctantly.

"If you need anything, let Monique know."

Not-so-secret code for Don't Bother Me.

They followed *Moniquelina* down the long corridor, past the first door, and beyond the design spaces. Two of the rooms were occupied by three or four people, another was set up like a conference room and filled with several more worker bees whose necks craned along with them as they passed.

"The code to the door," Monique told them as she punched it in, "is 76281."

Kat scrambled for her notebook and pen, scribbling a quick note.

"You don't have to punch anything before or after. Just the numbers."

"Got it," Kat replied.

"There's a desk in the corner," she said, pointing out the obvious about the large room with windows on two sides. "A cutting table. A sewing machine. A dress form. Various . . ." She wiggled her fingers toward a large cabinet built into the wall. ". . . design *accoutre**mah***. Is there anything else you'll need?"

Audrey jumped a bit. "Oh. No. I don't think so."

"Lunch is delivered every afternoon at two o'clock. If you want to order, tell Billie at reception by one. Stop and see her on your way out and she'll issue you a pass for the parking garage next door. If you parked in one of the lots on this block, Billie will also validate. See yourselves out when you're through."

Without another word, she spun around on her five-inch Jimmy Choos and made her exit.

"Well." Kat grimaced. "We're not inviting *her* to join us at the slumber party, are we?"

Audrey popped with laughter. "But it would be kind of funny to see what her jammies look like."

The two of them stood there surveying their surroundings. Finally, Audrey let out a chuckle. Kat giggled too.

"Can you believe this, Audrey?" Kat asked her.

"Hardly."

"We're in Weston LaMont's design studio. In a corner space."

"Yep. We sure are."

"It's way nicer than I imagined. How about you?"

"I'm still trying to wrap my brain around the fact that they order lunch for everyone every day," Audrey told her.

"Do you think we have to pay for it?"

"Just in case . . . we're on a diet."

"Agreed."

"Hey, Audrey," Kat said softly, moving in close as if to share a big secret. "What if he gets a load of what you've designed for Lisette, and he goes crazy for it and offers you a big job here, designing with him. Wouldn't that be bonkers?"

Audrey grinned. "Number one: *bonkers?* You're spending too much time with Russell Walker. Number two: there's only one designer at Weston LaMont Designs. If he offered me employment, it would be as a pattern maker or a seamstress, not a designer."

Kat looked around with a huge grin stretched across her face. "Well, you're here now," she said.

Audrey decided not to point out that she was there on a temporary visa.

"It's your opportunity to soak up the atmosphere," Kat said, and she squeezed Audrey's wrist. "Catch the vision of a big design business."

"A little something to keep me warm on those cold winter nights when I have to live under the Brooklyn Bridge?"

She poked Audrey's ribs with her elbow. "Stop."

Lisette stood in the middle of the room in her bra and slacks, her arms outstretched as Kat wrapped the tape measure around her waist.

"And I think my poor dad is about ready to go a little crazy with all of the last-minute details. Oh, but you should have seen him with the tailor last night, telling him all about the flowers and the cake. He's turning into a regular Colin Cowie."

"Oh, I love him," Kat remarked as she jotted the measurement down on the notepad.

Audrey twisted her hair into a knot, grabbed a pen from the desk, and fastened it in the bun like a chopstick.

"This hotel is really stunning," Lisette commented as Kat continued measuring. "I love the brick courtyard, and the ornate carved wood desk in the lobby. I'll bet the weddings held here are amazing."

"Where is your wedding venue, by the way?" Audrey asked. "I was surprised to hear that your dad and Jackson are friends but that you weren't booked here."

"Oh, I'd love to have a small enough wedding to hold it here."

"The main ballroom holds three or four hundred people, I think," Kat commented.

"My guest list is nearly five hundred."

Kat and Audrey looked at each other for a long, pregnant moment before each of them turned back to Lisette.

"Five *hundred*?" Kat exclaimed.

"Yeah. Gauche, right?"

"Well, no. I'm just . . . *Five hundred?* It must have been a logistical nightmare to find a venue for a wedding that size!"

"You have no idea. But the Omni is gorgeous. Plus they have accommodations for all of our out-of-town guests."

Audrey's heart began to race. No wonder Lisette had been more concerned with having the right dress than with the money it would take to commission it.

"I'm sorry. But . . . well . . . speaking of gauche, I hope this doesn't sound that way. But . . ."

When she paused momentarily, searching for the right words, Lisette chuckled. "Go ahead. Ask away."

"Jackson said your father is *an electrician*."

"He did?" Lisette tossed her blonde hair and grinned. "Well, I guess that's true in a slightly abstract way. Have you ever heard of Gibson Light & Magic?"

Audrey's racing heart began to tap like a bass drum. "That's your dad?"

"The special effects company?" Kat asked, and she tossed the pencil down on the notepad and whooped. "They're huge!"

"Yeah. That's my dad."

"They do effects for movies and concert tours," Kat told Audrey, as if she didn't already know. "They built that whole fireworks extravaganza for Sherry Pazone's last tour."

My dress . . . five hundred . . . out-of-town guests . . .

And Audrey had thought Kim Renfroe was her only avenue to a high profile wedding gown!

Audrey fell back on the bed, and she launched back up again with a shout when the pen holding her hair in place poked into her skull.

"Are you okay?" Lisette inquired.

"Fine. I just . . . Fine."

Kat broke free in response to a knock at the hotel room door, giving Audrey a few moments to control her breathing and claw her way back down to earth. When she glanced up again, a little munchkin in pink boots stood in front of her.

"Aren't you the lady who makes dresses for Barbie?"

"I am," Audrey said with a wide smile. "And you're Roslyn, wearing your very pretty pink boots."

"Mommy! Aunt Lisette's wedding dress-maker makes dresses for *Barbie!* Are you gonna make my dress for the wedding too?"

"Well, I'm not going to make it. But I'm going to fit it to you."

Roslyn leaned in closer and softly asked, "Could you make it sparkly? It's kinda plain."

"Sparkly is what I do best," Audrey whispered, and she raised her hand and high-fived the little girl.

"Are you serious? I thought we were just cutting the cake and taking some pictures! I never expected all of this."

Carly's astonishment lit up her face as they walked into the small ballroom. She reached behind her and squeezed Audrey's hand. "Can you believe this?"

Sherilyn had indeed outdone herself. A thousand twinkling lights created a canopy over the room, and rows of staggered-height electric candles flickered along three of the four walls. Three rectangular tables arranged in the shape of a large U and draped with deep blue linens displayed elegant china and crystal settings. Red and white roses flanked the exquisite cake on a side table next to a small dance floor, and a polished white Baby Grand piano sat angled into the corner of the room.

"What do you think?" Sherilyn asked them as she sauntered in the door.

Carly didn't bother to use her words; she just propelled herself at Sherilyn and tugged her into an enthusiastic hug.

Sherilyn giggled and rocked Carly from side to side. "I wanted you to have something special after all you two have been through."

"It's above and beyond," Devon told her over Carly's shoulder. "This is awesome."

"Your guests should start arriving in about ten minutes," she told them. "We'll set up a buffet on the far wall, nothing too fancy, just some tapas."

"You and Andy will be here, right?"

"We wouldn't miss it," she said with a grin. "This is Andy's night at Miguel's soup kitchen. He should finish up any minute and head over from there. We received responses from twelve of the fifteen people on your short list. So get yourself a beverage, and have fun."

Audrey caught Sherilyn by the arm and softly asked, "What's with the piano?"

"A little surprise," she told her, eyes glistening. "Stay tuned!"

Over the next few minutes, guests began to filter into the room. Audrey recognized most of them as wedding guests and hotel staff. For some reason, it didn't seem even remotely strange to find Emma and Jackson, Sherilyn and Andy, and Fee and Sean among the invited guests. The Tanglewood seemed to have a special magic about it; everyone who passed through ended up as some sort of extended family. Russell had fallen out of a tree and into their lives, for crying out loud, and now he had taken on the unique role of the crazy roaming brother.

J. R. had forged a place of his own as well, and Audrey watched him as he chatted with Emma and Fee, the three of them laughing and amiable. He looked so handsome in black jeans and a dark plum shirt, sleeves rolled to the elbow, and a same-tone dark plum tie knotted loosely around an open collar. She loved the shaggy layers of warm brown hair that skimmed that collar, the steel-blue eyes with a fringe of golden-brown lashes, even the colorful artwork just barely peeking out from the rolled cuff of his sleeve. She pretty much liked everything about J. R. Hunt, in fact.

And the thought terrified her.

Thankfully, Jackson crossed between them before she could read anything else into her growing feelings, and Audrey snagged him by the arm.

"Hi, Audrey."

"Hi?" she asked him. "Hi? That's all you have to say for yourself?"

The corner of his mouth tilted into a grin, and Jackson shook his head. "Why? What did I do?"

"Your friend Curtis is just an electrician?"

"Yyyyyeah. He's an electrical guru. Why? Oh, how did it work out with you and his daughter?"

"Amazing," she replied before slipping her arms around his neck, embracing him, and planting a sincere kiss on his cheek. "Jackson, I think it says a lot about you that this is how you see your friend, rather than the fact that he's the head of a multi-million dollar company."

He laughed. "Curtis is one of the most relatable guys I've ever met. He's not pretentious in the least, Audrey."

"No. I mean, I believe you. But you connecting me with his daughter, well, it's a huge step up for my business. And I can't thank you enough."

"Oh, well, you're welcome. I'm glad it worked out." He leaned forward and lifted Audrey's hand and squeezed it. "I really hoped it would."

Emotion misted her eyes, and she smiled at him. "I have no idea what it will mean for me in the bigger picture. But it came at just the right time, and I'm grateful."

Sherilyn tapped the microphone in the stand near the piano, and Jackson squeezed Audrey's hand again before he headed toward the empty seat next to Emma.

"Hi, everyone. Thank you so much for coming," Sherilyn said. "Devon and Carly, you've been through an awful lot. But I think I speak for everyone in this room when I tell you that you're an inspiration. And so we all thought you deserved a beautiful night where you can take a deep breath, relax into one another's arms, and celebrate your marriage."

Audrey glanced at them just in time to see Carly and Devon exchange a kiss.

"And to add to the celebration, we've asked someone very special to perform one of your favorite songs. I hope you'll all join me in welcoming this year's Grammy nominee, and a dear friend of us here at The Tanglewood Inn: Ben Colson."

Audrey's heart skipped a beat as Ben appeared from the sidelines and sat down at the piano.

"Congratulations to the happy couple," he said into the microphone as he adjusted it. "A little bird told me that the two of you have a very special song."

And with that, Russell stood up and took a bow. "It was me. I'm the bird."

"Why don't you come up here and sing it with me, Walker."

That was all it took, and Russell leaped over his chair and rushed the piano as Ben began to play. Carly clutched her heart at the first few notes of "Home," Michael Buble's song about a young couple separated by miles.

Devon stood up and offered his hand to his bride. As Russell and Ben Colson harmonized, the couple took to the dance floor while their closest friends looked on. Well, most of them looked on, anyway.

Audrey glanced over at J. R. to find that his eyes were fixed intently on her.

Top Five Most Popular First Dance Songs

1. "Unforgettable" by Nat King Cole

2. "At Last" by Etta James

3. "The Way You Look Tonight" by Frank Sinatra

4. "It Had to Be You" by Harry Connick, Jr.

5. "Endless Love" by Lionel Richie and Diana Ross

12

You're gawking again," Audrey said with a smile as J. R. strode toward her.

"I know. I'm sorry."

"Liar."

"What did you just call me?" he asked, and he wrapped his hand around Audrey's forearm. "Just for that, you'll have to dance with me."

"I have to?"

He shrugged. "That's the cost of calling me a liar, lady. Pay up or face the consequences."

Audrey chuckled and, as Ben Colson started a new song, she tossed back her head and sighed. "If I have to, I have to."

J. R. gladly wrapped her up in his arms and joined several other couples on the dance floor. Funny how she fit there so well, he realized, and he lowered his chin over the top of her head and inhaled the faint fragrance of her perfume.

"So Carly says—"

"Shhh," he hushed her. "Just enjoy the moment, would you, Audrey? Can you do that?"

He felt her smile against his chest. "I think so."

"Good," he said, his eyes closed, mid-sway. "No talking."

After a few moments of dancing, Audrey piped up. "You have a lot of rules, do you know that?"

"Shh."

"I'm just saying—"

"Sh."

And finally she went silent, leaving J. R. free to enjoy the sensory overload of this woman in his arms, her fragrance in his nostrils, her silky hair against his skin. As the music softly faded, J. R.'s disappointment crested, but he reluctantly released her.

Audrey looked up at him, her lips pressed firmly together.

He smiled. "You can talk now."

"Oh, good, because I can't wait to tell you about my day!"

"A good day or a bad day?"

"Very, very good."

"Do tell."

Over the next hour, the two of them floated in and out of quick chats with other people, watched the cutting of the cake and shared a piece of it, all amid an ongoing conversation-for-two about Jackson's friend the "electrician," Audrey's accommodations at Weston LaMont's elaborate offices, a 500-guest wedding, and the uncanny coincidence of happening across a familiar little girl with pink suede boots.

"She was so excited to have the woman who once made formalwear for Barbie altering and adding bling to her little dress," Audrey told him, and the way she smiled at him made J. R.'s pulse race. "She's so right-out-there and outspoken. She kind of reminds me of myself at that age."

"Somebody better warn her mother what's to come," J. R. teased.

"Hey!" she said and swatted playfully at his arm.

Carly stepped between them and smiled. "I think Dev has hit the wall. He's exhausted, so we're going to take off."

Audrey reached out and gave her friend a hug. "I'll call you in the morning."

"Okay," she said, pecking Audrey's cheek. "J. R., will you stop by before you head out?"

"Out?" Audrey exclaimed.

"He didn't tell you? He leaves first thing in the morning."

"I guess I forgot."

"I'll swing by on my way out of town," he said, and he embraced Carly. "You take care of my brother, huh?"

"It's my favorite thing to do."

"I know it is."

As Carly reached him at the table, Devon looked up and waved at J. R. "See you in the morning?"

J. R. nodded and watched the newlyweds say their thank-yous and good-byes and head for the door.

"You really have to go tomorrow?"

When he turned back toward Audrey, her face was curled into a disappointed pout. "What, you're going to miss me or something, Audrey?"

"No," she objected. "I'm just curious."

"Oh, well, yes. I'm shoving off to Austin. Remember?"

"It just got here so quickly. Will you come back after?"

"No, I'm planning to spend some time in Santa Fe before the exhibition in Vegas next month."

"Oh." She glanced away from him and stared with interest at nothing in particular. "So I guess I won't see you again. You know. Ever again?"

"Well, that's doubtful," he said with a chuckle. "My brother is married to your sister, for all intents and purposes."

"True."

It touched J. R. that she exhibited so much apparent emotion about his plans to leave. The truth was he hadn't thought she would care much, one way or the other.

"Could you . . . Would you come with me for a minute?" she asked him.

He leaned down toward her and very seriously asked, "Are you going to abduct me? Tie me to a chair with duct tape so I can't escape?"

"You'll have to come with me and see."

J. R. followed her, amused to no end. But the minute he rounded the corner into the hall, Audrey tossed her arms around his neck and hugged him so hard that he fell against the wall.

"Whoa," he exclaimed. "What's this for?"

Leaning back and looking him straight in the eyes, Audrey declared, "It was nice to meet you, J. R. You've been . . . really nice to me, and I enjoyed the bike rides and . . . well . . ." With a rumbly sigh, she sped through, "I'll miss you," and thrust a fast kiss to his lips. Before he even processed what had happened, she pulled away from him. "Take care," she said. "Be safe."

And Audrey Regan was gone.

She'd considered the notion a dozen times since getting out of bed that morning, and Audrey still couldn't justify a trip over to Carly's on the off chance of seeing J. R. one more time. She questioned herself. What was she hoping to accomplish anyway? A longer kiss good-bye? An epiphany on his part that he could indeed stay in one place long enough to pursue a relationship? Or a revelation of her own that she even wanted such a thing?

"Hopeless," she muttered as she ran her fingers over a bolt of batiste.

"Pardon?" Kat asked from the other side of the fabric table.

Audrey didn't even manage to say, "Nothing." She just waved her hand and uttered something indecipherable.

She glanced at her watch. Ten-thirty. He would have packed his bike, said his good-byes, and been on his way by then.

"Russell said J. R. left this morning," Kat remarked, unknowingly infringing on Audrey's private wonderings. "Did you have a chance to say good-bye?"

"Yeah," she replied casually. Well. *Mock-casually.* "What do you think of this?"

Kat's reaction didn't surprise Audrey when she crinkled up her nose and shook her head at the embroidered brocade wrapped around Audrey's hand. She didn't really like it either.

"I'm still partial to the beaded silk."

"Yeah," Audrey said. "In a perfect world, I would do the beading myself, but . . ."

"There's no time."

"Right. And this is really beautiful, right? I'll have it cut. Why don't you go and get a yard of that ruffled flower organza for the strap, and see if you can find something blingy for the embellishments on the shoulder we talked about. Oh, and we'll need pattern paper. A lot of it."

"I'll get everything we need. But only if you tell me what's going on with you this morning."

Audrey glanced up and did a double take at Kat's expectant expression. "What do you mean?"

"Come on. You look like someone shot your dog, Audrey."

"And yet I don't have a dog."

"What's going on in that head of yours, boss?"

"Go count beads, Katarina. Excuse me? Can I get some help with this fabric?"

"Certainly," the clerk said, and Audrey followed her without a look back at Kat.

"I need fifteen yards of the beaded silk, and six of the Habotai."

And thirty more minutes with this ridiculous guy I can't seem to shake.

"Audrey, look what I found. For the ruffled strap, they have this with tiny rhinestones hidden in the floral. What do you think?"

"She said she wanted bling," Audrey commented with a weary smile. "Let's see it against the beaded silk."

Kat set it next to the bolt of silk, and they both sighed.

"Perfect."

"Gorgeous."

"Spectacular," the clerk chimed in.

"J. R., are you sure you can't stay until after Devon reports to the base?"

"I'm sorry, Carly. This is a big job, and I need it."

He tried to resist the bitter taste of resentment building in the back of his throat. Didn't she know he would stay if he could? Any time Devon needed him, J. R. had always tried to be there. This kind of thing just cemented his drive to hit the open road and stay out there. The expectations of a significant other—or the wife of a *significant brother!*—could choke the life out of a guy's independence.

"Sweetie, stop nagging him."

Thank you.

"I'm not nagging, baby. I'm just—"

"We know what you're *just.* Give him a break now, all right?"

Carly flipped her hand and sighed before turning away and stalking out of the kitchen.

"Sorry, bro."

"Nah," J. R. replied, smacking his brother's shoulder. "She's just under the delusion that you'd benefit from me hanging around a little longer."

"Oh, that's no delusion," he remarked as he stared out the window.

"Dev, this job in Austin is—"

"I get it," he interrupted, and he turned back to look J. R. directly in the eye. "I get it. This is work, and you've got to follow it. It's just that, in general, I wish you would park it back in Atlanta for a while. It would be a huge relief to know Carly had someone looking after her while I'm gone. Not to mention when I get back, we could spend a little time together. Real time. Not this passing through town twice a year."

J. R. kept the volcanic groan that was building inside to himself.

"Look," Devon said with a sigh, "it's not like I don't already know this about you. Dad felt just like you do, and you're cut from the same cloth."

The two of them made a good pair. Carly made the cut, and Devon rubbed the salt into the wound.

"What a thing to say."

"I don't mean you're like him, J. R. Just in that wandering gene. I remember one time when he came back after one of those long disappearances, and he sat us down on that stone wall behind the house. You remember?"

J. R. nodded. "He said every time he tried to light for a while, things turned to garbage."

"Yeah, like he was some kind of computer and had to reboot on a regular basis so he could work up the gumption to stand being around us for a while."

"Dev. It's not like that with me. Not once have I thought I couldn't stand to be around you."

Devon smirked. "Yeah, I know."

"Do you really?"

His expression melted slightly. "I guess."

"I'm not a nine-to-fiver, Dev. This is what I do. I travel. I move from place to place. It's who I am. It has nothing to do with working up the gumption to be around you for any length of time."

"I get it, man. But what happens when you meet someone?"

"What do you mean? I meet people all the time."

"No. I mean, when you meet somebody special. Somebody you might want to settle down with. You're gonna, what—put her on the back of your bike and hit the road every few weeks? Who is the woman who would want that, bro?"

J. R. sensed the irritation growing. "I'm not looking for anyone, Dev. Maybe down the road."

"Well, that's the thing, J. R. A guy rarely comes across her when he's actually looking. She usually crosses the road right in front of him while he's on his way someplace else."

He sighed. "I'll keep an eye out then because," and he pointed at the door with his thumb, "I'm on my way someplace else right now. So stand down, soldier, and give your brother some love."

Devon stepped into J. R.'s open arms, tugging him into an embrace.

"Watch yourself over there," J. R. told him. "And no matter what else you do, do *NOT* get yourself shot . . . or hurt. Do you hear me?"

"Sir, yessir," he replied softly.

He pulled Devon into another hug and smacked him on the back. "Love you, man."

"Me too," Devon answered.

Audrey found herself wishing Carly had been able to join them as she and Kat strolled up the sidewalk to Sherilyn's house. She wasn't sure how much fun a "slumber party" was going to be when she barely knew anyone in attendance besides Kat. It seemed only fitting that, with Carly living in the next town over, a recapture-your-youth slumber party should be attended alongside the girl with whom she'd shared so many of them during their actual youths.

"This is going to be fun," Kat exclaimed, and the front door whooshed open.

Two unidentifiable women stood before them with hair slicked back from their terrifying faces. One of them opened her turquoise eyes wide as she peered at them from behind a neon green mask and said, "Finally! We thought you'd never get here."

Audrey recognized the timber of her voice and grinned at Sherilyn. "That's a new look for you, isn't it?"

"What do you think?" Emma asked from behind her own bright purple mask. "It's working for us, right?"

Audrey and Kat followed their lead into the sprawling family room where twin-sized air mattresses filled the largest part of the room like puzzle pieces set into perfect place. That huge dog of theirs—she thought she remembered his name to be Henry—lounged on the sofa next to Jackson's sister Norma, her bright green, wide-eyed greeting a perfect match to Sherilyn's. Fee's starker-white-than-usual face stared at them from the kitchen.

"What's your pleasure?" Fee asked, setting several thick plastic tubes on the counter before them. "The white is coconut milk for dry skin. The purple is lavender, for sensitive skin. And the green is mint julep," she added, grabbing the tube and reading the side of it, "for tired skin in need of refreshment."

"I want the purple," Kat said, snatching up the tube.

"Wait. Grab a headband from the basket," Fee directed her.

"There's a mirror and some makeup remover on the table over there," Emma added, and she followed Kat toward it.

"I guess I'll go for the green," Audrey said with a shrug. "I could use some refreshing."

And fifteen minutes later, the six of them (plus Henry) formed a colorful and jagged little circle in the center of the room, several snack bowls between them, and cans of soda placed in foam holders on the coffee table. Emma held one of the bowls with one arm like a basketball while she picked M&Ms out of the popcorn and peanuts and placed each of them on Sherilyn's knee. The moment a mound formed, Sherilyn scooped up the candies and popped them into her mouth while she waited for the next rejects to reach her.

"This reminds me so much of the slumber parties Carly and I used to have," Audrey shared with them.

"I wish she could have come," Sherilyn commented.

"My granny used to make pizza for us. They were way better than anything we could have ordered. And afterward, we'd make gooey pretzels."

"Gooey pretzels!" Kat chuckled. "That doesn't sound too appetizing."

"You have no idea!" she exclaimed. "They were the best. A slumber party tradition."

"Sweet, right?" Emma chimed in, her face twisted into a mop of disappointment and amusement.

"Of course," Audrey said with a tilt of her head.

"Of course."

"How did you make them?" Norma asked.

"You take pretzel sticks, the thick ones. And you dip them in chocolate and roll them in toppings."

"Like chocolate sprinkles?" Sherilyn asked, excited. "I could totally get behind that!"

"Sprinkles. Or coconut. Or chopped up nuts. Whatever you like."

"I nominate Audrey to bring the gooeys for our next slumber party!" Norma cried.

"I second that," Emma said.

"Done deal," Fee announced. "Gooeys it is!"

"We usually have a bigger group than this," Sherilyn said over a mouth full of chocolate candies. "But Pearl had to fill in for someone, and Susannah and Madeline had a charity thing." She looked to Emma and asked, "Is that what Georgiann is doing too?"

Emma and Norma exchanged glances before they both cracked up.

"What?" Sherilyn urged.

"George is over sleeping on an air mattress," Norma revealed. "She's not coming anymore."

"But she might stop by for breakfast," Emma added.

"Ohhhh, no!" Sherilyn cried. "There's no eggs and bacon without some slumber party shakin'!"

With that, she hopped to her feet and flicked on the stereo. In bare feet, she slid across the floor to the first few notes, just like Tom Cruise in *Risky Business*.

"It's Seger time!" Sherilyn called out, and she began doing her version of the Twist to "Old Time Rock & Roll." "C'mon, ladies!"

Emma filled her mouth with popcorn and peanuts before getting to her feet. "She's a Seger freak," she said to Audrey. "But it's her house, so we indulge her."

Sherilyn grabbed Emma's hand, and the two of them morphed into a strange and sort of spastic jitterbug. Norma popped up and joined in with a comical Watusi while Fee surrendered to an uninspired version of The Freddy.

"Come on, you two," Sherilyn said, tugging on Audrey's arm. "Show us whatcha got."

One corner of her mouth lifted in a tilt of a smile, and Kat beamed at her. Before you could say, "Today's music ain't got the same soul," Audrey and Kat were doing The Jerk.

Audrey tiptoed down the hall from the bathroom and stood at the edge of the family room, suppressing laughter as she surveyed the damage from the night before. Empty soda cans and water bottles and near-empty bowls littered the coffee table and the floor beside the couch where Sherilyn laid sprawled out, obviously ousted from the comfy sofa by the massive dog now sleeping there with his head on what was once her pillow.

Rumbling snores emanated from someone, and Audrey moved a little closer to discover that it was Norma. Fee lay flat on her back, her arms folded across her chest like a corpse, while Emma, curled into a semi-circle with her oversized Falcons jersey bunched up around her waist, occupied the mattress beside her. Face-down, Kat's arms and legs all extended into four different directions.

What a group, she thought, turning toward the kitchen, and she jumped when Andy unexpectedly appeared right in front of her. Henry flew from the sofa in an arch over Sherilyn and raced to Andy's side.

"Shh!" He grinned at Audrey as he scratched the dog's head. "Is my wife sleeping on the floor?"

"In deference to your dog," she whispered. "You scared me. Have you been here all night?"

He shook his head. "Spent the night at my mother's," he mouthed with only a breath of sound to accompany it. "Once a month, like clockwork. You ladies party, and I am fed like the prodigal son returned."

Audrey chuckled. "I was going to make coffee."

"I'll do it. I know where everything is."

She grinned at him, climbing up on one of the counter stools as he stealthily moved about the kitchen.

"Did you girls have a good time?" he asked.

"I haven't had so much fun—*or eaten so much junk!*—since high school."

Andy glanced at the pile of empty pizza boxes resting against the trash can and smiled. "Anchovies?" he asked.

"Afraid so. On one of them."

"My growing son or daughter appears to love anchovies," he told her with a shrug. "Which is odd because Sherilyn can't stand them."

"All evidence to the contrary," she cracked, and Andy held back a laugh with a snort.

One by one, he lined up individual K-cups of coffee on the counter. "I know who prefers what kind of coffee," he said, "with the exception of you and Kat. What's your pleasure?"

Inspecting the cups, she asked, "What do you have?"

He picked them up one at a time. "Decaf hazelnut for my wife. Crème brûlée for Emma Rae. Norma likes French roast. And Fee prefers extra bold." Pointing to a circular rack on the counter, he told her, "Sherilyn has every option known to man on there. It's like a portable Starbuck's."

"Oooh, Chocolate Glazed Donut!" she exclaimed, and she covered her mouth with one hand. "Sorry. I was blinded from courtesy by the promise of chocolate."

"It happens," he replied with a smile, and he took the small plastic container that she handed him and injected it into the machine behind him. He pushed a ceramic mug with a daisy emblazoned on it to the pedestal, pressed a button, and the brewed coffee began to spit into the cup. "Give it two minutes," he said. "I'm going to walk Henry before I get changed for work."

She thanked him, and Andy patted his thigh one time before Henry appeared, leash in mouth, ready for his walk.

Before the two of them returned, everyone was up and various coffees had been brewed. Emma and Sherilyn worked in the kitchen to get breakfast started while Fee and Kat set the large dining table, and Audrey sat at the counter with Norma.

"Jackson tells me you're working with Curtis Gibson's daughter on her wedding gown," Norma said as she sipped her French roast.

"Yes. I'm so grateful to him for making the connection between us."

"Lisette is a beautiful girl, isn't she?"

"Mm," Audrey nodded. "She really is."

"What are the challenges of creating something for her, in relation to a smaller woman? Is it very different?"

"It's different," she replied, accepting her awaited chocolate coffee from Sherilyn. "But I think it's going to be fun. We came up with a design that she loves, and she's going to look beautiful in it."

At first sip, Audrey closed her eyes and moaned softly.

"What kind?" Norma asked.

"Chocolate glazed donut," Sherilyn answered for her.

"Ohhh, that sounds tasty."

Audrey moaned again, this time more loudly. "It is."

"Audrey's design is stunning," Kat chimed in as she joined them at the counter. "It's this awesome fitted top with an asymmetrical ruffled strap, and the skirt is flared with beautiful beadwork and crystals."

"That sounds beautiful," Norma said. "I can't wait to see it when she walks down the aisle."

"Will you be there?"

"Oh, yes. Curtis and his wife are good friends to us. I've known Lisette since she was knee-high to a grasshopper."

Norma didn't possess the same deep southern drawl that her other sisters maintained, but Audrey spotted the twang in that last statement.

"When Jackson first told me about them, he said Curtis was an electrician."

Norma chuckled. "That sounds just like Jack."

"Then Lisette told us about her wedding plans," Kat added. "We were like, 'Isn't your dad an electrician?'"

"You wouldn't know it to meet him, but Curtis is quite a force in the business world. He's built that company from the ground up. It's going public next month, you know."

"What does that mean?" Kat asked.

"It means people can buy Gibson Light and Magic stock," Emma explained. "Like Microsoft."

"Will it be expensive?"

"I'd suggest buying quick and holding," Norma told her with a smile.

"You know, I had no real desire to break away from working to go to a grown-up slumber party," Audrey said with a laugh as she and Kat climbed the staircase toward the reception desk. "But I'm so glad I went. It was a great diversion. Those women are such a lot of fun."

"Can you believe Sherilyn and those anchovies, though?" Kat exclaimed. "I've never seen anyone put them away like that."

"It was kind of gross, actually."

"I know!"

The receptionist smiled as they approached her desk. "A delivery came for you a few minutes ago. I had them drop it in your work room."

"That will be our body," Audrey told Kat. "Thanks very much."

"Sure thing. Just let me know if you want in on the lunch order. We're getting Italian today, and I put a copy of the menu in there for you too."

"Thanks, Billie."

The moment they turned the corner, Audrey noticed that the door to their work room had been left open. Passing Monique's empty desk, she picked up the pace toward the end of the hall. She found Weston LaMont standing with one hand on his hip and the other scratching his chin as he gazed at the extra-large dress form before him.

"What on earth is this?" he asked as Audrey and Kat stepped in.

"It's a dress form," Audrey replied dryly. "Being a designer, perhaps you've seen them before."

"Not in this proportion."

Audrey chuckled, and she patted the shoulder of the form several times as she rounded it. "I'm thinking of calling her Mac."

"Mac!" he exclaimed.

"After Elle MacPherson. *The Body.*"

"Well, it's a body all right. I would think the name Bertha is a better bet."

Kat scowled at him as she dropped the load from her arms.

"Who is your client?" he asked Audrey. "The Rock?"

"All right," Audrey replied as she sank down into the chair behind the desk. "Try to be nice, will you?"

"These are my offices," he said with a smirk. "I'm not required to be nice."

"Couldn't you just try? Pretty please? A plus-sized bride is just like any other bride. She wants to look amazing, she wants the fairy tale. Her version is just . . . *Rubenesque*, that's all. There's just more to love."

"Seriously, Audrey. Who is your client?"

"Her name is Lisette, Wes. She's a plus-sized bride."

"I see that." He circled the dress form, inspecting every inch. "Where did you ever find a dress form this gargantuan?"

"Wes."

"Really. It's very resourceful. I didn't even know they made them."

"Kat found it."

When he looked at her, Kat answered without emotion. "Craig's List."

LaMont dragged a chair beside Audrey's desk and sat down. "Well, I have to see your design."

She thought it over for a moment, and a quiver of anxiety tickled her stomach.

"All right."

Audrey slid the leather portfolio across the desk and tugged at the zipper. "Here's the one we decided on."

LaMont scanned the page for nearly a full minute, a blank expression on his face. Audrey began to think that she had thumped down into a momentary world where the worst torture known to a designer had occurred: the thirty seconds where a fledgling waited for a response from a pro. If LaMont hated it, would the world hate it as well? If someone with his experience and expertise—

"There's something here."

"You think so?"

"Yes," he said, and he leaned back in the chair and looked at her over the top of his tortoise shell glasses. "I think you've really got something there, Audrey."

"Thank you."

"Not only is the dress interesting—I mean, you've taken a classic standard and infused some contemporary life into it—but you've also managed to weave a thread of couture into a market that doesn't have anything like it."

"Thank you, Wes." She wondered if he could hear her heart pounding.

"I'm not sure what kind of future there is in designing for a market of overeaters, but—"

Kat interrupted him with a throaty groan. When Audrey looked up at her, Kat raised a hand and said, "Fine. I'm going to go and talk to Billie about lunch."

LaMont sighed. "I've offended her delicate sensibilities."

"Insensitivity tends to do that to her. It's a flaw."

He laughed out loud. "Hasn't she heard I'm a creative genius? We don't have to be . . . *sensitive.*"

"I'll try to remember that," she teased. "Should I write it down?"

"What are your plans today?" he asked, ignoring the barb.

"Finishing up the pattern so we can start to cut."

"I'll leave you to it then," he said, and he rose to his feet and crossed to the door. Turning back, he added, "Good work, Audrey. Congratulations."

"Thank you."

"Oh. If you're given to a heavy lunch, the eggplant sandwich at Caruso's is quite good. Perhaps you can order a few if your client's coming in."

Audrey spun her chair around, faced out the window, and clamped her eyes shut. "Later, Wes."

She listened as the click of his shoes on the marble floor faded. What a miserable man Weston LaMont was. She wondered what had possessed him to summon enough compassion to agree to lend her some work space! It certainly wasn't his huge, open heart.

"The man is despicable," Kat said as she returned to the office and closed the door behind her. "I hope God forgives me, but I'd like to just slap him silly."

Audrey chuckled. "Let's get busy, shall we?"

For the next hour, Audrey finished up the pattern pieces that she'd begun the previous day, and Kat helped her to adjust the dress form so that they fit perfectly into place. To make sure they were on the right track, Kat measured the mannequin to compare Lisette's measurements.

"By George, I think we've got it!" Kat said in a thick English accent.

"Very good. Let's start cutting."

They stopped for a quick lunch before spending another couple of hours smoothing out yards of fabric atop the cutting table so that Audrey could apply the patterns and, with meticulous caution, cut out the pieces. When Audrey finally stood back and admired three stacks of carefully folded sections of fabric, each of them still attached to their paper pattern, Kat grinned at her from the other side of the open laptop.

"Nice work."

"Thanks."

"Why don't you sit down and relax a few minutes so I can show you something."

Audrey folded into the chair, crossed her legs, and rested her arms on the desk before her. "What's up?"

Kat swiveled the laptop screen toward her. "What do you think of this for Lisette's bling?"

"Oooh," she said, leaning forward to inspect the rhinestone vine of flowers more carefully. "This is beautiful. Where did you find it?"

"Well—"

"Not on Craigslist!" she exclaimed.

"No."

"It's too bad it's not just a little longer. It would work perfectly, wouldn't it?"

"It could be extended."

"Yes? Do they have any larger pieces?"

"It's one of mine," Kat stated.

Audrey looked up at her over the top of the screen, and Kat didn't even blink.

"You made this? When?"

"A few months ago," she replied.

"Where is it?"

"At my apartment. I had my friend Staci go in and take some photos of a few pieces I thought might work, and she emailed them to me."

Audrey leaned back and folded her hands in her lap. "Can I see the others?"

Kat enthusiastically spun the laptop around again, punched several keys, and flipped it back toward Audrey. Three different photos lined the screen in a perfect row.

The center photo caught her eye immediately: a brooch resting on a swatch of deep purple velvet. Pastel pink rhinestone tulips just on the verge of wilting, sat atop a clear crystal stem that curved downward toward pale green rhinestone leaves.

The third photo showed Audrey's favorite of the three in the context of Lisette's wedding gown: a large bouquet of rhinestone flowers in the shape of hearts.

"This last one," she said, tapping the screen. "What are the measurements?"

"It's about five inches long, no more than three inches wide."

"Do me a favor? Email all three over to Lisette and ask her what she thinks. I like the last one for her, the bouquet of hearts. Let's see what she thinks."

"Are you serious?"

"Of course I am. Kat, these are exquisite!"

She hopped up from behind the desk, hurried around to Audrey, leaned over, and embraced her.

"Why haven't you shown me any of your work before?"

"I have."

"No. You've worn a cute pair of earrings or a great bracelet, and when I've asked about them you've told me you made them. But you've never shown me anything like this."

"It's my passion, Audrey. The way your designs are for you."

Audrey gazed at Kat, her wide eyes misted with emotion and brimming with excitement.

"I wish I'd known this, Katarina. You're really gifted."

"Thank you," she said, hand to heart. "I'll send these over to Lisette right away."

While Kat tapped away at the computer, Audrey took the time to give more thought to the idea that her valued, organized assistant had been carrying around a dream of her own, and Audrey had never noticed. A running parade of earrings, bracelets—and that stunning choker Kat had worn to the bridal show last spring!—flew past her mind's eye, and Audrey found herself looking at Kat with a fresh perspective.

Sherilyn had encouraged her several times since they'd arrived in Atlanta about taking her jewelry designs to the mass market.

"I have a profession," Kat had told her, and Audrey had added that she could never survive without her. But maybe she would have to.

Even if Lisette's gown acted as a stepping-stone that garnered a bigger opportunity for Audrey, the realization could not be ignored; she might have to continue her journey as a designer without Kat.

The thought choked her slightly, and she had a rough time breathing around the massive lump of emotion resting in the hollow of her throat. She'd been working hard to ignore the tickle at the base of her heart, the one that relentlessly reminded her almost every hour that J. R. had ridden away from her, off into the sunset. The thought of Kat doing the same thing was almost too much for her now.

"I'm due at Carly's for dinner in an hour. Are you ready to call it a day?"

"You bet."

Audrey dropped Kat at The Tanglewood before continuing over to Carly and Devon's house. It had been a long time since she'd driven in the Atlanta area, and the little black Cobalt she'd rented for her three weeks in town zipped nicely through Roswell traffic. She tuned the radio to a classic oldies station, and she found herself smiling and singing along when Bob Seger's "Old Time Rock & Roll" hit the airwaves, reminding her of the teenage dance party she'd attended at Sherilyn's house.

Tapping the steering wheel and singing along as she rounded the corner into the driveway, Audrey suddenly gasped, the next lyric to the song frozen on her lips as she jammed on the brakes.

She just sat there in the driveway, staring at the familiar Harley-Davidson parked behind Devon's big truck.

The Top Five World-Class Designers of *Bling*

1. Tacori

Tacori is known for platinum and diamond jewelry combining heirloom elegance with contemporary detail. The company's signature is a crescent silhouette design.

2. Neil Lane

While Lane is most widely known for his red carpet bling, his personal taste is demonstrated in his lavish personal collection of Tiffany jewels, as well as Renaissance pieces and nineteenth-century gems.

3. Harry Winston

Winston is responsible for the tradition of lending out jewelry to stars for their appearances on the red carpet. Since the 1930s, Harry Winston is a name most equated with luxury, exquisite craftsmanship, and rare stones such as those he donated to the Smithsonian.

4. Tiffany & Co.

Since the 1800s, Tiffany's has established many FIRSTS in the industry, from the first retail catalog to setting the purity standard for platinum in the United States. While the company offers a stone and setting for virtually every occasion, it is famous for the one-carat diamond engagement ring in the Tiffany setting, and its blue box is universally recognizable.

5. Cartier

With more than a century of artistry to its credit, the French-based Cartier brand is synonymous with luxury jewelry. Once labeled by royalty as "Jeweller to Kings, King of Jewellers," the Cartier name has also been attached to a diverse array of products, from leather goods to fragrance to fine timepieces.

13

Audrey pushed the front door open, walked tentatively inside, and stood there listening to the voices in the kitchen. One note from J. R. and she inhaled sharply and hurried to the wood-framed mirror in the entry. She fluffed her hair, checked her lips, quickly ran her index finger over her front teeth, and vigorously shook off the nervous electricity suddenly coursing through her. Taking one more deep breath, she passed through the arched doorway.

"Oh, good! Aud, you're right on time. And look who's here!"

J. R. swung around in his chair and smiled at her, his steel-blue eyes piercing. "Hey, Audrey."

"Hey, J. R. What are you doing here? Shouldn't you be half-way to Austin by now?"

"He was nearly to Louisiana before the guy he was meeting called and canceled," Carly interjected. "Can you believe the nerve of that guy?"

"I'm so sorry. And . . . you decided not to go back to Santa Fe. I thought that was your plan."

"My new sister-in-law presented a compelling argument for me being here until Devon ships out. I figured it might be a sort of sign that I needed to come back."

"He has no idea how much it cost me for Carly to pay the guy off," Devon said, pulling a mock-serious face.

"Oh, stop it," Carly retorted. "I did not."

Audrey swallowed hard. "Well, if we have to put up with you a little longer, I guess we can manage, right?"

Devon cackled at that and squeezed Audrey's hand. "How are the new digs working out?"

"Weston LaMont is a pity," she said as she rounded the table and sat down across from J. R. "But the offices are unbelievable. Marble floors, walls of windows, and you should see the women's restroom, Caroline. It's the size of the bridal suite at The Tanglewood."

"And they order lunch from a different restaurant every day," Carly told them as she delivered a glass of iced tea to Audrey.

"Yeah, nice start to it too. Today was Caruso's."

"Fancy," Devon said.

"What did you have?"

"Chicken Caesar salad."

"Oh, shoot. We're having chicken for dinner."

Audrey exchanged grins with J. R. "I think I can manage chicken twice in one day. What kind?"

"Barbecued. It's Dev's favorite."

"Do you need any help?"

"No. Just sit there and tell us about your day."

"There's not really much to tell," Audrey replied, and she shrugged one shoulder at J. R. "Fit the form, cut the fabric. The usual . . . Only in some pretty amazing surroundings."

"Right," he chimed in. "I can't tell you how many times a day I do the same thing. Form after form. Fabric after fabric."

Devon cracked up and playfully smacked J. R. on the arm.

"Stop it, you two," Carly reprimanded with a grin. "When will you start to sew?"

"Tomorrow."

"And you'll be able to finish and fit the dress to the bride in plenty of time for the wedding?"

Audrey crossed her fingers and held them up. "Here's hoping."

"It was a real stroke of luck that this job kind of fell into your lap, wasn't it?" Devon asked her.

"The funny thing is," she said, and she tripped momentarily over the intensity of J. R.'s eyes. "Uh, I . . . Well, just before it happened, I said a prayer that God would provide some sort of answer because my design business was rolling downhill fast."

"You prayed, Aud?"

She noticed all eyes on her, and she giggled nervously. "Well. Yeah. I pray. What's with the shock and awe about it?"

Carly smiled. "I'm just happy to hear it, that's all."

"I came across this verse in the Bible—"

"The Bible?"

Smacking the tabletop lightly with her hand, she laughed. "Yes, Caroline. They're in every hotel room, or hadn't you heard?"

"But you were reading it?"

She looked from Carly to Devon to J. R. "Yes. I was restless, and . . . Oh, never mind."

"No, no, I want to hear it," Carly said, and she sat down in the chair beside her. "You were restless, and you opened the Bible. That's good. Go on."

After a long moment of silence, Audrey raised her hand and pointed over her shoulder with her thumb. "I'm going to . . . go and get cleaned up."

In the bathroom, Audrey stared at her reflection for a few seconds before leaning forward on the edge of the sink, her eyes clamped shut, shaking her head.

In a hotel room, praying, reading the Bible. Why did I say that out loud? How desperate and sad can I make myself look?

She pumped a dollop of soap to her hands and rubbed it into a lather beneath the running water, cringing as she played the conversation over in her head.

It's official. I'm 100 percent dork now. No doubt about it.

She dried her hands on the fluffy terrycloth guest towel with a big yellow **H** embroidered on it. She figured, in that moment, **H** was for Humiliation rather than Hunt.

Audrey jumped when she opened the bathroom door to find J. R. standing on the other side.

"Sorry. Didn't know there was a line."

He grinned. "There's not. I was waiting for you."

"Oh?"

"Carly says there's half an hour before dinner."

Audrey tilted her head slightly. "And this information is important because . . ."

"Time for a quick ride, if you're interested."

The appealing offer acted as a catalyst for a slow-moving smile that spread across her entire face and up to her ears.

"Let's go."

She realized as she climbed aboard J. R.'s Harley that something about sneaking away on a motorcycle with a guy transported her back to a time when the biggest thing she had to worry about was what to wear to the lake on Friday night and whether Joe Rossi would finally kiss her. Shaggy-haired, leather jacket-clad J. R. Hunt represented *Escape* to Audrey, with a capital **E**.

When he emerged out of the garage with the second helmet and handed it to her, Audrey smiled at him.

"What?"

"Could we maybe, just this once, go *without the helmet*?"

"No."

"Please?"

J. R.'s brow furrowed, and he asked her, "Why?"

"Didn't you ever just need to feel the wind in your hair?"

He grinned. "Sure."

"I need that today."

He considered the request for a long moment before he set the helmets on the grass and straddled the front portion of the black leather seat. "We are not leaving the suburb," he told her over his shoulder.

"Got it."

"Just a little wind in your hair, and back here for dinner," he declared, turning the key.

"Right."

"You know," he said as he gripped the gears. "Not too many girls enjoy the whole wind-messing-up-my-hair experience."

"I know. But sometimes you just have that sort of day where you need a lot of fresh air, all at once. Do you know what I mean?"

She felt the inward draw of a chuckle as she wrapped her arms around his mid-section. "You're preachin' to the choir, sister."

J. R. had the idea of offering Audrey a ride with the intention of getting her alone and telling her there was really no need for her face to turn three shades of red over the admission that she'd said a prayer or turned to the Bible for comfort. He did it all the time. In fact, he had planned to tell her it was the only thing that got him through sometimes, like each time Devon shipped out.

But he didn't tell her any of that.

They just rode along in silence, thirty miles per hour in a residential suburb, the cool twilight air pushing away all thoughts of the day, cleansing them. He caught a glimpse of Audrey in the mirror, her eyes gently closed, waves of light blonde hair dancing on the breeze, and her pinkish lips angled upward in a contented smile.

She's exquisite, he thought as he watched her for a moment before he dragged his attention back to the road ahead.

Her eyes were still closed when he pulled into the driveway and turned off the engine. "Nooo," she cried softly without opening them. "It's not over yet."

"Just for now," he promised, looking at her reflection as she opened those gorgeous russet eyes.

She caught sight of him right off, and she grinned into the mirror. "Thank you," she said, and she nuzzled her chin against his shoulder.

He couldn't break the connection by looking away. The two of them just sat there—he didn't know for how long—their eyes locked together through the reflection of the side mirror. He could feel her heart pounding against his back. He wondered if she had any clear idea how gorgeous she looked just then. Never mind the blazing sunset in the sky behind her. It was Audrey who took his breath away; Audrey who caused his pulse to pound.

"Are you ready for barbecued chicken?" he asked her, and she closed her eyes.

"No. Are you?"

"No."

"But we're going in anyway, aren't we?" she asked, her nose wrinkled up.

"That we are."

She planted a quick kiss to the side of his neck before clumsily climbing down. "Thank you again," she said, and she extended her hand toward him.

J. R. stepped over the bike and accepted her hand. Their fingers entwined like they belonged there, and the two of them strolled up the sidewalk as if they had nowhere specific to go.

At the front door, Audrey turned toward him and smiled. She stood so close that he could feel the warmth of her breath.

"I'm really happy that you came back."

"I am too."

"You're a good guy, J. R."

"I like to think so."

"Oh, you are. There's no question. You're a very good guy."

"You're quite pleasant also," he offered with a smile.

"I . . . kinda want to kiss you now."

"Do you?"

"Really a lot."

"Then I think you should."

Audrey inched toward him, and J. R. wondered if she had planned the tease or whether perhaps she might just be shy about it. Before he could decide, her lips pressed softly against his in a sweet and tender kiss.

"Dev," came the whisper from the other side of the door. "Come and see. They're making out."

Audrey pulled back slightly and raked her fingers through her hair. "We can hear you, Caroline."

"Oooh!" The skitter of shuffling feet faded as Carly called back to them from the general direction of her kitchen, "Sorry!"

Audrey shook her head. "This can't go well for us, you know."

"Ha! I'm inclined to agree."

With a giggle, her amber eyes flashed. "Sorry to drag you into harm's way."

"No apologies necessary," he replied, and he pulled her into a final kiss.

They walked into the kitchen, straight-faced and ignoring Devon and Carly's animated curiosity.

"So . . ." Devon began, but Audrey raised her hand and cut him off at first syllable.

"J. R. has not proposed, and neither have I. We're just two people who went for a motorcycle ride on a great Georgia night. We exchanged a kiss, and now we're here at your table hoping to have a pleasant dinner. Period. New paragraph. Capisce?"

Devon and Carly exchanged glances.

"Or," she continued, "we can leave you to your barbecued chicken, and we can bounce out of here and stop for a burger somewhere. Your choice."

J. R. worked hard to disguise his amusement. In lieu of failure, he simply lowered his head and brushed some imaginary dust from the thigh of his jeans.

"Fine." Carly was first to surrender, and she curled up her face like she'd just taken a bite out of an old lemon. "We'll never speak of it again."

"Excellent!" Audrey rewarded her. "Let's eat."

"I'm in awe," J. R. remarked.

"It's all in the wrist," she stated as she unfolded a napkin into her lap.

Conversation cruised around the odd jobs Devon hoped to tackle before leaving, took a left at Russell's visit that day where he brought three pints of fresh strawberries from a produce stand he'd apparently visited near the site of his new Atlanta home—both of which J. R. had a rough time picturing—and meandered around to an all-girls' slumber party that Carly had evidently missed.

"I was still stuck on the picture of Russell Walker buying produce at a roadside stand," J. R. told them. "But now you have me at slumber party. I think I speak for my brother as well here. We want details."

"Down, boy," Carly teased. "They have them over at Sherilyn's."

"Why didn't you go, sweetie?" Devon asked.

"Because I only have you home for a limited time. I'm not going anywhere or doing anything that I don't go or do with you."

Devon reached across the table and caressed her hand.

"They have them every month," Audrey chimed in. "You can go next time."

"Oh, I don't think I'll be invited again. I think it's just for that little circle of girls."

"You're part of the family now," J. R. told her. "I'm sure they'll ask you next time."

"Well, how was it?" Carly asked as she spooned a second helping of red potatoes to Devon's plate.

"Quite fun, actually. Kat and I had a ball."

"Really? What did you do?"

"Yes, Audrey," Devon teased. "Tell us all about it."

"Well," she said with a grin. "We had facials. Mine was mint julep, for refreshment."

"La-dee-dah!" he commented.

"And Sherilyn put on some music, and we all got up and danced around."

"Seger?" J. R. asked.

"To start, yes. Then the Beatles, some Van Morrison, a little Sam Cooke."

"Eclectic," Devon cracked, shooting J. R. a smirk.

"I love Sam Cooke," J. R. replied.

"And we watched some old *I Love Lucy* shows, ordered pizza, baked some cookies, and had some general girl talk. It was fun."

"Who's Sam Cooke?" Carly asked them.

J. R. sang the chorus of "Bring It On Home to Me," and Devon followed it with a chunk of "Twistin' the Night Away."

"'You Send Me,'" Audrey said, leaning back into her chair with a sigh, and she and Devon began to sing the song.

"I know that one!" Carly exclaimed, and she joined in.

A moment later, Devon hopped to his feet and led his wife to her feet as well. The two of them danced across the kitchen floor while all four of them belted out the song. It surprised J. R. that he knew all the words. It surprised him even more that the sing-along in his brother's kitchen had lifted his mood in such a profound way. He hadn't felt so lighthearted in . . . he wasn't sure how long.

And the shiny smile Audrey tossed at him from across the table? Well, that certainly didn't hurt either.

"If this was a Nora Ephron movie," Kat said as they stood back to admire Audrey's work, "the last ten days would have been the music montage."

Audrey chuckled.

"While the love song plays, moviegoers see quick shots of you on the back of J. R.'s bike, me furniture shopping with Russell for his new house . . ."

"With flashes of Lisette's wedding gown coming together, and your jewelry design making it to the final version."

Kat cautiously removed the brooch from the velvet bag that protected it, placing it in her palm and running a finger gently around the bouquet of heart flowers.

"I'm so glad she picked that one," Audrey told her. "It's my favorite."

Kat held it up to the gown before them, and Audrey placed the ruffled strap over the shoulder of Mac, her headless dress form.

"It's going to be stunning."

"Thank you so much, Audrey. It's my first official sale."

"Well, you would have sold something much sooner if you'd actually shown them to anyone but your friend Staci."

"Do you really think I stand a chance? Making it as a jewelry designer, I mean."

Audrey sighed as she removed the ruffle trim and coiled it around her hand. "I would love to think I could keep you as my assistant forever, Kat. I can't imagine doing all of this without you. But you do have a gift. You have to do something with it."

"Wait!" LaMont exclaimed from the doorway. "Let me see it again."

Audrey unrolled the ruffle over the shoulder of the form, took the rhinestone bouquet from Kat, and held it to the spot where the asymmetric strap met the dress.

"What do you think?"

"Love the lines," he commented. "Good silhouette. I'd like to see it on the bride-to-be."

If he thought she would bring Lisette there during working hours and subject her to—

"Have you had a fitting yet?"

"Not yet."

"When?"

"Soon."

LaMont grazed her with his eyes. "Here?" he asked.

"Not sure yet. It really depends on my bride."

Okay. A tiny fib. But for a good cause.

"Well, it's lovely. You've surprised me. And that's not an easy thing to do."

Audrey grinned. "Then my work here is done."

"And the bling? Is that original as well?"

Audrey extended her palm toward him for a closer look. "It's Kat's design."

He darted his focus to Kat. "Really."

"It's spectacular, isn't it?"

"And you have her answering your phone and holding your straight pins and fabric samples?"

"Only for the moment," Audrey confessed. "Until she realizes she's the next big thing."

"Perhaps you're both the next big thing," he surmised, and Audrey's heart began to race at the thought. "Before you're finished here and pack up to leave us, I think we need to have a conversation, the two of us."

"Oh?"

Hold it together. Hold it together.

"I've given some thought lately to branching out. I would like to get your take on that."

Audrey tipped her head casually, despite the fact that there was nothing *casual* about the way she felt just then.

"Something to think about," he added. "We'll talk in a day or two."

Audrey strolled to the door and closed it behind him. Given that the office was made of glass, she couldn't leap into the air and scream the way she wanted. Instead, she meandered back toward the desk, grabbing Kat's hand on the way, squeezing and shaking it as Kat whimpered with excitement.

"Audrey!" she whispered, leaning across the desk as Audrey sat down behind it. "This could be *IT* for you!"

"He didn't make any offers," she reminded Kat. "He just said he wants my take."

"I know, but he's going to. Can't you tell he's going to?"

Audrey growled with enthusiasm. "It did sound that way, didn't it? It's not the same as having my own design firm, but House of LaMont is a great name to be associated with, Kat."

"It's a done deal," she beamed. "I could just tell. He looked at Lisette's gown, and he realized how talented you really are. You could almost hear him say it! 'How can I cash in on this?'"

"Okay, let's focus," Audrey said, as much to herself as to Kat. "You call Lisette and ask her to come over here tomorrow morning."

"You want her to come here? What if she runs into him?"

"I don't want to take a chance on transporting the dress back and forth if we don't have to. Bring her in early. We'll get her in and out of here before Wes ever arrives."

"Eight?"

"Good. Meanwhile, what are you and Russell doing tonight?"

"I don't know. Nothing so far."

"I'll call J. R. Let's have dinner together, the four of us."

"Ooh, fun."

"I'll ask him to get in touch with Russell, and we'll all meet at Morelli's around seven. I feel like celebrating."

Kat hurried around the desk and squeezed Audrey's shoulders. "I'm so happy for you, Audrey!"

"Let's wait and see what he offers." Her caution melted into a broad, giddy grin. "But I'm sort of happy for me too."

"Aud, I thought you couldn't stand Weston LaMont."

"Well, he's certainly not one of my favorite people," she said, twirling several long strands of pasta around her fork. "But he's a brilliant designer. And all things considered, it might not be a terrible idea to align myself with his house."

"Really?" Carly looked from Audrey to Kat and asked, "What do you think about this, Kat?"

"I think I'd rather see Audrey Regan Designs affiliated with House of LaMont than to see it swirl the drain."

"Well, don't beat around the bush or be gentle, Katarina. Just tell us how you feel," Audrey exclaimed.

"Sorry. But just two weeks ago, you were trying to figure out how to keep from surrendering. LaMont can help."

"Okay, okay," Audrey told them, using both hands to simulate leveling out. "Let's not get ahead of ourselves. Let's just wait and see." In an effort to bring things back around, she asked, "J. R., how is your lamb chop?"

"First rate," he replied, exchanging glances with Russell and Devon.

"Rightie-oh, mate," Russell egged him on. "Just stand back and let the women go at it."

"It's the only safe choice," Devon added, and the three men shared a laugh.

Audrey shook her head at them and stared Devon down. "Are you enjoying yourselves?"

Devon shrugged and nodded. "Yeah. Kinda."

Russell, Devon, and J. R. all looked at her, wide-eyed and straight-faced.

"Oh, please. Innocent doesn't work on any one of you."

Russell snorted, setting the other two loose.

"Very mature. Oh . . . What. Ever."

Which only set them to laughing all the harder.

"Children!"

"Ah, Audrey, it's . . . amazing."

"You look remarkable!" Kat said, angling the full-length mirror so that Lisette could see the back of the gown. "It looks so much better on you than on Mac!"

Lisette chuckled and leaned toward the dress form. "I'm sure she meant no offense, Mac."

"I'm glad we went with the chapel-length train," Audrey commented. "I think it's perfect for this silhouette. We still need to add a little something to the boning at the base of your torso, and I'll take it up right here." She gathered small sections at each shoulder blade. "And here. See how much better that looks?"

"Yes. It's just right."

"The strap is a little loose too. Hang on while I re-pin."

Audrey glanced at the metal clock on the wall. Nearly nine. She would have to push things along if she planned to shuffle Lisette out of the office before people started arriving at ten.

"I was surprised to see that you're sharing work space with Weston LaMont," Lisette said as Audrey pulled a straight pin from the cushion wrapped around her wrist.

"Why's that?"

"I read about his new venture in the *Journal* this morning. To tell you the truth, it worried me a little. I don't want to see my one-of-a-kind dress showing up next year on every plus-sized bride in the country."

Audrey smiled. "What do you mean?"

"The new line. What's it called? Rubenesque?"

Audrey's eyes made a beeline to Kat's, and they stared at one another until Kat blinked.

"He's starting a new line?" she asked.

"You didn't know?" Lisette asked. "I read about it in the car on the way over here. Have a look. The paper is in my bag, on the chair."

Kat zipped toward it and yanked the newspaper out of the tall camel tote.

"On the front page of Fashion and Style."

Audrey finished pinning and looked at Kat expectantly.

"Here it is," she said, and a moment later she gasped. "That snake!"

"Kat, what?!"

"Next season's runways will have to be a little wider," Kat read straight from the paper. "Weston LaMont, renowned designer and a definitive name in bridal and red carpet trends, will now add plus-sized design to his repertoire. Rubenesque Couture, an offshoot of LaMont House of Design, will begin creating high-end fashion for the discriminating curvier woman later this year."

Kat slapped the newspaper section down to the desktop with a stifled scream. "That snake!"

"This can't be right," Audrey said. "How can this be right?"

"Audrey, do you remember what you said to him? You told him that the plus-sized bride was like any other bride, she's just slightly more *Rubenesque*."

"You didn't know about this?" Lisette asked, and she suddenly winced. "Ooh. Can I get some help here?"

"Sorry."

Audrey finished unzipping the gown and gingerly lifted it over Lisette's mane of blonde hair. While she slipped into the long gray cashmere sweater she'd worn over her black leggings, Lisette bounced her gaze back and forth between Kat and Audrey.

"So what does this mean?" she asked. "You didn't know about it?"

"No," Audrey declared. "He never mentioned it."

"Maybe that's what he wants to talk to you about," Kat suggested. "Maybe he's going to ask you to design the Rubenesque label."

"Maybe," she said, a little lost in her overload of speculation.

"You wouldn't include my dress, right?" Lisette clarified. "I mean, I really wanted—"

"No," Audrey said, raising her hand. "No, of course not."

After a moment, "But you wouldn't really design for him either, right?"

Audrey glanced at Lisette to meet an expression of consternation.

"I . . . don't know. I'm . . . Why do you ask?"

"I kind of thought you were in business for yourself. I mean, when I checked you out after our first meeting, I read on the internet that Audrey Regan Designs is an up-and-comer, and I just thought you were sort of creating your own name."

"Well. That was the plan."

"Until?"

Rather than explain her financial woes to a paying client, Audrey smiled at Lisette. "No offer has been made to work with Wes. It's pointless to talk about a possibility that hasn't reached the light of day."

"Still, I hope you'll turn him down and keep pursuing your own dream instead of his, Audrey. You're very talented."

Audrey hoped the smile she gave Lisette in return for the compliment didn't look as tired as it felt. So many scenarios wove through the maze in her head, crashing into dead ends and bumping into sharp edges.

Kat walked Lisette downstairs and, after she left the building, Audrey must have read the *Journal* article over five times. For someone with such little regard for human imperfection, it struck her as strange that LaMont had chosen to go this route with his designs.

"I just don't get it," she said aloud as Kat returned to the room.

"Well, you'll get the chance to ask him about it in person in about three minutes. His car arrived just as Lisette's pulled away from the building."

"Too close for comfort."

"I'll say."

"I just . . . don't . . . get it," she repeated, shaking her head. "I wonder how long this has been in the works."

Before the speculation could go any further, LaMont stepped into the doorway.

"Nice article," Audrey blurted before he could say a word.

"Oh, you saw it," he replied, and he crossed the room and sat down in the chair across from her desk. "So what do you think?"

Behind him, Kat opened her mouth to speak, and Audrey silenced her with the raise of her hand. "Katarina. Can you check with Billie about that delivery, please?"

Kat wrinkled her brow and stared at her for a moment before spinning on her heel and leaving the office.

"What do I think?" Audrey said. "I think it's a little strange that you would start a plus-size line when you clearly can't stand plus-size people."

"Ironic, isn't it?" he remarked. "Frankly, I had been thinking of expanding my demographic for quite a while. I was right in the middle of working on a business plan when I saw what you had done right here."

She wanted to stop him from even glancing at Lisette's gown, but LaMont stood up and walked toward it where she and Kat had placed it on the form. She found herself wishing she'd never been so foolish as to ask this man for help of any kind.

"It's exquisite, really."

Audrey leaned back in her chair and watched him. His words and tone didn't quite match.

"For me to inspire a designer of your caliber," she said cautiously, "is a highlight of my career."

"Your short career."

"I'm sorry. What?"

"You've been designing for, what? Three years?"

"If you count Barbie couture, it's been more than twenty." He didn't appear to find the amusement in her statement. "But professionally, since I graduated five or six years ago."

"Still so many dues to pay," he commented.

What you don't know about the dues I've paid could fill several of your glass-encased offices.

"I'd considered asking you to join my house. Did you know that?"

"No," she fibbed.

"What would you have said?"

The way he looked at her made Audrey antsy somehow.

"If you'd extended an offer that you've clearly decided now not to extend?" she clarified with a push-up smile. "I normally save my brain cells for actual problem-solving rather than the hypothetical variety."

"I suspect you would have accepted," he observed as he folded back into the chair.

"Oh?"

He nodded, looking at her over the bridge of his glasses. "Mm-hm. Because Audrey Regan Designs is, for all intents and purposes, ready to capsize. In fact, it should have already if not for a fluke break here and there. And although you would prefer to navigate the fashion world under your own name, you might have accepted a position working for me just to keep the dream going a little longer."

"You seem to have given this a lot of thought, Wes."

"You're talented, Audrey. You have a good eye and a fresh perspective."

"Thank you for saying so."

"But you still have years of hits and misses before you're ever going to be able to stand on your own two feet. My taking you under the considerable banner of House of LaMont would just make your trip around the mountain that much longer, and my investment in you futile."

Audrey vowed silently not to show him reaction of any sort. She would not lower her eyes, nor would she take one breath that might be mistaken for a sigh of resignation or disappointment.

"I don't happen to agree with you," she finally said coolly. "Regardless of that, we are at least on the same page. I don't see working for you as something in the best interest of my design career. So if you had made the offer, Wes, I would have . . . respectfully declined."

His grin seemed to slither across his face.

"That being said, I appreciate so much that you opened your doors to me while I worked in Atlanta." She knew better than to continue, but she couldn't manage to stop herself. "I hope you'll reconsider and allow me to reimburse you for the office space we've occupied?"

Audrey gulped. The empty offer hovered over her like thick morning vapor on a very still lake.

"Certainly not."

Oh, thank God!

"I have you to thank for the new direction with Rubenesque. You're my muse, Audrey."

He rose from the chair and just stood there looking at her for a long, uncomfortable gap of time before he finally turned and clicked across the floor and out the door.

Audrey inhaled sharply, holding the air inside her lungs for several seconds before releasing it slowly. On her second shot, Kat scurried into the room and closed the door behind her.

"He has pictures."

Audrey blew out the air from her lungs before asking, "Sorry, what?"

"I was just talking to Billie, Audrey. LaMont has digital photographs of Lisette's gown. He had her upload them to his laptop yesterday when Monique was out sick."

"And Billie just *told* you this."

"She can't stand the bugger either," Kat revealed, her eyes open wide and her expression so serious that Audrey almost laughed.

"Will she help us to—"

"Yep."

"Are you sure?"

Kat nodded emphatically.

"Let's pack up then. We'll need to vacate quickly once the deed is done."

Rather than stop and examine this new information and try to figure it all out, Audrey leapt to her feet. She and Kat sprang into action. While Kat packed several boxes with remnants of fabric, beading, thread, and pattern paper, Audrey draped a garment bag carefully atop the gown and dress form.

When she picked up her cell phone from the desk and began to dial, Kat asked her, "What are you doing?"

"Calling for reinforcements."

A moment later, J. R. had agreed to drive into Atlanta with Devon's truck. The bed would be plenty big enough to house a couple of boxes and a super-sized body with no head.

Top Four Types of Bridal Gown Trains

1. Sweeping Train

Also known by the term "brush train" because it barely brushes the floor, this is a good choice when the goal is an elegant but simple statement gown.

2. Chapel Train

Usually about four feet from the waistline, this choice can be used for either formal or informal gowns, dependent upon the silhouette of the dress.

3. Cathedral Train

Nearly twice as long as the chapel train, this option is most often used for a formal affair, or for that fairy-tale wedding with the big impact.

The cathedral train is often detachable for freedom on the dance floor.

4. Royal Train

Think Kate Middleton.

The royal train falls eight feet or more from the waistline, and it usually enters the church a minute or more after the bride's entrance.

14

You brought Russell?"

"I thought we might need some extra muscle."

"And . . . you brought *Russell*?"

J. R. laughed. "Not that kind of muscle, Agent 99. Muscle for lifting boxes."

"But he's . . ." Audrey raised an eyebrow as she whispered, "a loose cannon."

The four of them managed to get the boxes out of the office, down the stairs, and into the back of Devon's truck without much notice. But as they emerged with the real treasure, every eye in the building seemed to be focused on them.

Audrey had removed Mac's stick leg and metal stand, and she balanced them clumsily as she led the way down the corridor toward the stairs. J. R. and Russell followed, one of them on each end of the headless, gowned torso sealed inside the vinyl bag.

"What on earth!" Monique exclaimed from where she stood in front of Billie's desk. "Are you leaving?"

"Well, Mac is," Audrey replied, and she stepped aside on the stairway for J. R. and Russell to continue with the getaway.

"Was that . . . *Russell Walker*?"

Audrey's antennae perked, and she stopped at the top of the stairs and smiled. "Yes. Yes, it is. Would you like to meet him, Monique?"

"Could I?"

"Of course. We'll be right back," she said, waving her hand over her head and descending the stairs at a speedy clip.

With the truck parked in the loading zone just outside the front door, and Kat already standing in the back of the truck to guide the precious cargo to a safe landing, Audrey whispered, "Make sure she's secure. If anything happens to this dress, I'm done."

Kat grinned at her. "There's a *tarp!*"

"Excellent. Can you and J. R. manage? I need to steal Russell for a moment."

"I knew it," Russell cackled. "The ladies can never resist an Aussie."

"Oh, stow your ego for thirty seconds, will you? I need to distract someone, and you're just the eye candy to do it."

"Did you hear that?" he asked J. R. "I'm eye candy."

Audrey snagged his wrist and tugged Russell back into the building. At the bottom of the marble stairway, she turned and stared him down.

"No nonsense," she warned in a raspy whisper. "There's a woman at the top of these stairs named Monique. I need you to charm her and do everything you can to get her to follow you back into the office we just cleaned out. Do you understand?"

"I do," he said, mock-serious. "My mission, should I choose to accept it—"

"Russell, please. This is so important."

"Calm down. I've got it."

Halfway up the stairs, Audrey stopped and grabbed Russell's arm. "The other woman. Billie. Do *not* engage her. She's doing me a favor once you get Monique out of the way."

"Rightie-oh."

"So it's Monique only."

" 'Kay!"

Russell started up the stairs again, but Audrey snagged his arm one more time.

"Down the hall and out of the way."

"Yes, Audrey. Now shouldn't we get on with this?"

She sighed. "Sorry."

Just as she suspected, Monique stood waiting at the very top of the stairs. Audrey glanced at Billie over the woman's tailored shoulder, and Billie nodded.

"Monique, this is Russell Walker. Russell, this is Weston LaMont's right arm. The place would be a dysfunctional machine without Monique."

"Oh, Audrey, really."

Monique grinned at Russell like a hungry cheetah. Thankfully, Russell lunged before she did.

"Monique," he repeated, and he grabbed her hand, slowly walking her down the hall. "What a beautiful French name. And it's perfect for you because it stems from the Latin word *monere*, which means to advise. You were deemed a leader from the time you were born."

Billie jumped up from her chair and rounded the desk. "Oh, he's good," she whispered to Audrey. "I'll just need three minutes."

Audrey touched Billie's arm as she rushed past her. "Thank you so much."

Through the glass, she watched Russell charm the woman, realizing Monique had no idea what had hit her. She found herself worrying for a moment that perhaps Russell's keen abilities with women might end up breaking Kat's heart in the long run. What was to prevent him from—

"Billie tells me you're leaving us."

Audrey reeled around to find LaMont standing behind her. "Y-yes. And I want to thank you for everything, Wes. I don't even have words to tell you . . . what it was like to get to know you."

She didn't want to, but Audrey shook his hand enthusiastically.

"Really. Thank you so much. For the work space and the lunches. And the tip about the eggplant sandwiches at Caruso's."

Okay. Now you're babbling.

"Anyway, thank you."

"I wish you the best of luck, Audrey."

"And you too. I mean with the Rubenesque line. I hope it . . . soars to the heights that you deserve."

"That's very gracious."

"Oh. Well." Audrey glanced down the hall over LaMont's shoulder for the hundredth time. Where was she? "Gracious. I don't know. What is gracious, really? But—"

At last, Billie raced into view and gave her the A-OK.

"Where is that Russell?" Waving her arms at him through the glass, she exclaimed, "Time to go! Let's go now."

She watched as Russell kissed Monique's hand. She couldn't hear her moan as she swooned, but she certainly could see it. The woman melted like a wax candle on a sunny window sill.

"LaMont, isn't it?" Russell said as he moved toward them. "How are you, mate?"

Russell extended his hand, but Audrey snagged it from the air between the two men. "J. R. is waiting downstairs, Russell. We've got to go."

"Oh. All rightie then."

"Thanks again for everything," Audrey said as she pulled him toward the stairs. She turned back and shot Billie a covert smile. "Really. Thank you."

And with that, they headed down the stairs.

Near the bottom, Audrey told Russell, "If you're using that false charm of yours on Kat, and you're not genuine with her, I'm going to hang you by your ponytail from the second floor balcony. When you fall out of The Tanglewood sky this time, you'll do it without your hair."

Russell winced as they burst through the front door. "Thanks for that visual, love. Very effective."

"Why?" Carly asked. "Why did he have photographs of Audrey's gown?"

"We can't be sure," J. R. replied. "But since he was in the paper today announcing his big plus-size clothing line, I have my guesses."

"What a slime!"

"Kat made friends with the receptionist while they were there. A young girl named Billie. And she went in and deleted the photos from his desktop. But Audrey says there's no telling if there are other copies out there. Maybe he emailed the photos to someone, and he could retrieve them from his sent mail."

"Or he could have backed up his hard drive," Devon suggested.

"Right. But she took the only shot she could."

"What a slime!"

J. R. grinned. "Easy there."

"I can't help it. That just makes me so angry. Audrey works so hard, and she's so talented."

"No argument here."

"Is she all right? Do I need to call her?"

"Sweetie, you'll see her in an hour."

Carly's expression deflated. "I can't believe it's your last night."

"I know," Devon answered softly. "C'mere."

She took two long steps toward Devon's chair and melted into his embrace. "I need more time," she whimpered into his shoulder.

"I know."

"Look, maybe you two would rather spend tonight alone," J. R. suggested. "I think everyone would understand if you didn't want to socialize tonight."

"No, we're going," Carly said.

"We might just bail early."

"I'm going to head over there now," he told them. "You two follow when you're ready."

J. R. hardly remembered the ride over to Sherilyn and Andy's house once he arrived. It had been a blur of disjointed thought: Devon shipping out again; Carly left behind; recollections of his big adventure with Audrey. Like that unmemorable ride, the world just kept right on turning whether he kept up or not.

"J. R.'s here," Emma announced when he walked through the door behind her, and she touched his arm. "Devon and Carly came separately?"

"Yeah, they're right behind me."

Andy, Jackson, and Sean stood out on the deck, hovering over the grill like mother hens. Fee, Emma, Kat, Audrey, and Sherilyn buzzed about the kitchen, passing plates and filling bowls and setting them out in a buffet line on the counter, perfectly-synchronized gears in a well-oiled machine.

Audrey looked up at him quickly and shot him a smile that he felt in his knees before the action drew her back in.

"Here you go," Sherilyn said, handing over a large stainless steel spoon.

"Where's Russell?" J. R. asked no one in particular.

"Outside with the boys," Kat replied.

Once out on the deck, J. R. saw Russell on the lawn below, pitching a ball that Henry chased with vigor. With fur flying and a huge red tongue dangling out of the side of his mouth, the dog raced across the yard in pursuit, and he returned to drop it at Russell's feet, looking up at him with hope.

"Play date?" J. R. asked Andy as he stepped up beside him and watched.

"Two peas in a pod," he answered.

Andy tipped open the roll-top and tended to the steaks and chicken breasts sizzling on the grill. Enormous cobs of corn peeked out from husks on the other side next to large foil packages.

"This a new grill?" J. R. noted.

Andy lit up. "The Aztec Premium Prestige."

"Ah, geez," Sean muttered, and he turned around and walked into the house.

"We've heard it a time or two," Jackson said with a grin.

"Dual head stainless steel gas grill," Andy continued without notice, "with forty-five thousand BTU, full rotisserie, and eleven hundred square inches of cooking surface. It's the champion of excellence and precision in grilling, my friend."

As Andy set about turning the steaks, J. R. and Jackson shared an amused glance. "Good to know," J. R. said, and he smacked Andy on the back before turning toward the house.

"You're driving them away in herds, Drummond," Jackson commented.

"Don't care," Andy declared, spatula firmly in hand. "This baby is worthy of a little praise."

"Yeah, okay." And Jackson followed J. R.

Devon and Carly stood at the counter with Audrey and Sherilyn as he walked in. J. R. patted Devon's arm on his way past. He approached Audrey at the sink and caressed her shoulder.

"Nice to see you, Agent 99."

She snickered as she sprinkled fresh Parmesan cheese over the top of a large bowl.

"What is that?" he asked, leaning toward the bowl.

"Seafood orzo," she told him. "Sherilyn taught me how to make it. Orzo with shrimp, fish, peppers, tomatoes, basil. All the good stuff."

"Ooh, I love orzo," Carly said, peering over the counter at the bowl.

J. R. picked up a fork from the open drawer, but Audrey pulled the huge bowl away before he could grab a bite.

"C'mon. Just a taste. I'm starving. I didn't have lunch. I was off doing espionage with you."

She tilted her full lips into a crooked grin. "Just a taste."

The dish lived up to the anticipation. "This is amazing."

"Thank you," Sherilyn said, snatching the fork from his hand. "And you can have all you like when dinner is served. Now go get yourself something to drink and tell my husband the guests of honor have arrived."

"Do I have to?"

Sherilyn scowled at him.

"I won't get a word in, and I've already heard everything about the new grill."

"Several times over," Sean called out from the other room.

Her frown turned into a broad grin, and Sherilyn laughed out loud. "It's a new toy. He'll get over it."

Jackson and Sean groaned their good-natured skepticism from the sofa in the living room.

"I can just hear him out there in the snow this Christmas," Sean mocked as Jackson cackled with laughter. "Aztec Premium. Four billion BTUs, and *Look!* A rotisserie!"

"Oh, hush. Go get Russell and help Andy bring in the food, you slackers."

"Go on," Fee told them. "The sooner you do, the sooner we can serve dinner and keep Andy's mouth full so he can't talk about the grill."

That drove Sean and Jackson immediately to their feet.

"Here, Henry!" Sean called through the open door. "Here, Russell! Come here, boys!"

"You're awful," Emma said with a chuckle.

J. R. used his fingers to pluck a chunk of fish from the bowl of orzo, and he plopped it into his mouth before Audrey could stop him.

"What is that? Halibut?"

"Yes," she told him. "But if you don't get out of here, it's going to turn into *snapper*!"

He laughed as he scurried through the back door.

"How we doing, Chef?" he asked Andy. "The natives are restless and hungry."

"Hold your horses, it's on its way."

And ten minutes later, dinner buffet for twelve hit the counter.

"Before we overload our plates and dive into this feast," Sherilyn announced, "I thought it might be nice if we joined hands and said a little prayer of thanks."

J. R. took Fee's hand on one side and Audrey's on the other. When everyone settled into a jagged circle, he and the others bowed their heads.

"Lord Jesus," Sherilyn said, "Andy and I want to thank You for this exceptional group of people that You've put into our lives and brought into our home. We ask for Your blessing on each and every person in this prayer circle, but especially on Devon."

J. R.'s heart squeezed slightly.

"Send Your angels of protection with him as he travels where You send him. Keep him safe from all harm, and redeem the time so that it seems like nothing flat before he's back here with us."

J. R. opened his eyes long enough to glance at Devon as Carly curled into him and nestled beneath his chin.

"And Lord, we ask for ministering angels for Carly, to bring her peace and comfort, to remind her every day and every night that her future, and Devon's future, is safe with You."

"Protect them and keep them, Lord God," Andy added, "until You bring us all back together again, celebrating Devon's return."

"And we ask," Carly chimed in, "that You would bring peace to the Middle East, Lord. Bring all of our sons and fathers and husbands and brothers home safely. And let them stay here."

Agreements sounded all around, and Russell added a prayer rhyme of his own.

"Not to be rude. But please bless the food."

"That's quite a number."

"Yes. It is."

"It's . . . big."

"Huge."

Audrey tossed the page to the bed beside her and collapsed backwards into the pile of pillows.

"I can't charge her that much, Kat."

"You have no choice," Kat said as she picked up the paper and sat down next to her. "Lisette is the one who told you to make whatever arrangements you needed to make in order to stay here in Atlanta, to rush her gown, to . . ."

"I know, I know. But there's no way she's expecting it to have cost this much, Kat. And I can't afford to charge her any less."

A light rap on the door drew Audrey straight upright.

"That's her."

Kat opened the door and greeted Lisette. She looked lovely in an emerald green silk blouse and black pleated trousers, her long blonde hair twisted back into a loose braid that fell over one shoulder.

"All ready for your final fitting?" Kat asked, and Lisette beamed at the gown on the dress form in the corner.

"What I'm ready for is my wedding day."

"Well, it's almost here," Audrey reassured her.

"Can't get here soon enough. I just want to be married to Griffin and on that plane to Costa Rica."

"Oh, that sounds perfect!" Kat exclaimed. "Have you ever been?"

"Twice. But Griff never has. I can't wait to get him down there where we can lounge on our private beach and sip little drinks with umbrellas in them for two weeks."

"I can't even imagine," Audrey said with a chuckle. "Let's get you into your dress, shall we?"

"Can we have just a minute?"

Audrey paused. "Of course."

"Will you sit down with me for a minute?"

Audrey crossed to the bed and sat down on the corner. Her heart started to pound harder while she imagined all sorts of scenarios.

"I'll give you some privacy," Kat said, heading toward the door.

"No, Kat. Please. I'd like to talk to both of you."

Kat's eyes grew wide, locking into Audrey's for a couple of seconds before she sat down on the chair.

"I can't stop thinking about what we talked about the other morning."

Audrey shook her head. "I . . . don't know . . ."

"Sorry. When I showed you the article in the *Journal* about Weston LaMont, and I got the impression that you thought he might offer you a job designing for him."

"Well," Audrey began, and she popped with one slightly bitter chuckle. "That's not an issue after all."

"No?"

"No. It seems Mr. LaMont thinks I still have years of crawling through the desert before I'm deemed worthy. I mean, I might be his *muse*, but inspiration is one thing. I'm certainly not good enough to—" Regret sliced her words in two. "I shouldn't have said that. I'm sorry."

"So he got the idea from you," she surmised. "And now he's going to run with it."

"That about covers it."

Lisette flicked the hem of her blouse with one pink fingernail. When she looked up, Audrey saw something strange in Lisette's eyes, and she grinned at the sight of it.

"I know. It's ironic."

"No," Lisette said. "I've been thinking a lot about it, and now . . . talking to you . . . I'm pretty sure I'm on the right track. But I'm a little nervous to say this to you."

"You want to change the gown, right? Just tell me, Lisette. Whatever it is, I'll do my best to—"

"No," she interrupted, this time on a string of giggles. "No, that's not it at all."

Kat shrugged when Audrey looked at her.

"So what is it?"

"My dress is perfect, Audrey. Absolutely perfect. I wouldn't change one thread."

"Oh, good."

"So perfect, in fact, that it got me to thinking about what a talent you are."

"Well. Thank you."

"And Kat. That awesome brooch you designed. It's just amazing."

Kat's smile didn't quite reach her eyes. Instead, curiosity roiled.

"The thing is . . . I had been thinking about talking to you about maybe investing in you."

"Investing in me?" Audrey cocked her head slightly, and she felt her entire forehead furrow.

"Well," Lisette sighed. "I was thinking that a really high-end bridal design line seemed like a great idea. But I took it to my dad, and we talked it over, and we both came away with the feeling that this economy just doesn't support that kind of move."

"Welcome to my world," Audrey said, and she chuckled. "The economy doesn't seem to have much interest in supporting me at all."

"I wouldn't be so quick to say that," Lisette corrected. "Maybe you won't even be interested in this, but what do you think about going in another direction with your talents? Expanding on them."

Audrey took a long moment to listen to the rushing sound in her ears before replying. "What do you have in mind exactly?"

"I've been full-figured my whole life," she explained. "And every time an important event has come up, I've struggled to find something really nice to wear."

Audrey nodded.

"But Audrey, you have such a great sense of style. And what you did with my gown, taking something that might be found for a small woman and adjusting it to fit the curves of a larger body, it was kind of miraculous."

She glanced at Lisette's dress in the corner. Mac wore that gown like the blueblood of dress forms!

"And you know, it was really this place that got my dad and me to thinking with a broader view."

"This place? The Tanglewood?"

"Yes. It's a one-stop shop for destination weddings. They have it all covered. So why couldn't we do that, except with garments?"

Audrey's wheels began to turn slowly, but she knew she hadn't quite caught up with Lisette just yet.

"We offer an experience for brides, size fourteen to thirty. You design bridal gowns and dresses for bridesmaids and mothers of the bride, no matter what size they are. We could even supply coordinating dresses for the flower girls. Are you following me here?"

Audrey nodded. "I think so."

"I think plus-sized brides would fly in from all over the country to an Atlanta showroom specializing in a couture experience with a retail pricetag. And with the showroom, we also offer different shops where they can choose veils and shoes, jewelry accessories—which is where you come in, Kat. And we contract high-end make-up artists and stylists to give tutorials on the glamorous wedding day look, even contract them out to travel to the locations if they choose that. We give them a one-stop opportunity unlike anything else out there in the bridal market. What do you think?"

"Are you joking?" Kat said, leaping to her feet. "This is brilliant!"

"You think so too? Because I'm really—"

"Wait, wait a minute!" Audrey exclaimed. "Let's just slow down and think about this."

"Look," Lisette said, "I realize this is a brand new idea for you, and you need time to think it over. Dad and I have been sitting with it for a week now. He owns an enormous warehouse over in Alpharetta, near North Point Mall. It's just sitting there empty, and I think it would be an amazing location. Why don't you talk it over, really think about it, both of you? When Griff and I return from our honeymoon, we'll talk again. I was thinking that in the first year, we may all struggle a little. But we can build this thing, Audrey. The three of us together."

Audrey opened her mouth, but nothing came out. And if something had, she couldn't even imagine what it might have been.

"I've been looking for something that excited me like this for a really long time. Will you consider it?"

"Of course," she said, nodding. "Yes. We'll think about it, and I'd like to run it by a business consultant of some kind."

"Good. Do that."

"And we'll talk after Costa Rica."

Lisette jumped to her feet, pulling Audrey along with her, and she embraced the two of them at the same time.

"I just have a feeling about this," she told them. "I think it's meant to be."

Kat piped up. "So do I!"

"You know what I'm hungry for?"

"What?"

"Seafood orzo. Sherilyn showed me how to make it the other night, and I think I might be able to do it on my own. Would you eat some if I made it?"

"I guess."

Audrey leaned backward on the bed and stared at the ceiling. "I think I'll make a shopping list and make some for dinner . . . Anyway, I was saying before that I made enough on Lisette's job to pay my bills for next month, so I don't have to rush back to New York. And J. R. has agreed to stick around town long enough to be my date at Lisette's wedding this weekend. But I can't help wondering whether you're entirely sure you want to let me and Kat both move into the house with you, Caroline. If the new business venture takes off, it might be a while before we have time to find our own places and get—"

"Aud?"

"I know, I know, you're sure now. But what about a month from now when—"

"Aud."

"Just hear me out, Carly."

"No," she belted out from the other side of the bathroom door. "You need to hear me out."

Audrey tipped sideways on the bed and folded her arm beneath her head. "Well, I really can't thank you enough. Sherilyn said the best move is to put everything down on paper, and then she suggested talking to Jackson. Apparently, he's—"

"Audrey!"

"What?"

"Stop talking."

"Fine. You don't have to be—"

When the bathroom door swished open and Carly just stood there staring at her, her eyes as wide and shiny as quarters, Audrey immediately fell silent.

"Aud," she whimpered, and she lifted a small plastic stick into the air and held it there.

"What is that?"

"It's a pregnancy test."

"A what? . . . Why are you . . . A pregnancy test?"

"Yes."

"And you took the test?"

"Yes."

"Well, did you pass or fail?"

Carly finally blinked. "I guess that depends on how you look at it, but I'd say it's a pretty big passing grade!" She began to hop up and down, twirling around in the air. "I'm pregnant!!"

Sherilyn's Seafood Orzo

1-pound package orzo
½ pound medium shrimp, peeled and deveined
6 ounces halibut, cut in bite-sized chunks
¼ cup fresh Parmesan cheese
1 small green pepper, diced
2 bunches scallions
2 medium-sized Roma tomatoes, diced
1 white onion, diced
1 bunch fresh parsley, chopped
1 bunch fresh basil, chopped
1 clove garlic, minced
3 Tablespoons extra virgin olive oil

Prepare orzo according to directions.
Drain and stir in 1 Tablespoon olive oil.
Heat remaining oil in large sauté pan.
Add diced pepper, onions, tomatoes, and minced garlic, and sauté for 2-3 minutes.
Add chunked halibut and shrimp, and sauté until cooked.
Add parsley, basil, orzo and ¾ of the Parmesan cheese.
Mix well and sprinkle the top with remaining Parmesan cheese.

15

"Do you, Lisette Margaret Gibson, take this man, Griffin Earl Jenkins, to be your husband?"

"I do."

"And do you, Griffin Earl Jenkins, take this woman, Lisette Margaret Gibson, to be your wife?"

"I do."

"That's what we waited to hear," the minister told them with a smile. "In that case, I do now pronounce you, before God and this congregation, husband and wife. Griff, kiss your bride."

Audrey reached over and squeezed Kat's hand before they joined J. R. and Russell, and about five hundred others, in applauding the new Mr. and Mrs. Jenkins. When the couple headed down the aisle past them, Lisette locked eyes with Audrey, placed a hand to her heart and mouthed, "Thank you."

"You look stunning," Audrey returned.

"Do you have any idea how long it will take for all these people to make their way into the reception?" Russell asked J. R. "It's like a cattle drive."

"Let's just hang here for a while then," Kat suggested, and they all agreed.

The four of them took their seats again until the crowd began to thin.

"John Robert!" In the next instant, Lisette's little flower girl Roslyn tossed herself onto J. R. and hugged him. "I didn't know you'd be here. Did you come with Audrey?"

"I did," he told her. "And I got to see you walk up the aisle. Nice job with the rose petals, by the way. Very even tosses, no stragglers."

"I know, right?" she exclaimed. "And guess what." Before he could ask, she raised the skirt of her dress slightly to show the pink boots she wore underneath. "Check it out, Audrey. Aunt Lis said I could."

"Very nice, Roslyn!"

"I told you they were cute, right?"

"Yes, you did," Audrey replied. "But those are even better than I thought."

"Are you guys coming for supper?"

"You mean the reception?" she asked with a smile. "Yes, we are."

Roslyn raised an eyebrow and looked around before whispering, "There's going to be a lot of cake for dessert."

"Excellent."

"Do you like cake, John Robert?"

One side of J. R.'s mouth tilted upward as he replied. "A lot."

"Oh good! I'll see you guys in there then?"

"See you there."

Audrey watched the little girl skip down the aisle to catch up to her mother near the door.

"I didn't get to tell you earlier," J. R. said, leaning toward Audrey. "I spoke to Carly this morning."

Audrey smiled. "She told you then? Spectacular news, isn't it?"

"It is." He nodded. "I just wish she'd discovered it earlier so Devon could have known before he left."

"He'll be over the moon when he hears."

"And worried sick."

She hummed her agreement and added, "No doubt."

"It makes me feel a little conflicted."

"About leaving tomorrow?"

He glared at the chair in front of him. "Yeah."

Trying to disguise the hope already climbing up the back of her throat, she suggested, "Maybe you should rethink it then." When she finally glanced over at him, their eyes clicked together like a key in a lock. "Maybe."

"I know it's beginning to look like the entire universe revolves around the nucleus of Atlanta," he said with a crooked tilt of a smile. "And in particular, around the hotel. But it's not like that for everyone."

"I know."

But she didn't really.

"I'm considering a business opportunity that would bring me back here," she pointed out. "And Kat was already planning to move here. Carly and Devon are here. And there's Sherilyn and Emma and everyone at The Tanglewood. For crying out loud, even Russell is relocating to Atlanta."

His voice was soft and somewhat tender as he asked, "And?"

Audrey twisted the strap of her small beaded purse around her index finger, and she sighed. "It just seems like something to think about, that's all."

"Audrey." J. R. took her hand between both of his and held it until she lifted her eyes and looked at him. "Angel, I'm not moving to Atlanta."

"Okay."

"I have a home. In Santa Fe."

"All right," she said, easing her hand away from him.

"But that doesn't mean I won't be back."

She glanced at him again. "You will?"

"Of course I will. I have family here, and friends."

Is that what I am? Your friend?

"And you."

She smiled. "Well, you better not become a stranger . . . because you can be replaced, you know."

J. R. chuckled as he draped his arm loosely around her shoulder. "Replaced, huh?"

"Yep. There are ten thousand other Harleys on the road . . . a *hundred thousand* other guys who might just enjoy doing a little espionage."

"You make a good point. I'll keep that in mind."

She swallowed around the lump in her throat before asking, "So tomorrow morning?"

"First thing."

Before she could think of an appropriate reply, Russell leaned forward around Kat and asked them, "Want to set out on our trek?"

J. R. nodded, and the four of them stood up and stepped out of the row to the white aisle covered in scarlet red rose petals. Audrey rested her hand on the back of the gold ladder-back chair in front of her until J. R. offered his folded arm. She smiled as she looped her own through his.

"So what are you thinking about the business deal with the bride?" he asked as they strolled toward the door.

"I'm not sure yet. Lisette has a huge vision, and it makes me a little nervous."

"How so?"

"She's not involved in fashion. An undertaking like what she has in mind is massive under the best of circumstances. But without the expertise to back it up . . . I'm just not sure it's a good idea to dive into it with a complete novice and attach my name to it in good faith. Does that sound ungrateful?"

"It sounds cautious. And there's nothing wrong with that."

Audrey smoothed the narrow skirt of her dress. She hadn't been certain about the choice for Lisette's wedding, but it had been one of the last-minute extras she'd added to her luggage before leaving New York. Shimmering pale pink fabric overlaid with a deep plum lace; she remembered wondering where she might wear the dress, but it had turned into fashion kismet. Audrey loved when that happened.

As she and Russell passed them, Kat adjusted the translucent cap sleeve that had turned slightly.

"I'm afraid it will break Kat's heart if I decide it's not the right move. She was so excited that Lisette included her jewelry designs in her plans. I just don't know . . . you know . . . if it's right for *me*. But at the same time, I did ask God for an answer, and there was Lisette . . . On the other hand . . ." Audrey stopped herself and turned toward J. R. "Sorry. I'm normally a much more fun date."

"Yes, I know," he said, and he tapped her hand where it rested on his forearm.

"Sherilyn suggested I meet with Jackson and talk it over with him. I think I'll feel a lot better once I get his business perspective."

"That's very good advice."

"You think so?"

"I do."

"Careful, lad," Russell teased, turning around in front of them. "Saying 'I do' out loud at a wedding? You're playing fast and loose with your freedom, if you ask me."

Kat playfully smacked his arm and giggled. "No one did."

The Omni ballroom teemed with guests finding their way around white-on-scarlet linen draped tables set with fine bone china, tall rose centerpieces and shimmering crystal goblets. The uniformed wait staff appeared almost synchronized in their movements.

"It looks like the front tables are the only ones with assigned seating," Kat told them.

"The rest of us peasants can sit wherever we like," Russell teased. "It's every man and lady for themselves."

Russell excused himself for interrupting a conversation in progress at a nearby table.

"He's a force of nature," Audrey observed, and J. R. laughed.

"You have no idea."

"C'mon!" Russell called, motioning to them. "These chairs are open."

Audrey inched around the table and sat down next to one of the guests already occupying it. She'd seen the woman at the ceremony, and she'd been wearing a beautiful wide-brimmed hat wrapped in copper tulle and silk flowers.

"Where's your hat?" she asked with a smile.

"I beg your pardon?"

"Oh, I noticed the stunning hat you wore to the wedding."

The elegant woman grinned. "It might have needed its own chair, so I took it upstairs and left it in my hotel room."

"That's a pity. I'd have enjoyed meeting it."

"Perhaps I can arrange an introduction later," she retorted, and they shared a chuckle.

"It's vintage, isn't it?" Audrey inquired. "1930s?"

"It is. Good eye," she replied, and she seemed surprised that Audrey recognized it. Leaning toward her, she revealed, "I have an addiction."

"I'm pretty sure there's a secret handshake for people like us."

"You too?"

"Afraid so." Extending her hand, she said, "Audrey Regan."

"Really," the woman commented over their handshake. "The wedding dress designer."

Audrey inhaled sharply. "Yes!"

"Riley Eastwood," she told her with a grin. "The designer cast-off."

"Riley Eastwood?" Audrey exclaimed. "It's such a pleasure to meet you."

Riley glanced down at their clasped hands.

"I'm sorry," Audrey said with a chuckle, dropping the handshake.

"Lisette's dress is a stunner," Riley said. "Really beautiful work."

"Thank you so much!" Audrey said with a sigh. "That's . . . I mean, I'm really sorry it didn't . . . you know . . . but . . ."

Riley touched her arm and smiled. "I'm just not in touch with the curvy woman. You obviously are, and I think what you were able to do for that silhouette is phenomenal. As I watched her walk down the aisle, I was actually a little in awe."

Audrey had to find her breath. "Thank you."

"I'm not saying I didn't want to scratch your eyes out for a quick minute," she teased, "but seriously. She looks stunning."

Audrey's hand jerked to her heart, and the beat pounded against it. "She's a beautiful woman. She wore the dress well."

"Still," she said, rolling both hands. "I salute you."

Audrey could hardly contain herself as she turned to J. R. and exclaimed, "Riley Eastwood just saluted me."

"Audrey?" Riley said, angling toward her. "Is that Russell Walker with you?"

"That's the last of it," J. R. announced, and he dropped three suitcases to the bed in the guest room.

It wasn't hard to figure out which of them belonged to Audrey. The large rectangular bag and the smaller round one, both upholstered in pink plaid with pink leather trim and chocolate brown ribbons dangling from the handles, screamed Audrey Regan.

"This one's Kat's," she said, cluelessly confirming his suspicions as she picked up the red one. "It goes in the office."

"It's going to be a tight fit around here," he observed. "You ready for that?"

"I think the larger question is whether Caroline is ready for it," she replied.

J. R. felt his resolve tank in a big way when she turned around and smiled at him. "I guess it's time I hit the road," he said anyway.

Her expression diffused into unabashed disappointment, and her full red lips took a downward dip at the corners. She pushed back her waves of platinum hair, clicked her tongue, and thumped her denim-clad thigh with her fist. "Okay then."

Almost against his own will, J. R. opened his arms to her, and Audrey walked right into them. With her head nestled into the curve of his neck, she wrapped her arms around his waist and groaned sweetly.

"I can't believe I'm telling you this," she said. "But I'm really going to miss you."

"Color me astonished," he commented.

"Yeah. Imagine how I feel."

J. R. laughed and kissed her hair.

"Will you keep in touch?" she asked him.

"Audrey. Even if you weren't living with my brother's pregnant wife, you would still hear from me now and again." She muttered something that he couldn't discern. "What was that?"

She looked up at him, those remarkable amber eyes wide and misted with sincerity. "Please be careful on the road, J. R."

"I will."

"And wear your helmet."

"I always do."

"Oh, that's right. It's me who doesn't," she realized with a giggle. "Well, zip your jacket and all that."

"Will do. And you do the same."

Without a trace of warning, Audrey slipped her arms around his neck and rushed forward into a kiss. Almost before he could respond, she withdrew, reeled around, and scurried out of the bedroom.

"Take care, J. R.," she called back to him.

"Don't be nervous. Jackson is a really level-headed businessman. He's agreed to hear you out and tell you what he thinks."

Sherilyn's warm smile almost put Audrey at ease.

"Go on in. Just show him what you have on paper, and see what advice he has."

"This is just so out of my comfort zone," she admitted. "I'm a creative type. I can handle business decisions on a small scale, but this is just . . ."

"Enormous!" Sherilyn finished for her. "And an enormous opportunity stands the chance of providing an enormous blessing, right?"

"I suppose."

"Breathe a minute. Then go in and talk to Jackson. He's wonderful."

Audrey obediently drew in a deep breath and held it for a few seconds. As she slowly released it, Sherilyn tugged on her sleeve before leaving her standing there alone outside of Jackson's office.

"Are you ready for me?" she asked, peeking in at him. "Susannah isn't out here."

"She's running an errand with Norma this afternoon," he replied. "Come on in, Audrey."

Tucking the yellow pad of notes under her arm, she crossed the office and sat down across the desk from him, wondering how to get the conversation underway. Jackson handled that for her.

"So tell me about this business dilemma."

"Okay." She took a deep breath. "Your friend Curtis's daughter came up with an idea . . ."

It took her thirty minutes to unroll the whole thing, and Jackson didn't interrupt her once. Leaning back in the leather chair, his elbows propped on the arms and his hands folded, he simply listened. When she was finally through, Audrey groaned and laughed.

"So that's it. What do you think?"

"Well," he said thoughtfully. "A few key questions come to mind, but I'm sure you've already asked them yourself. What is Lisette's background in business? And even if she's well-equipped to start a business, does she know anything about the bridal industry? Also, where is the capital coming from? Is it her investment, or is it her father's? And where does he play in all of this?"

"Yep," she said with a smile. "Those are my questions, and a few more."

"Let's just start with one issue at a time," he suggested. "Why don't you tell me your gut feeling about this. Not what your logic tells you, but what your gut tells you."

"My gut is in knots," she admitted.

"Because it's such a big change?"

"No." She thought it over for a moment then felt confirmed. "No. Not at all. I'm ready for a big change. I mean, my business has been suffering for a while now. I just can't seem to make a go of things. And I really don't like New York much at all, so I'm open to a move. It's just that . . ."

Jackson smiled. "Now we're getting to the heart of it."

". . . I'm a designer, you know? And a very specialized one at that. I want to focus on design. Building a broad business like this one from the ground up doesn't really get me as excited as . . . panic-stricken."

"There's your answer."

She frowned curiously.

"Everything else aside, Audrey. Are you passionate enough about this idea to change your whole life to pursue it?"

She knew the answer, but she didn't say it out loud.

"It's just that Kat has her heart set on it. And I really want to be excited about it with her, I really do. I just can't get past the thoughts of how massive the undertaking really is. Starting from a completely empty warehouse with no inventory or equipment or . . ." She paused and released a low growl. "My granny used to tell me all the time that the secret to finding happiness in your work is finding that one thing that you're really good at, and then doing that one thing to the very best of your ability. I'm really good at just one thing, and that's only a tiny slice of what Lisette has in mind."

"Here's what I can tell you from my own experience," Jackson said. "My late wife dreamed of owning this place when it was just a small local business. She had this whole vision of making it into a wedding destination hotel. After her death, I bought it thinking I could honor her memory by chasing her dream. And it was the hardest thing I've ever done. I entered a field where I had no experience. Everything went wrong, and I had no idea what I was doing. If it hadn't been for my sisters, and then God dropping Emma into the mix, I would have run for the hills."

Audrey chuckled. "But you stuck with it, and it eventually turned into something really spectacular."

"Yes. Through very little fault of my own." Jackson leaned forward and looked into Audrey's eyes. "I wouldn't trade the things this place brought into my life. And I have no doubt that you can do whatever you set out to do. But look, I didn't take the easy road. It was costly, and it was painful, and it literally took a village of people to drag me and this place to our feet. I don't recommend taking on that kind of endeavor because Kat needs it or Lisette wants it, or any other reason outside of your personal passion and commitment to it. Does that make sense?"

She nodded. "It does."

"I'm not telling you that it's a mistake to try something really big and altogether new. I'm just telling you it would be a mistake if you're not completely convinced, deep down in your soul, that it's the path you're meant to take."

Audrey sighed and collapsed back into the chair.

"I have a buddy who can help you with working out the logistics of things. He's a consultant for new business ventures, and I'm sure he would be willing to sit down with you and map it all out. But first I recommend you take a few minutes to breathe."

"Ha! That's what Sherilyn said, to just breathe."

"It's good advice. Breathe. Relax. Pray. And wait. Don't make a move of any kind until you're convinced it's the right one."

"Thank you, Jackson."

"Hey, I don't pretend that this is any great service I've provided here today, Audrey. But it's the best advice I've got."

"And it's more than I had when I walked in."

"That's something then, right?"

Jackson's warm smile put Audrey at ease. She had no doubt that she would be reacquainted with the former anxiety at some point but, for that moment, she would concentrate on just following the best advice she'd been given.

She would breathe.

"Here you go. Can I get you anything else?"

"No. Thank you."

Audrey creamed the cup of hazelnut coffee and absently stirred it for much longer than necessary, allowing the slight breeze to caress her harried thoughts. The last time she'd taken a table in the courtyard, she and J. R. had been together.

Macaroni and cheese.

She'd been craving comfort food that night. Picking up the chocolate-dipped cookie from the plate in front of her, she realized comfort came in all forms—so many of them edible.

Audrey looked up. A patch of blue sky hid behind the tree branches, and a cottonball cloud ambled across the view. She'd really fallen in love with this place in the short time since her arrival.

Short time. Long on activity.

So much had happened since that day she'd climbed out of the taxi and walked through the front doors of The Tanglewood Inn. She'd expected to stay a couple of days. Carly and Devon would get married, and she would return to New York to pack up her life. The road had taken a few hard twists, but there she was again . . . thinking about the unrelenting future.

"Hello, dear."

Audrey dragged her attention from the shimmying leaves overhead.

"Have you been waiting long?"

She chuckled, more out of surprise than amusement. Emma's elderly aunt had taken the chair across from her.

"Hi, Sophie."

"Those look divine," she said, her attention focused on the plate of cookies.

"Help yourself."

"I have such a sweet tooth."

Her captivating smile warmed Audrey somehow, and she couldn't help returning it as Sophie chose a flower-shaped butter cookie and demurely bit off one of the petals.

"Is he joining us?" she asked Audrey.

"Who?"

"Your young man."

Audrey realized she meant J. R. She'd forgotten that they'd met the day of Jackson's birthday party, and Sophie had taken quite a shine to him.

"Oh, no. J. R. has left town."

Sophie thought that over for a moment. "I'm so sorry to hear that, dear. You must miss him horribly."

She lifted one shoulder in a shrug. "You know," she admitted with a smile, "I didn't expect to miss him this much, in fact, but I really do."

"There, there," the woman said, and she reached across the table and consoled her with a pat to Audrey's hand. "He won't be away for long."

"I'm afraid he will, Sophie. He's gone home to Santa Fe. He has a life there."

"Nonsense." She grinned at Audrey as she plucked another cookie from the plate. "That's not home. It's just one stop on the road back to you."

A little flutter inside her chest drove Audrey's hand to her heart.

"You might help him along though," Sophie advised. "You might give him a little incentive to put the pedal to the metal."

"Like what?" She felt silly for asking, but not silly enough not to wait with hope for the answer.

"A man who wanders just needs a little purpose. He's like a bumble bee. He'll light if the right flower calls his name."

Audrey giggled and squeezed the woman's hand. "You're a very uplifting person, Sophie. I'm glad to know you."

"Well, we'll have plenty of time to get to know each other even better," she declared. "I've seen all of your movies, you know."

"My . . . movies?"

"Aunt Soph, what are you doing?" Emma asked, scurrying toward the table, shaking her head. "Audrey, I'm sorry. I got tied up on the phone."

"It's fine," she said. "Your aunt has been giving me some wonderful advice."

"Look, Emma Rae. It's Carole Lombard, right here in Jackson's hotel."

Emma grinned and took Sophie's hand into hers and kissed it. "I think Miss Lombard was having some private time, Aunt Soph. Let's go visit Jackson and leave her to her coffee, shall we?"

"Jackson? Oh, yes. I'd like to see Jackson."

Sophie braced herself on Emma's arm to get up from the table, and she wobbled slightly on her feet. Turning back toward Audrey, she beamed.

"Clark will come back to you, dear. He never could stay away from you for long. Remember what he said? He trusts you, and he knows you wouldn't even know how to think about letting him down."

Audrey glanced at Emma.

"Clark Gable and Carole Lombard. We just saw a piece about them on AMC last week."

"Give him a reason to come home. He'll come back to you."

Emma shrugged and gave Audrey a crooked little smile. "Come on, Aunt Soph. Let's get upstairs and see Jackson before his next meeting."

"Take care," Audrey told them. "And thanks for the advice, Sophie."

"Anytime, dear."

"Do you think she's right? Maybe all J. R. needs is a little incentive?"

"Oh, Kat, I don't know," Audrey replied with a chuckle.

"Well, you'd like to have him back, wouldn't you?"

"Of course she would," Carly piped up from the kitchen. "Do you mind if I get pineapple and ham?"

"On pizza?" Audrey exclaimed. "You hate Hawaiian pizza!"

"I know. I always did. But it sounds so good to me right now."

Kat and Audrey exchanged grins.

"We've moved into a house with a walking trunk of hormones."

"Oh, Aud! What a thing to say."

"You know, I'll bet Russell could get him to come back," Kat suggested.

"To what?" Audrey cried. "I told you—and I'm sorry, Kat, I really am—but I'm just not feeling this deal with Lisette."

"Stop it. It's fine. Besides, Russell says he knows someone who might be able to help me get my own line going."

"Are you serious?"

"We'll see how it goes. But you're making the right decision for you, Audrey. I get that, and there's no hard feelings."

"Thank you, Kat. It would have been so great to keep you right by my side, but I'm really happy for you. Meanwhile . . . I don't know."

"If you could have one door open for you, what would it be?" Kat suggested, drawing her feet underneath her on the chair.

"I've already put so much time and energy into my own design business. Aside from that paying off at last?"

"Right. Anything else that would make you feel happy and fulfilled. Would you want to design for someone else who is already established?"

"Well, yeah," she admitted. "If he wasn't such a tragic human being, being taken in with House of LaMont would have been a great opportunity. But he's such—"

"A snake," Kat completed for her, and they exchanged a smile.

"I couldn't work for someone like him and be happy. But in a perfect world, where he would be a normal human, I could make my mark with his dollars and brand behind me."

After a gap of throbbing silence, Kat finally broke it. "Something is going to turn up for you, Audrey. I just know it. We're all praying for you, and I just know there's something around the corner."

"Yeah?" She tilted her head and tried to smile again. "Any idea when?"

"None at all."

The three of them shared a desperate kind of amusement, the kind of laughter friends often share when one of their lives heads over a cliff and no one knows what to do or say.

"Meanwhile, I have no idea what's going to become of me or where I'll—"

"I told you," Carly said as she plunked down on the chair across from her, "you'll be here. You said yourself you can't afford to keep things going in New York City. Kat will be here because of Russell. I'm here, and *I'm pregnant!*"

"Which you have made abundantly clear by mentioning it every thirty-six seconds in the last two days."

"Where else would you go to regroup? Here. And if J. R. were here too . . ."

Audrey raised her hand to try to cut Carly off before she could continue.

"I'm just saying, it might help if you reached out to him, Aud."

"So you're suggesting I somehow lure J. R. back to Atlanta—after him clearly telling me he has no desire whatsoever to relocate here, by the way—so that he'll be around on the off chance that the next opportunity I find will keep me here too?"

Carly pulled a face at Kat. "She makes everything so dramatic."

"Look who you're telling."

Carly crossed the kitchen with the phone to her ear. "Yes, I'd like to order a large Hawaiian."

Audrey and Kat both jumped, startled as Carly pulled open one of the cabinets and yanked on the door several times until the top hinge gave way.

"Caroline! What are you doing?"

"Some cheesy bread too," she told the person on the other end of the phone line. "A large order. And could we get some of that chocolate lava cake I saw on your commercial?" Pulling a butter knife from the drawer, she bent down to the floor and used it to begin prying up one of the linoleum tiles. "Forty minutes? Any chance you could put a rush on it? Hungry pregnant lady on the phone . . . Thank you so much!"

"Carly, what on earth—"

"Shh," she said as she returned to the table and sat down.

Audrey frowned at Kat. "She's lost her mind."

"Apparently."

"You know what would be so good right now, Aud? Gooey pretzels!"

"Oh yeah. She's pregnant," Audrey said with a giggle.

As Carly began to dial once again, Audrey reached out for the phone and missed. Carly beamed as she pressed the handset to her ear.

"Hey, J. R.," she said, and when Audrey gasped, Carly jumped from the chair and crossed to the doorway. "How are you doing?"

"Oh, no." Audrey cringed and dropped her head into her hands.

Suppressing laughter, Kat whispered, "This is going to get so good."

"I hate to bother you with this, I really do. But I'm just about going out of my mind. You've got three women in one house that is literally falling apart around us. I just about knocked myself out five minutes ago when the cabinet door came right off the hinges. Not one of us has skills with a hammer or a screwdriver, and the place is a hazard, J. R. Are you sure you can't come back to Atlanta for a while once you finish up whatever you're working on? I wouldn't ask except that Devon always kept things in such great shape, and I'm overwhelmed with planning for the baby. I mean, I need to get the office converted to a nursery, and I don't think you're supposed to paint when you're pregnant, are you? . . . See, I didn't think so."

Carly held Audrey and Kat captivated, and she hung up the phone a few minutes later with a triumphant smile. "He's going to see what he can work out."

"Caroline. You are evil."

"I am not evil. I am inventive."

As she dialed yet again, Audrey flew to her feet.

"Step away from the phone, Caroline!"

"Don't worry. Just one more call, then the pizza will be here." Carly turned sideways in the chair, crossed her legs, and smiled. "Sherilyn. Hey, it's Carly. Listen, I need your help with something. A little project I'm working on."

Granny Beatrice's Gooey Pretzels

About half a 12-ounce bag of semi-sweet or milk chocolate chips
1 bag rod-shaped pretzels
Various toppings, such as:
Chocolate sprinkles
Crushed pecans
Ground walnuts
Shredded coconut
Cinnamon and sugar mixture

Melt chocolate chips and pour into a tall container, such as a glass.
Prepare several plates, each with a thin layer of selected toppings.
Dip each pretzel in the chocolate.
Roll the pretzel in the desired toppings.
Munch!

16

No joke, mate. I want to hire you."

J. R. tilted his head against the phone, took a swig from his cold coffee, and grimaced. "Hire me."

"Yeah. I'm closing on the house way sooner than expected, and it needs all kinds of work around the grounds, and I need a shelving unit built in too. I have these awesome plans for it, but you know I don't know what I'm doing when it comes to all that."

"And you want me to come and build you some shelves."

"Rightie. And help me get it fit for human habitation so Kit-Kat will want to come over and won't feel like she's trapped in some bachelor money pit."

J. R. sat there, weighing Russell's words. "Why don't you hire a contractor?"

"Because I don't want some Joe I don't know telling me what I should do. I want you doing that."

He laughed. "Since when?"

"C'mon, mate. This is new territory for me, settling and making roots. I'm in my thirties, and I've never owned anything bigger than a Hummer! This is a big deal for me. I need your help."

First Carly, and now Russell?

Call waiting beeped in, and J. R. sighed. "I've got another call. I'll get back to you in a bit."

"Don't leave me hanging now."

"Hello?"

"J. R., how are you? It's Jackson Drake."

"Jackson," he exclaimed. "I'm good, man. How about you?"

"Well, I'm much better since I just learned that you have some experience as a builder."

"I'm in carpentry. But I only worked with a builder for a few summers when I needed the extra income. How did you know about that?"

"Here's the deal, J. R. I'm hoping maybe there's a lull in Harley restoration for a few months. If you're interested, we're doing some construction here at the hotel, and I could really use someone to oversee things for me. Make sure I'm not being taken for a ride."

J. R. narrowed his eyes thoughtfully. "Seriously?"

"Yeah. Sherilyn mentioned that Carly had asked you to come back to help her get ready for the baby. I got to thinking maybe you could use a paying gig to help you do that, and I'd really appreciate the expertise."

Oh, come on. Et tu, Jackson?

"I should reach Atlanta at the end of the week. How about I drop by and talk to you about it then."

"Sounds good. Listen, I really do appreciate it, J. R."

"Sure."

J. R. shook his head as he disconnected the call and slid his phone across the table. Suddenly, he had a vision of the whole lot of them, gathered around Sherilyn and Andy's dining table, laughing and concocting their plan.

"Let Carly call first," Russell had probably devised. "Then I'll follow it up."

"But he won't come for no reason," Sherilyn likely pointed out. "We need something solid, like a job offer."

"Oooh, Jackson can take care of that!" Emma no doubt exclaimed. "You'll do that for me, won't you, Jackson?"

And there was Audrey in his mind's eye, sitting in the corner, taking it all in, hoping for their success but not willing to participate. And why would she? If she turned down the new business deal, as he suspected, she would be off to New York again, maybe even before he reached the state of Georgia.

He wished he hadn't phoned Carly and agreed to return, in fact. He had an inkling that she might have been playing him in the first sixty seconds of their conversation, but he couldn't deny the gravitational pull toward the obligation of doing for her what Devon could not. And the idea of his pregnant sister-in-law standing on a ladder and painting a wall . . . Well! That wasn't going to happen, no way and no how. So he acquiesced.

They should have quit while they were ahead. Talk about overkill!

First Russell's call, and now Jackson! The poor guy. They'd obviously roped him into making a job offer, the point at which J. R. felt he had no choice but to draw the line. It shouldn't cost Jackson money out of pocket to help their scheme along.

So maybe he would go ahead and make the trip, after all. He owed Devon that. He could help Carly in whatever way she needed to prepare for the baby, and maybe he could build a shelf or two for Russell. But he slammed on the brakes at the idea of a pity job, from Jackson or anyone else.

Still, the idea of seeing Audrey again . . .

Audrey dragged the last box across the cement floor of Carly's basement and pushed it into a neat line with the others while Kat relocated Mac to the far wall.

"There we go! I can ship these later if we have to."

"Thanks, Kat." Audrey sat down on the edge of one of the boxes. "Remember storage?"

"No," Kat teased. "I haven't been able to afford a basement, or even a free closet for that matter, in my entire adult life."

Audrey laughed. "Me neither."

"Aud," Carly called from the top of the stairs. "Your harp is singing."

"Can you see who it is?"

"Unknown caller."

"That's the third time today," she told Kat. "I'm coming."

"Too late. It went to voice mail," Carly said. "You can check for a voice mail later. Now come on up here, both of you. I have a few paint sample cards."

Audrey and Kat clomped up the stairs and shut the basement door to find dozens of color cards spread across the tabletop.

"A few?" Audrey teased.

"Well, maybe more than a few. Help me choose."

"How can you choose the nursery color before you know what you're having?" Audrey asked, and she grabbed an apple out of the bowl on the counter and took a bite as she plopped into a chair.

"I was thinking green or yellow," she replied. "Something that would work for a boy or a girl."

"Caroline, you're only eight weeks pregnant. Don't you want to—"

"Don't say it, Audrey." Carly's face curled up like a fist. "I want to focus on our little boy or little girl, so I don't have to think about . . ."

"Okay. Okay, I'm sorry."

"I like this shade of green," Kat interjected, and she pulled one of the cards from the stack and slid it toward Carly. "My friend in New York did her nursery in this color on the bottom part of the wall, with a really pale butter yellow on the top, and they were separated by this adorable border with ducks on it."

"I want sheep," Carly said, drying her eyes. "I like the idea of comparing our baby to a little lamb."

Audrey's chest squeezed as she watched her friend cling to whatever hope she might be able to get her spiritual hands around.

"Why don't we go shopping tomorrow," she suggested. "We can look at borders and wallpaper, and see what strikes you. Once you pick your little lambs for the room, we'll match the paint color to them."

Carly smiled gratefully. "Leave it to you to organize it all. That makes sense."

A light rap at the front door drew their attention, and Kat hopped up to answer it. A moment later, she returned to the kitchen with a strange expression on her face, followed by an even stranger sight.

"Hi, Audrey."

Riley Eastwood?

"Riley. What are . . . How did you . . . ?"

Riley grinned. "My assistant has been trying to track you down for me ever since Lisette's wedding."

"Um, you remember Kat. And this is my friend Carly. It's her house. Carly, this is Riley Eastwood. The designer."

"Oh." Carly's eyes widened. "It's nice to meet you."

"I hope you don't mind the intrusion," she replied. "Audrey, we tracked you down at The Tanglewood, and Cynthia spoke to a young woman there this morning. Sherilyn Drummond?"

"Yes."

"I've been trying to call your cell, and I just thought maybe it would be better if we spoke in person."

"It's no intrusion at all," Carly answered for her. "Why don't you two go out to the patio and have a seat. I'll bring iced tea."

Audrey couldn't help it, and a chuckle rolled out. *The consummate hostess.*

"Would you give me a few minutes?" Riley asked.

Audrey's brain couldn't stop running scenarios, and Kat poked her in the back with her index finger.

"Of course," she finally answered. "Let's go outside."

Once they settled at the patio table, Riley raked her dark hair. "It's gorgeous out here, isn't it? It's already so cold in Chicago."

"Oh. That's right. You're from Chicago."

She nodded. "I'm flying back home tomorrow, so I'm very happy Cynthia was able to find you before I have to go."

"What did you . . . want to talk to me about?"

"Lisette's gown."

"Oh." She mulled it over before adding, "What about it?"

"The draping, the construction," she said. "And the way it fit Lisette. You inspired me. And that's not easy to do anymore."

"I'm . . . Thank you."

Carly seemed to tiptoe through the door, and she placed two glasses of tea on the table. "Don't mind me," she said, disappearing again.

"I'll get right to it," Riley said. "Have you ever been to London Fashion Week?"

Audrey chuckled. "No."

"Well, I have a show there next February."

"Really!" she exclaimed. "Congratulations."

"Thank you. I'll be showing my spring and summer line, and I normally finish with a couple of statement pieces."

"I know. I saw your New York runway show two years ago when you had that Latin-inspired wedding gown with the feathers and that train. Oh!" she moaned. "It was spectacular!"

"Thank you. Well, this year, I'm thinking of something a little different. And I wondered if you might be interested."

Interested!

"Interested?"

Riley slid forward to the edge of her chair. "What if my statement piece at the finale of my show in London is to introduce . . . *my new plus-size label.*"

Audrey's heartbeat fluttered. "Your new . . ."

Riley used both hands to create an imaginary marquee over them. "Audrey Regan. For Riley Eastwood."

"Are you joking?" *Because it's not very funny, if you are.*

"No. Of course not." Riley snickered and shook her head. "Audrey, I told you. You inspired me. You did for Lisette what I wasn't able to do, and it got me to thinking. What if we blended our skills? You, the up and coming new designer—and me, the established one. You infuse new blood into my line while I expand into a niche market. What do you think?"

Audrey wondered if she could. *Think.*

"I have to warn you, Audrey, I'm not much of a gambler. I want to start out with two or three pieces. Say, three gowns. One of them understated, another more elaborate one. And then a third over-the-top, set-their-eyeballs-on-fire stunner to close the show. What do you think?"

There was that word again. *Think.*

"Audrey, say yes!" Carly cried from the other side of the tiny opening in the door, and Riley burst out laughing.

"Privacy?" Audrey called, and the door clicked shut behind her. "Sorry, Riley."

"It's fine."

"Look, Carly's husband is a Marine, and he's just shipped out to the Middle East. To make matters worse—or better, I guess!—she's just discovered that she's pregnant."

"What wonderful news."

"I can't pick up and move to Chicago right now. I'm still planted with one foot in New York, and—"

"Audrey. Wait. Listen. You can work wherever you want to. If things take off like I hope, we may have to revisit that next year. But for the moment, I'm not asking you to change your whole life on the crazy chance that the fashion world is ready for what we have to offer them."

Audrey felt torn. She loved the work she did in creating Lisette's gown. But branding herself as a couture designer specifically for plus-sized women? That had been part of her concern with Lisette's Wedding Central idea. What if it didn't work? Would she be painted into a corner that allowed no escape?

Audrey rubbed her temple and smiled. "Can I think about this, Riley?"

"Of course."

"I mean, the opportunity to work with you in any way is just a dream come true. But I really need to give this some thought."

Riley produced a business card from the front pocket of her bag, and she handed it to Audrey. "I'm leaving tomorrow afternoon. If you have any questions, or if you want to discuss it some more while I'm here, give me a call. Maybe we can have dinner."

"Thank you," she muttered, looking down at the glossy blue card with Riley's recognizable logo embossed in the upper corner.

"If I don't hear from you, I'll call you next week for your answer."

Riley had already gone inside the house before Audrey realized it and hopped to her feet to follow.

"Thank you so much, really," she said at the door.

"Whatever you decide, Audrey, I think you're incredibly talented. You're headed for great things. I hope you'll let me be part of it."

"Talk to you soon."

The moment the front door closed, Carly threw herself at Audrey. Kat joined them, and Kat and Carly jumped up and down with their arms around Audrey, bouncing her until she felt like one of those rubber balls attached to a paddle with an elastic band.

"Stop it, stop it," she cried.

Carly grabbed her by the shoulders. "What is wrong with you? This is fantastic, Aud!"

"Just give me a minute to process."

"There's nothing to process. Tell her, Kat! Tell her."

Kat looked Audrey in the eyes so hard that it burned, and she nodded. "Audrey. This is the one. Weston LaMont was a no-go. Lisette wasn't for you. But this is Riley Eastwood. It's a no-brainer."

Think. Trying, but. Frozen.

"Audrey," Carly said, shaking her. "Are you kidding!"

No brainer. Riley for-goodness-sake Eastwood.

Kat caught her again. "Right?"

Audrey built to a slow nod.

"Yes!" Carly exclaimed.

"Yes," Audrey repeated.

As realization pressed down on her like a heavy ray of scorching sun, a low rumbling groan emanated from deep within her.

"Yes!" Kat and Carly both shouted, and Audrey pointed at the door with a question stuck in her throat. "Yes!" they both repeated.

"Go!" Carly added.

Reminded of a cartoon character with wheels spinning but getting nowhere, Audrey pushed herself into action and ran out the front door in time to see Riley's car backing out to the street.

"Wait!" she shrieked, tearing across the lawn toward the car. "Riley, wait!"

And in the fashion of the aforementioned cartoon character, her feet took on a life of their own, and she crashed directly into the car and flew across the hood.

"Do you need some help with that?" Riley asked, cringing as Audrey struggled to keep her fork in hand.

"No, no," she said, adjusting the sling on her arm and trying again. "I think I've got it."

"Are you sure?" With a half-laugh, half-groan, she added, "Because you really look awful."

"Thank you, Riley. Feel free to be honest. Don't hold anything back."

"Oh good," she replied with a chuckle. "Can I get you some more Neosporin for your nose?"

A grin rose on Audrey's face, and she winced as it did. She'd scraped her nose and cheek on the gravel when she flew off the car, and she hadn't had much luck camouflaging the shadow of tomorrow's black eye with cover stick. And the ugly blue and white sling cradling her sprained shoulder did nothing for her carefully-chosen outfit. But none of that took away from the fact that Audrey Regan and Riley Eastwood were now colleagues. And fast friends.

"So do you want to tell me what that was this morning?" Riley asked as she cut her salad into smaller bites.

"Not at all." They shared a laugh, and Audrey sighed. "I've been in a real time of flux these last couple of months. A lot of things have crossed my path, but none of it felt quite right. I think I became sort of like a deer caught in headlights about making a decision on direction."

As she looked up from her pasta, Audrey blinked to make sure of what she saw.

"That's a good analogy," Riley stated seriously. "I've seen a scared deer before. That's just what it looked like." Noticing Audrey's expression, she added, "And so is that. Are you all right?"

Audrey's jaw dropped slightly as he approached their table in Morelli's restaurant, and her entire face tingled as a wide grin spread over it.

"Hi, angel."

"J. R.?" she exclaimed, but when she tried to hop to her feet, pain yanked her back down to the chair.

"Audrey, what have you done to yourself?" he asked, caressing her shoulder.

Recognition dawned and he grinned at Riley. "Riley Eastwood, right?"

"Yes. Good to see you again."

"You too." J. R. folded into the empty chair next to Audrey. "What happened?"

"Riley ran over me with her car," she said, dead serious.

"Hey!"

Audrey popped with laughter.

"If anyone ran into anyone else," Riley objected, "I would say it's the other way around."

"What are you doing here so soon?" Audrey asked him. "Does Carly know you're here?"

"Not yet. I came straight here to see Russell."

Audrey's heartbeat thumped in her ears as she looked at him. "It's so good to see you."

Riley wiped her mouth with the corner of her napkin, then laid it across her plate. "I'm going to let you two reconnect."

"Oh, don't go," Audrey said.

"I have to get packed for an eight a.m. flight tomorrow. I'll call you in a few days. You take care of yourself, please. And J. R., it was great to see you again."

Audrey leaned on the table edge to push up to her feet. Rounding the table, she hugged Riley with her good arm. "Thank you so much, Riley."

"I'm thrilled to be working with you."

"Same here."

Once Riley left the restaurant, J. R. helped Audrey get settled back into her chair.

"You are a sight for sore eyes," she told him, shaking her head and grinning like a ridiculous schoolgirl.

"Back atcha," he teased. Gingerly touching her cheek, he asked, "Does that hurt?"

"Like you can't believe."

He leaned forward and placed a careful, gentle kiss on the corner of her mouth. Her pulse tapped in the hollow of her throat, and Audrey smiled.

"You're working with Riley Eastwood?"

"Oh." She grinned. "Yes."

"That's great."

Audrey nodded. "It really is. I finally feel like . . ."

"The road smoothed out?"

"Exactly."

"I'm glad for you, Audrey," he said. "Does she have anything for me?"

She tilted her head and raised an eyebrow. "Pardon?"

"I've been getting a lot of offers lately. I thought maybe you wanted to make one too."

She chuckled nervously. "What are you talking about?"

"The call from Carly . . ."

Audrey's face felt suddenly warm, and both palms went instantly damp. *He knows.*

". . . and from Russell. And then Jackson. Funny how *everyone in Greater Atlanta* needs me so much, all of a sudden like that. Don't you think so?"

"I guess . . . you're a likable guy."

"Yeah, that must be it, huh?"

"Well, frankly, I don't see it so much. But I guess so." He remained silent for several stomach-wrenching moments before Audrey glanced over at him. "So if you knew, why did you come? You could have just called them all out on it and stayed in Santa Fe."

"Well," he began. "There are two reasons."

"The first?"

"Carly. Especially now, Devon needs to know she's being looked after. And I want to be there for them both."

"You're a good brother." She touched his hand and smiled. "And second?"

"The place kind of grows on you. Have you ever noticed that?"

A noisy pop of laughter came out of somewhere deep in her throat. "Yes," she said, nodding. "Indeed it does."

"The people here are. . ."

"Unforgettable."

"Yes."

"I know. It's kind of hard to think about leaving them behind."

"It is," he remarked.

"Yeah, all of them. Sherilyn and Andy, Emma and Jackson . . ."

Me? Am I one of the unforgettable ones?

"Yes, Audrey."

She turned and looked into his steel-blue eyes. "What?"

"You."

"Me?"

"You. You are hard to leave behind. I admit it, okay? I want to be here because you're here."

She melted into another one of those J. R.-driven schoolgirl smiles. Completely against her will, J. R. Hunt had driven her to . . . *giggle?*

Oh, good grief. Get ahold of yourself, girl.

"Oh, and now you're going to get all cute and cuddly over it," he teased. "There will be no living with you now."

"If it irritates you so much, maybe you should go back to Santa Fe then."

J. R. curled his arm behind her neck and gently pulled her toward him.

"This is it," he whispered into her ear, and Audrey's eyes jerked upward to meet his.

"What do you mean?"

"You. Me. This is it."

"It is?"

"I realized it somewhere outside of Birmingham," he commented.

J. R. took her face into his hands and carefully pressed his lips against hers. A rush of electricity skittered up Audrey's back and brought goosebumps to the back of her neck.

"Just to be clear," she said as their lips parted, and J. R. laughed right out loud.

"Yes, Audrey. I'll say it slowly to be sure you understand. *I . . . love . . . you.*"

"You do?"

"I do."

She had to ask. "Are you sure?"

"Yes, I'm sure. I don't know how great a deal it is for you, or whether I'll be any good at this at all, but it's done now. I'm in love with you."

"Do you think maybe we should get you a second opinion?"

"You are such a pain in the rear end."

"I know," she admitted with a grin. "I'm sorry. I just want to enjoy the moment. Do you mind?"

"No. Go ahead."

"Oh good. So! About these feelings you have for me. Love, you called it?"

Discussion Questions

1. Audrey is very different from the other women in the book. How do you think her unique qualities serve the story?
2. What do you think solidifies the growing attraction between Audrey and J. R.?
3. J. R. isn't your typical leading man. What depth do you think is derived from his personality and appearance?
4. Do you think J. R.'s lifestyle affects his ability to commit to Audrey?
5. There are many peripheral characters in the book. Which ones do you think had the greatest impact on Audrey and J. R.?
6. How does the long-standing relationship between Audrey and Carly affect them and contribute to the advancement of the story?
7. What do you think of the family dynamics between J. R. and his brother? Do you think it plays an important part in the future of J. R. and Audrey's relationship?
8. How did you feel about the way faith and prayer was approached in the telling of the story?
9. How did Audrey's faith mature over the course of the book, and how did the people around her contribute to her spiritual growth?
10. What did Kat symbolize through her role in Audrey's life?
11. Sherilyn and Andy provide a homestead in the background of the story. How does the one provided by Carly and Devon compare, and what specific purposes do both couples provide for the advancement of the story?
12. What did you think of Lisette, and specifically how she was perceived by LaMont?
13. How did you feel about the ultimate decision Audrey made regarding her future as a designer?

Want to learn more about author
Sandra D. Bricker and check out other great
fiction from Abingdon Press?

Sign up for our fiction newsletter at
www.AbingdonPress.com
to read interviews with your favorite authors, find tips
for starting a reading group, and stay posted on what
new titles are on the horizon. It's a place to connect
with other fiction readers or post a
comment about this book.

Be sure to visit Sandra online!

www.SandraDBricker.com